By JOE COSENTINO

The Naked Prince and Other Tales from Fairyland

BOBBY AND PAOLO'S HOLIDAY STORIES
A Home for the Holidays
The Perfect Gift
The First Noel
The Bobby and Paolo Holiday Stories Anthology

IN MY HEART
An Infatuation
A Shooting Star
In My Heart Anthology

Published by DREAMSPINNER PRESS
www.dreamspinnerpress.com

THE
BOBBY&PAOLO
HOLIDAY STORIES

JOE COSENTINO

Published by
DREAMSPINNER PRESS

5032 Capital Circle SW, Suite 2, PMB# 279, Tallahassee, FL 32305-7886 USA
www.dreamspinnerpress.com

This is a work of fiction. Names, characters, places, and incidents either are the product of author imagination or are used fictitiously, and any resemblance to actual persons, living or dead, business establishments, events, or locales is entirely coincidental.

The Bobby and Paolo Holiday Stories
© 2018 Joe Cosentino.

Cover Art
© 2018 Adrian Nicholas.
adrian.nicholas177@gmail.com
Cover content is for illustrative purposes only and any person depicted on the cover is a model.

Trade Paperback ISBN: 978-1-64080-773-0
Library of Congress Control Number: 2018941006
Trade Paperback published December 2018
v. 1.0
A Home for the Holidays originally published by Dreamspinner Press, December 2015.
The Perfect Gift originally published by Dreamspinner Press, December 2017.
The First Noel originally published by Dreamspinner Press, December 2018.

Printed in the United States of America
∞
This paper meets the requirements of
ANSI/NISO Z39.48-1992 (Permanence of Paper).

Table of Contents

A HOME FOR THE HOLIDAYS

JOE COSENTINO

To Fred, for everything over all these years;
to the staff at Dreamspinner Press;
and to everyone seeking a home for the holidays.

Acknowledgments

To MY parents, sister, niece, nephew, and cousins for insisting I take a trip to Italy. You were right!

"BOBBY, EVERY Christmas your father and I buy you a nice gift and you return it. So this year before we go shopping, I'm asking you. What do you want for Christmas, exactly?"

I was tempted to answer, "How about the new Zeb Atlas DVD, Mom?" No longer reading my law textbook, I pressed the cell phone against my ear and responded, "My red sweater is getting frayed. I guess I could use a new one, Mom."

"I don't like red on you. I'll get you a green sweater. It will go nicely with your eyes. You'll be twenty-four in June. Nobody ever caught a husband wearing red clothes, except for Mrs. Klaus, and then look how overweight *he* was."

I adjusted the heavy book on my knees and leaned back against the headboard of my narrow dorm room bed. Since fall semester of my third year of law school was over, my roommate had already gone back to Utah to be with his father and three mothers. Normally I would go home for the holidays.

As far back as I can remember, every December twenty-third through the twenty-fifth my mother works herself to exhaustion while forbidding anyone to help her. Since I am not married, I am seated at the kiddie table, where I dodge meatball and manicotti grenades courtesy of my little nieces and nephews. Then the gifts are bestowed with price tags on them so we all know "how many hours your father and I had to work to be able to buy our children such beautiful things." This is followed by "oohs" and "ahhs" for every gift except the presents from me, which garner comments from my parents and two sisters like, "Oh well, I can wear that for dress-down day at work… if I keep on my coat." After the extended family of aunts, uncles, and cousins arrive for dessert (cannoli grenades at the kiddy table), my mother's side (the Mascobellos) eat the pastries, and my father's side (the McGraths) drink the liqueurs, while I sit upstairs in my old bedroom reading law case decisions on the Internet.

This Christmas is going to be different. Throughout my childhood I heard stories about my mother's now-deceased father who had a first cousin in Capri, Italy. Mom, "too exhausted from taking care of all of you to survive such a journey," had recently spoken on the phone to her deceased father's cousin's daughter-in-law (got that?), and the two women had arranged for me to spend this Christmas with my Italian relatives. This led to my Christmas in Italy with my Italian cousin, Paolo Mascobello. More on that later!

"Don't worry, Mom."

"How can I not worry? This is the first time you won't be with us for Christmas. You'll be halfway around the world."

"But you made the plans with your relatives."

"That's what I'm worried about. Please don't embarrass me, Bobby," Mom said, followed by a maternal sigh. "And do everything they ask you to do."

"I will, Mom, except I'm not eating octopus."

"Eat anything they put in front of you! And say 'Thank you.'"

"Okay, Mom."

"And bring extra underwear. For all I know they do their laundry on a rock in the Mediterranean. What? Oh, Dad says to put your money in your underpants in case somebody tries to rob you."

"What if the robber reaches into my underpants?"

"Hey, don't talk dirty to me. I'm your mother."

I glanced at my watch. "Okay, Mom."

"And don't spend all the money I sent you in one place."

"You didn't need to send me money, Mom."

"Take it. And don't tell your sisters. I'm not a bank."

I closed the book and rose from the bed. "Okay, Mom."

"And call me the minute you get there."

I reached for my luggage. "Okay, Mom."

"And be careful crossing the streets, and don't forget to bring your coat!"

After promising to be good more times than a criminal facing the parole board, I said "Arrivederci" to Mom and was off to meet my Italian relatives.

On the plane next to a three-hundred-pound snoring woman with apnea, I contorted my lean, strong body (thanks to being a lifeguard every summer) in my miniscule seat and read four law journals over the eight-hour flight. Since the Italians ran the airline, the food was good and plentiful, but the seats would have been a squeeze in a doll house. I am five feet ten inches tall with long arms and legs, frizzy ginger hair, and a long penis. As you can imagine, using the tiny bathroom on the plane was like one of those circus acts, where ten clowns come out of the small car. True to the stories I'd heard about Italian drivers, the plane took off late but arrived early.

At Naples International Airport I whizzed through customs, thanks to years of studying Italian in high school and college and the Italian customs officer, who liked redheads.

Next was a *Speed Racer* taxi ride from the airport to the boat terminal that would have made a racecar driver nauseated. Then came the three-hour boat ride to the island of Capri's Marina Grande. Though I had seen pictures of it, the sight of the enormous cliffs sitting majestically on the water literally took my breath away. Tired of looking out of the cappuccino-stained windows, I walked onto the deck of the boat to get a better view. It was fifty degrees in Capri, typical for December, so I whispered a "Thanks" to my mother for reminding me to bring my brown leather jacket.

From the *funiculare* (cable car) I marveled at the stunning views of the island below and Mt. Vesuvius in the distance.

At the Piazzetta (main plaza) I boarded an island bus that zoomed around harrowing, tight corners like a car in a fun house.

After a long walk up a steep hill surrounded by boulders, I finally reached the intertwining gold leaves on the front gate of the Villa di Mascobello. It was a large white stone villa with a terra cotta orange roof and matching shutters. With suitcase in hand I approached the orange double doors, feeling like Kunta Kinte at the start of his familial journey.

I released the large brass knocker in the shape of an *M* and was greeted by a young woman in a flowery housedress. After I introduced myself, Lucia led me through orange and blue marble columns past an entranceway of white marble to a double-story sitting room with views from its many windows of the island and the Mediterranean Sea. Overstuffed sofas, love seats, and chairs flanked three tiled fireplaces stationed around the luxurious room. Lucia told me (in Italian) the mistress of the house would be down to greet me shortly. I thanked my Italian teacher in high school, who had drummed the language into my brain.

I expected Lucia's boss to be an overweight, scowling woman wearing a long black dress with rosary beads dangling from her weather-beaten hands. I also assumed, like Lucia, she would speak to me in Italian. So I was quite surprised when an attractive middle-aged woman with auburn hair, wearing a stylish blue dress with matching shoes and a silver necklace, dismissed Lucia with my suitcase, kissed both of my cheeks, and said in perfect English, "Bobby, I am Caterina Mascobello. It is a pleasure to meet you. Thank you for visiting us. Did you have a nice trip?"

"Yes, thank you, Mrs. Mascobello."

She smiled. "Please call me Mama. Everyone does."

I liked her right away. "Thank you, Mama."

"What did you do on the long plane ride?"

"I read four law journals."

She laughed like a young girl. "I hope we can find more amusing things for you to do while you are here."

"Thank you." I tried to remember my family lineage. "According to my mother, you are my grandfather's cousin's daughter-in-law. Did I get that right?"

"All that matters is you are family." She hugged me. "I so enjoyed speaking with your mother on the phone. Is she well?"

"Probably not, until I call to report I'm here alive and well."

"Then you must do so immediately."

As we started to leave the room, I admired the enormous, beautifully decorated (in gold) Christmas tree in the corner of the room. "What a beautiful tree."

"Thank you, Bobby. Paolo says he is going to decorate it every year, but the task seems to fall to Lucia."

"Is Paolo your husband?"

Caterina laughed again. "Paolo is my son. You will meet him and the rest of the family at lunch in the dining room at 1:00 p.m."

Back in the hallway, Caterina pointed up the wide marble staircase. "You will find a phone in the hallway. Your bedroom is the third on your left. By now Lucia will have unpacked your things. Take a nap, and I will see you at lunch."

Feeling like Little Orphan Annie at Daddy Warbucks's mansion, I said, "Thank you… for everything, Mama."

She pinched my cheek; then she was off.

At the top of the stairs, I picked up the ivory phone and called my mother. I wasn't surprised when she answered after only one ring.

"Hello, Mom."

"So you made it there alive?"

"I'm alive. Caterina's very nice."

"Is she thinner than me?"

"Yes."

"Are you calling your mother fat?"

"No, but she's thinner."

"Is the villa gorgeous?"

I glanced at the elaborate gold mirrors and sconces displayed on the hallway walls. "Yes."

"Are you being polite to everyone?"

"I'll meet everyone at lunch." I looked at the heavy wooden doors with their ornate molding. "Now I'm headed to my room to unpack."

"What? Oh, your father says not to talk to anybody outside of the family so you don't get kidnapped."

My jet lag kicked in, and my eyes started to close. "Bye, Mom. Give Dad my love."

After swearing on my dead grandfather's grave that I would behave at the Mascobello's villa like a visiting prince at Buckingham Palace, I agreed to call my mother the next day. After I finally hung up the phone, I walked down the wide, long marble hallway, counting doors to my bedroom.

Upon entering my room, I noticed Lucia had unpacked my things into a large mahogany wardrobe out of C. S. Lewis. Exhausted from my trip, I stripped off my clothes, leaped onto the gigantic, canopied four-poster bed, and slept until I felt a firm nudge on my shoulder. As I opened my still jet-lagged eyes, I wasn't sure if I was dreaming or awake. Standing next to my bed was the most gorgeous man I had ever seen. About my height and age, his wavy chestnut hair framed piercing sapphire eyes, a straight nose, and full red lips. Wearing a skintight button-down red shirt, black pants, and black loafers, he gave Michelangelo's *David* a run for his florin. To say his body was strong was like saying the Catholic Church had a little wealth and power. His taut, perfectly shaped muscles sprouted additional muscles of even greater magnitude. Bulging shoulders led to mountainous pectoral muscles, a narrow waist and hips, and a prominent lump between his sculpted thighs. His skin was olive colored and so smooth it appeared as if he had no veins in his body.

"Mama said you should come down for lunch."

Covering my rapidly growing erection with my thigh, I responded in a daze, "Who are you?"

He spoke perfect English. "I am Paolo."

Next to Paolo, even with a swimmer's body, I felt incredibly white and skinny. "Hello, Paolo. I'm Bobby. I think we're related." As I rose to get dressed, Paolo seemed to check out my body, or was that wishful thinking?

"Your grandfather and my grandfather were cousins."

Doing the math quickly, I said, "So that makes us third cousins?"

"I guess it does." He shook my hand. It felt warm and comforting. "We look nothing alike."

I laughed at the understatement. "No."

"Is this your first time in Italy?"

"Yes."

"Do you like it here?"

"Yes."

"Do you answer every question with 'yes' or 'no'?"

"No." I felt like a teenager at his first dance.

Paolo shrugged his massive shoulders. "You better get down to the dining room. Mama doesn't like to hold lunch."

Once dressed in a light blue sweater and dark blue pants, I said, "I don't know how to get to the dining room."

He smiled. "Follow me."

Lunch in the dining room was like an Italian wedding at a catering hall back in Philly. We sat around an enormous oak table under a multitiered crystal chandelier, surrounded by french doors leading to a roomy balcony overlooking a vast garden full of statues, fountains, and lemon trees. The orange walls were adorned with gold-framed pictures of various saints and Italian celebrities.

The table was laden with huge ceramic platters filled with antipasti, garlic bread dipped in olive oil, gnocchi in pesto sauce, Caesar salad, pasta marinara, veal piccata, chicken cacciatore, cod in olive oil and garlic, stuffed calamari, eggplant, and broccoli rabe. Two large sterling silver carafes were full to the brim with red and white wine.

After Paolo and I joined the others, Mama introduced me to everyone sitting at the table, starting at the head and moving clockwise. Everyone, including Mama, spoke in Italian.

"Bobby, may I present Luciano Mascobello, your grandfather's cousin. Please call him Nonno. Next is Luciano's wife, Franca. She is Nonna. Luciano's son and my husband, Guiseppe, is Papa. Our daughter Francesca, Francesca's boyfriend Bruno, and our son Paolo."

The men, except for Paolo and me, wore dark suits. Nonna was dressed in a black housedress. Mama wore a pretty red dress with pearls, and Francesca sported an attractive beige business suit that matched her bleached blonde hair.

Everyone smiled and welcomed me to their home. I tried not to be rude to the others, but sitting next to Paolo, I found it difficult to take my eyes off him.

An enormous German shepherd raced into the room and planted his drooling face in my lap. Mama smiled and said, "This is Pino."

"Pino seems to have made a new friend," Francesca said, followed by a giggle in my direction.

After I let out a sneeze, Mama said, "I hope you aren't allergic to Pino."

Nonna responded with a wave of her wrinkled hand. "How can you be allergic to Pino, Bobby? He likes *you*."

After filling his tall crystal glass with wine, Nonno reached for the antipasti platter, and his wife slapped his hand. "Say grace first, Nonno!"

Raising his gaze to the chandelier, Nonno said rapidly, "Father, heaven, grace, bless, let's eat," then dove into the food.

Nonna tucked a stray gray hair back into her bun. "Such a rushed grace so near Christmas, the day Jesus was born to start the Roman Catholic religion!"

Ignoring his wife, Nonno filled his plate. "I never thought I would see the day when my dead cousin Sergio's grandson would come to my home." He wiped a tear from his eye. "I thank God I lived to see it."

Nonna added, "I will ask the priest to do a special blessing over you, Bobby."

Paolo whispered to his sister, "I bet the priest would like to do a lot of things over him."

Paolo and Francesca shared a laugh. I blushed.

Between spearing large bites of food, Papa waved his sterling silver fork. "What does your father do in the States, Bobby? Like most Americans, he must be rich."

Stifling a laugh, I responded, "My father manages the largest department store in Philadelphia. My mother is a bookkeeper. We're what Americans call middle class."

As he licked olive oil from his fingers, Papa explained, "Nonno is retired, so I head the family business now. We own a wind and solar power company. Francesca is my second in command."

Mama added proudly, "Paolo works in the warehouse."

Laughing and throwing a piece of bread at Paolo, Francesca said, "When Paolo works."

Paolo threw the bread back at his sister. "Mama arranged for me to be off this week."

"Mama arranges for you to be off *many* weeks." Francesca turned to her mother. "While Papa and I run the company, Paolo draws pictures in his room."

"It gets me away from my tyrant boss," Paolo responded.

Francesca stuck her tongue out at her brother, and he crossed his eyes at her.

"Enough, you two," Mama said with a raised eyebrow.

After tasting the mouthwatering food, I gave the dog a handful of veal, and he ate it in a corner of the room.

Obviously proud of his legacy, Papa ran a hand through his thick black hair. "This entire villa, and much of our country, is run by clean energy. You see, Bobby, solar and wind energy keep our families… and our environment safe." Looking over at Bruno's full plate, Papa added, "I hope one day Bruno will come to work for the company."

Francesca glared at her father. "Bruno *has* a job, Papa."

"Working for the mob," Papa grumbled.

"Bruno does not work for the mob, Papa! He's a salesman for a liquor company."

Undaunted, Papa said, "Where he *persuades* store owners to sell his products."

Francesca said defensively, "Papa, Bruno doesn't bribe or strong-arm anybody."

Bruno added with a wink at me, "Except for that one guy we shot in the restaurant."

Revealing a straight pure white smile, Paolo seemed to enjoy his family's antics.

Not wanting to be left out of the discussion, Nonna held up her St. Mary ceramic napkin holder. "I made this in church." She addressed her family. "When I die I want every one of you to look at this, think of me, and cry."

Paolo and Francesca laughed openly.

Changing the subject, Mama said, "Bobby is in law school."

"That's a wonderful field, Bobby," Papa said, helping himself to more chicken. "The lawyer for our company makes a fortune."

"We have a lawyer working for our liquor company. He got us out of a lot of tough—"

Francesca's elbow stifled Bruno's remark.

Speaking with my mouth full of delicious food, I said, "I brought my books along with me so I don't miss any study time."

Mama said, "Why don't you show Bobby around the island, Paolo?"

"I have plans to go to the gym, then meet some people for drinks," Paolo responded with a glance at his watch.

Mama displayed her Italian tenacity. "You can do that anytime, Paolo. Bobby will only be here for a week. Your sister can't do it since she has to work."

Nonna took a second helping of pasta. "You go out too much with your friends, Paolo. You should settle down and get married."

Teasing her, Paolo replied, "Maybe I will move in with one of my friends, Nonna."

With a hand to her heart, Nonna replied, "A boy should leave home in the hands of his wife or in a coffin!"

Not wanting to impose, I said, "Mama, Paolo doesn't have to—"

"It's all settled, Bobby. Paolo will be your guide," Mama said, wiping her mouth with her silk napkin.

"When does the tour start?" Paolo asked, his mouth full of smirk.

Mama replied, "How about after lunch?"

Paolo pushed away his plate and glared at his mother. "Your wish is my command."

After eating more food than I thought possible and receiving kisses on my cheeks from each of my Italian relatives (except Paolo), I excused myself and went upstairs to my room. Smiling at the antics of my quaint Italian relatives, I realized it was time to get to my studies, so I gathered my law books from my suitcase, then headed back downstairs.

I found an empty powder-blue sitting room and sat on a high-backed chair next to a blue-tiled fireplace, then opened my books on my lap. After a few minutes had passed, I looked up and found Paolo leaning on the fireplace mantel. He was wearing a stylish purple shirt and gray pants—both skintight.

"Why are you studying?" he asked in English.

The books slipped and hit the orange-and blue-tiled floor as I replied. "I take my bar exams this summer."

He turned up his full upper lip. "It is December."

"There's a lot to study."

Paolo sat on the window seat and looked out over the stunning landscape. "Did you not hear Mama at lunch? I am your designated tour guide."

I rested the books on a sturdy end table. "You don't have to do that. Go out with your friends."

The rays of sun from the window made his sapphire eyes glisten. "Mama does not take no for an answer."

Looking at the dancing flames in the fireplace, I said, "I'm fine here. Thank you anyway, Paolo."

He shrugged his huge shoulders and started to leave. Halting at the doorway, he said, "Why did you come to Capri?"

"To spend Christmas with my Italian relatives."

Paolo pointed to himself, smiled, then held out his hand to me.

Returning his smile, I said, "I don't want to be a burden to you, Paolo. We can tell Mama you took me out."

He leaned back as if he'd been shot. "Lie to Mama? Never!"

I laughed.

Paolo held out his hand again. It was smooth and strong. I couldn't resist taking it. Paolo pulled me up to stand next to him. He smelled of clean sea air. I grabbed my books, and we went upstairs to unload them and put on our jackets. Then I followed Paolo to a courtyard next to the villa, where we stopped next to a motor scooter.

Two helmets rested on the seat. Paolo placed one over his thick, wavy hair, then handed me its companion. When I couldn't figure out how to fasten it, Paolo did it for me, like a mother putting a snow hat on a toddler. Then Paolo instructed me to climb on the scooter behind him, and he took off.

As we sped down the rural road, I held on to the back of the scooter, looked out at the amazing view, and shivered from the cool air.

Paolo called out, "Put your hands in my jacket pockets."

Obeying Paolo's orders, I enjoyed the warmth of the leather fabric and the touch of Paolo's abdominal muscles against my hands.

Like most drivers in Italy, Paolo sped along the windy roads. When we reached a zigzag or a turn in the road, I held on tighter.

Paolo shouted, "Do not worry, cousin. You are safe in my hands."

Somehow I knew that was true.

When we arrived at Via Krupp in the southern part of the island, Paolo parked his scooter in a parking area. We walked through what Paolo called, "the villas of the rich and famous," underscored by the sparkling turquoise sea below, which perfectly matched Paolo's eyes.

"What do you do in America besides study law, cousin?" Paolo asked with a teasing grin.

"Spend time with my family, much like you," I responded.

"What about your friends?"

"They're in law school like me and don't have a great deal of time for friendship."

His red lips formed an adorable pout. "That is a shame."

"According to Nonna, you spend too much time with your friends."

"According to Nonna, I should never leave the house."

As we entered the cobblestone walkway of the Augustus Gardens, we passed array after array of beautiful flowers. Paolo explained there were nine hundred different species of vegetation on the island.

"Even in the winter I can smell the delicious scents," I said, inhaling.

"It never gets really cold here, even in winter."

"Why is that?"

He pinched my chin. "Because Italians have warm hearts, cousin."

After walking over a stone bridge, we sat on a bench looking out over the white Faraglioni rocks, perched majestically in the twinkling azure sea.

"This is the most beautiful sight I have ever seen!"

He smiled. "Better than your law books?"

Returning the smile, I answered, "*Much* better."

"You look relaxed now. Not like when you arrived at our door."

I did a double take. "You saw my arrival?"

Paolo's dimples appeared. "Our villa has windows, cousin. I like to look out at the beautiful surroundings."

He walked on, and I followed.

"How come so many of these statues depict muscular, naked men?"

"The artists obviously had good taste."

"As do the art lovers in Italy. Art isn't censored here like it is in parts of the US."

Paolo laughed. "We only censor people, not art."

I took in the gorgeous panorama. "Thank you for being my guide today. Everything is so beautiful. I'm sorry Mama twisted your arm, but I have to admit, I'm glad she did."

He winked at me. "Mama is always right, cousin."

As we walked back to Paolo's scooter, I said, "I'm sorry if I took you away from your friends."

He responded, "My friends will wait."

When we returned to the scooter, Paolo again fastened my helmet and his, and we were off to the next location. If it was scientifically possible, Paolo drove even faster. With each twist and turn in the road, I clung onto him tighter. He smiled back at me, enjoying my reliance on him.

Upon arriving at Marina Piccola, a gorgeous white sand beach surrounded by artistic white stone formations, I noticed Paolo's sapphire eyes again perfectly matched the color of the water. After hanging his jacket on the scooter, Paolo kicked off his loafers, then unbuttoned his shirt, revealing perfectly sculpted shoulder, pectoral, abdominal, and back muscles. Then he unbuttoned his pants and displayed mountainous thigh and calf muscles and an incredibly long and thick uncircumcised penis. Paolo ran toward the water and called out over his shoulder, "Join me, cousin."

I shouted after him, "It's only fifty-five degrees!"

Paolo turned toward me and unleashed an intoxicating grin. "But the sun is shining, and we are the only two people on the beach." He jumped into the water, came up to the surface, then called out with a twinkle in his eyes, "I am your guide, cousin. Let me guide you."

With Paolo frolicking in the water, I threw caution to the wind (the cold wind), stripped off my clothes, ran across the white sandy beach, dove into the water, and swam to Paolo.

Paolo greeted me with a splash of water, which landed across my chest. I splashed back, and Paolo said, "Ah, so my American cousin has some spunk."

I sent a splash of water to Paolo's face, and he dove on top of me in an attempt to hold my head under the water. After swimming under his legs, I lifted Paolo up onto my shoulders and flipped him backward into the water. Laughing in delight, Paolo did the same to me, and we wrestled and splashed in the sea. Then Paolo wrapped his strong arms around me and pinned my arms behind my back. As our bodies connected, Paolo's firm, mountainous chest pressed against mine, and his raging erection brushed against my thigh. My pulsing erection rubbed against his eight-pack abdominal muscles. We froze, staring into each other's eyes, experiencing the heat and comfort of each other's bodies. Suddenly Paolo released my arms as if they were on fire, and he swam back to shore. Not quite sure what had happened, I swam after him.

When we got to his scooter, Paolo snapped open a side compartment, pulled out a towel, dried himself, then threw the towel to me. By the time I was dry, Paolo was dressed and waiting on his scooter. I dressed quickly and we were off.

Paolo drove us to a coastal hiking path of seventeen kilometers that looked out over the twinkling turquoise sea toward the Faraglioni. After Paolo parked the scooter, we walked for a while, until I finally broke the silence.

"I'm sorry if I offended you at the beach, Paolo."

"You did not offend me, cousin."

"Then why did you run away from me?"

"We are what we are. It is as simple as that."

"I don't understand."

Paolo looked up at the cottony clouds. "Do you have a boyfriend in the States?"

Shaking my head no, I noticed my red hair was frizzier than usual.

A line formed on Paolo's smooth forehead. "Why not?"

"I guess I've been busy studying. How about you? Do you have… anyone?"

He smiled. "I have had many boyfriends, cousin."

"Oh."

He looked at me. "Does that shock you?"

"No."

"Do you think less of your Italian cousin?"

"No."

"Are we back to yes-and-no answers?"

I smiled. "Were any of your boyfriends serious?"

"Not for me."

"How come?"

"It is not my way."

I searched his handsome face. "Do you have a boyfriend now?"

He smirked. "I think I like the yes-and-no conversation better."

We continued walking, then rested on a low stone wall, enjoying the captivating views and salty sea breeze.

Changing the subject, I said, "I like your family."

"They like you too, especially Pino," Paolo responded, revealing a sexy dimple over his right cheek.

I stretched out my leg muscles from all the walking. "Kudos to your family business."

"I don't understand that word, 'kudos.'"

"It means congratulations."

"What for?"

"Wind and solar power save the environment… and many people's lives too."

"If you say so."

"It's been harder to convert to clean energy in the US, due to wealthy oil and coal companies supporting conservative political candidates."

Paolo ran a thick hand through his luxurious hair, and the sun lit up his sienna-colored highlights like a halo. "I do not follow politics in Italy or in the US."

I felt guilty for taking time away from my law books, but at the same time I didn't care. "Do you like working in the warehouse?"

He shrugged. "It is okay."

"What do you do there?"

"Move boxes."

"Is there a different job you'd like to do at your family's company?"

"Not really."

"Aren't you interested in harnessing clean energy?"

He batted his long eyelashes. "I have my own energy to harness." Then he added, "I leave the family business to Papa and Francesca."

"Does that disappoint your family?"

"They are disappointed in many things about me," he said with a melancholy smile.

After filling my lungs with the crisp sea air, I said, "Francesca said you are an artist. What do you draw?"

"Silly pictures."

"Of what?"

"Nothing important."

"Then why did Francesca mention them?"

"Why does Francesca do anything?"

"Please tell me, Paolo."

Paolo sighed, as if appeasing a small child. "They are designs… for men's clothing."

"Given your amazing wardrobe, I'm not surprised you're into men's clothing."

He grinned seductively. "Both on and off."

I smiled. "Can I see your designs sometime?"

"They are not for show. Just for fun. What is it you say in America? It is my… hobby." Rising, he reached out his hand to help me up, and we were back on our walk.

"It's interesting how different each generation is in your family."

Paolo nodded. "Nonna and Nonno live in the past when the family was rich and powerful. Mama and Papa exist in a fake reality, where everyone in the family is perfect. Francesca is very much like Papa—tough and determined."

"And who are you like?"

He winked. "I'm like me."

"Does your family expect you to marry and have children one day?"

Paolo laughed. "Nonna talks about nothing else, except her funeral. Mama knows better."

"She knows—?"

"Everybody knows except Nonno and Nonna."

"How come?"

"They wouldn't understand."

"Are you sure?"

"I'm sure."

"And the rest of your family is okay with it?"

"We don't talk about it."

"Not even when you go out on dates?"

Paolo laughed. "They don't know about my 'dates.'"

"Why not?"

"Because my 'dates' aren't that important." Eager to get off the hot seat, Paolo asked, "How about your family in America?" He pinched my cheek. "Do they know their little law student likes boys?"

I felt relaxed and light-headed under the warm rays of the sun. "My mother is the president of our local chapter of PFLAG."

"What is PFLAG?"

"Parents and Friends of Lesbians and Gays."

He laughed. "We don't have such things in Italy. We all just do what we do, then put money in the collection plate on Sunday."

"That sounds dishonest."

"We lie to the priest and the priest lies too. So we are even."

I stopped walking. "Doesn't it bother you that Italy is practically the only country in Europe where same-sex civil marriage is illegal?"

"No."

"Why not?"

"I have no plans to get married."

"How come?"

"Why should I get married? To have a marriage like Mama and Papa's, where he puts girlfriends up in apartments she pretends she doesn't know about, or like Nonno and Nonna who talk of nothing but family and death, or my sister and her boyfriend who will soon be saddled with kids under threat from mobsters?"

"But don't you want a partner and children to share your life?"

He laughed. "You will make a good lawyer, cousin. You ask many questions."

"As a good lawyer, I'd like to note you didn't answer my last question."

"I think I liked you better when you said 'yes' and 'no.'"

Having passed a number of opposite-sex couples on our walk, I was pleasantly surprised to see two men walking by us arm in arm. "Are those two men lovers?"

Paolo smiled. "Our culture is different from yours, cousin. Italian men kiss each other on the cheek, walk arm in arm, put their arms around one another. It is a sign of friendship." He put his hand on my shoulder. "It is a good thing… for people like us."

Paolo put his arm through mine, and we continued our walk.

I enjoyed the feeling of Paolo's high-peaked bicep against my arm. "Did you go to college, Paolo?"

"Of course."

"What did you study?"

"Not much."

"How did you graduate?"

"By majoring in art… and flirting with the teachers."

"Didn't it bother you… spending all that money and not learning anything?"

"It wasn't my money, and I learned a lot."

"What did you learn?"

"That my cousin from America asks too many questions."

He pinched my side, and I giggled. Delighted at finding my sensitive spot, Paolo tickled the sides of my stomach, and we both laughed uproariously.

By the time we got back to the scooter, the sky had turned gray.

"Is it going to rain?" I asked, putting on my helmet (no longer needing Paolo's help).

"It gets dark early in the winter, cousin."

"So I guess it's back to the villa."

As we climbed onto the scooter, Paolo said, "No, cousin. Nighttime is when Capri comes alive. Hold on and get ready for a wild ride. The tour has just begun."

Paolo sped southwest to Faro di Punta Carena, a beautiful wavy beach surrounding a little bay overlooked by a lighthouse guarding the Tyrrhenian Sea. After reaching into the scooter's side compartment, Paolo pocketed a bottle full of yellow liquid and led me up to a white ledge overlooking the sea. As we sat on a grassy knoll, the gray-blue sky around us suddenly burst forth with ribbons of pink, orange, and purple, like fireworks.

Paolo said, "Just in time for sunset."

"It's so beautiful, Paolo."

We rested with our backs against the rocks. Paolo took a sip from the bottle, then handed it to me. "Try some."

As I drank, my mouth was rewarded with a sweet and sour lemony surge of flavor. "It's delicious. Is it made from lemons?"

He nodded. "It is our most favorite liqueur, Limoncello."

We sat and listened to the crashing waves on one side of us, then watched the peaceful bay on the other, both illuminated by the powerful glow from the ancient lighthouse.

"I come here quite frequently."

Impressed with Paolo's fluent English, I asked, "When did you learn English, Paolo?"

Taking back the bottle of Limoncello for another sip, Paolo responded, "They teach us as children in school."

I said with a smile, "I guess you didn't flirt with the teachers in grade school."

He kissed his fingers, then released the kiss into the night air. "You guessed wrong, cousin."

After another delicious drink from the bottle, I said, "I didn't start studying Italian until I was in high school."

"You learned well too."

"But I didn't flirt with the teachers."

He patted my cheek. "Somehow I knew that, cousin."

A light breeze encircled us, and I buttoned my leather jacket. Paolo put down the bottle and wrapped his arm around me. "Better?"

I nodded and rested my head on his strong shoulder as we gazed at the finale of the gorgeous sunset. Then we stared at each other under the moonlight and our lips grew closer. When they were nearly touching, Paolo abruptly stood and picked up the half-empty Limoncello bottle.

"The sunset is over. I will take you out to dinner."

"Can't we stay here a little while longer?"

"We need to get a table before they are all full."

After a quick ride, we dined al fresco at Ristorante Lido del Faro with its gorgeous views of the sea. I looked out at the lighthouse standing majestically as a beacon to the passing boats. Paolo ordered for us: white wine, marinated salmon and anchovies appetizer, green salad with goat cheese, linguini with prawns, pezzogna fish with tomatoes and herbs, and torta caprese (a moist flour-free dessert made with butter, chocolate, and almonds). Each course was brought out separately, so Paolo and I relished the taste of each delicious dish. When we were eating the garlic-laden pasta course, Paolo asked, "Do your dates back in America take you to such nice places?"

I choked on a prawn. "I told you I don't date much, Paolo."

Paolo took a sip of wine, rolled it around in his mouth, then swallowed. "Doesn't your flag mother want you to have a boyfriend for the cause?"

"That's PFLAG, and as a matter of fact she does."

He looked me over. "Don't the boys in America like your adorable white body, red hair, and green eyes... the colors of the Italian flag?"

Blushing, I responded, "I dated a few guys back in college and one later on in law school, but nothing stuck."

He smirked. "I bet things got sticky."

"Actually, they didn't."

Paolo flung his wide back against his chair. "Cousin! Do you mean you have never... you are a virgin?"

Hoping nobody else in the restaurant spoke English, I responded softly, "That's me. A twenty-three-year-old virgin."

The candlelight illuminated the look of shock and disbelief on his handsome face. "We are *very* different, cousin."

Turning the table (not literally), I said, "But you said you don't want a partner."

He sounded like a college professor giving a lecture. "This dinner is delicious, is it not?"

"Absolutely," I replied, grateful the conversation was no longer about my virginity.

Motioning to my plate, he asked, "But would you want to eat this *same* dinner every night for the rest of your life?"

Given the mouthwatering meal, I had to take a moment to think. "I guess not."

"Ah!" He raised his palms to the sky like a magician at the end of an illusion. "That is how I feel about the boys on Capri."

I dug into the fish course with its fragrant herbs, rich extra virgin olive oil, and sweet tomato topping. "But food and sex are two different things."

"Not for me. Both are a necessary but *temporary* pleasure." He squeezed my knee. "You should try it some time, cousin."

Looking at Paolo's amorous grin, I adjusted my napkin to fully cover my lap.

For the rest of our dinner we discussed the wonderful food and breathtaking environment. With Paolo's talk about numerous boyfriends, I was surprised he never once looked at anyone in the crowded restaurant and instead focused solely on me.

After finishing our amazingly rich desserts, I offered to pay the bill. Paolo insisted on treating me, noting Mama had given him the money before we left the villa.

When we arrived back at the villa, Paolo and I walked up to the second floor and stopped at the doorway to my room.

Brushing his strong fingers through his thick dark hair, Paolo said, "I hope you had a better time sightseeing than studying."

"Capri is phenomenal! Thank you for showing me your amazing island, Paolo."

Paolo looked like a little boy starved for approval. "Did you really like it, Bobby?"

"I really liked it."

We were only inches apart. I could feel his warm breath caressing my cheeks, and his scent of white sand and foamy waves infiltrated my nostrils. Our eyes met, and we shared a warm, comforting smile.

"Pleasant dreams, cousin." Paolo kissed each of my cheeks and turned away.

To my amazement, I reached up, held him by the side of his face, and kissed him on the lips.

Paolo tottered backward, as if he'd had too much to drink. "Why did you do that?"

"I wanted to."

"Do not do that again."

"But—"

"Good night, cousin." Paolo walked down the hall and closed his bedroom door.

I couldn't sleep that night due to visions of Paolo dancing in my head. Tossing and turning in bed, all I could think about was my enigmatic cousin. One moment he seemed like a worldly adventurer and the next a lost boy. He was passionate but apathetic. Strong but languid. He seemed to have all the answers except what to do with his life. He was attentive and affectionate with me, but when I responded he became disinterested and distant.

I turned on the Tiffany lamp next to my bed and opened one of my law books. After reading the same sentence three times, I closed the book. Staring into space, I saw Paolo's muscular body, thick penis, olive skin, haunting eyes, and pouting lips in front of me. Lying back in bed with the sheet over my head, I realized what I had been afraid to admit. I was falling in love with my cousin. I jumped out of the bed in my birthday suit, opened the wardrobe, and put on my robe. Pacing the room, I asked myself if being in love with Paolo was incest. What would my family think? What would

Paolo's family say if I told them? I would no doubt be thrown into the funicular and sent back to Philly pronto.

When morning finally came, I lay in bed awake and watched my bedroom door open. Paolo entered and stood next to my bed wearing a tantalizing silk shirt that matched his eyes and skintight jeans. Looking like a child on Christmas morning, Paolo tousled my hair. "Hurry up and get dressed, cousin. I will meet you at my scooter." And he was gone.

After hurriedly washing and dressing, I raced down the stairs and leaped onto Paolo's scooter. He took off as I fastened my helmet. Still groggy from my sleepless night, I slipped my hands into Paolo's coat pockets, rested my head on his strapping back, and closed my eyes as he sped down the road.

When we arrived at Piazza Vittoria in Via Caposcuro, Paolo took a bag from the scooter's compartment and led me to a chairlift, which hoisted us into the sky. With my legs dangling over the dark Tyrrhenian Sea, I felt as if I were flying through a black hole. I waved to Paolo in the seat behind me, and he smiled like a proud parent at an amusement park.

When we arrived at Mt. Solaro, we stepped off the chairlifts. Paolo looked down at the homes nestled on layers of rocks. "This is the highest point on the Isle of Capri, five hundred and eighty-nine meters above sea level."

"All I see in front of me is a thick blanket of fog. Is that because it's been warm for winter?"

"Wait and watch."

Paolo sat me down next to him on a flat section of the mountain, then nudged my side with his elbow and pointed to the fog. As if he was Moses parting the Red Sea, Paolo looked triumphant as the sun came up and the wind blew the vapors of fog upward, crowning the clouds and revealing stunning views of the Bay of Naples, the Amalfi Coast, and the mountains of Calabria in the distance. As we looked out over the turquoise water, white mountains, and azure sky, I felt like I was in heaven.

I pressed my shoulder against his. "It's sheer magic, Paolo! And pretty amazing science."

"We call it Acchiappanuvole, the cloud catcher."

I leaned back and took in the scent of ripe lemons. "What an amazing smell!" I scanned the mountaintop. "I don't see any lemon trees up here."

He pointed like a daycare teacher with a color chart. "That is the erba cetra. It grows wild all over Mt. Solaro."

Paolo opened the bag, and we shared a breakfast of soft cheese, crusty bread, crunchy apples, and sweet orange juice as we enjoyed the view.

Thinking back to the hallway the night before, I said, "I apologize for kissing you last night."

"Why would you do that?"

"Apologize or kiss you?"

"Both."

"I feel comfortable with you, Paolo."

"I feel comfortable with you too, which is a good thing since we are cousins."

After finishing breakfast we walked around Mt. Solaro. Upon reaching the statue of Caesar Augustus, Paolo explained that the Italian hero was the first person to land on Capri Island.

"Augustus is like your Christopher Columbus, cousin."

I wondered if Augustus had killed off the natives already living there before claiming to have discovered Capri. Looking at the statue's rippling muscles, wavy hair, and piercing eyes, I heard myself say, "He reminds me of you."

Paolo did a double take. "I think I am better looking."

"And obviously more modest."

Sitting on a bench near the statue, Paolo explained, "Italians do not believe in modesty. As you say in the States, we tell it like we see it." He rested back on the bench, and his pectoral muscles swelled.

I sat next to him. "How do you see it, Paolo?"

"What?"

"My visit so far."

"I see my cousin from America, a bookworm who I complained to Mama would cramp my style." He pinched my nose affectionately. "But who turned out to be a young man with *many* surprises."

I followed Paolo down a long stone walkway to a quaint stone country chapel.

"This is Santa Maria a Cetrella, cousin."

"It's beautiful, Paolo, and so old!"

He nodded. "Unlike in the States, we don't knock anything down in Italy. We renovate to savor our history." He pinched my cheek. "And to share it with tourists."

Paolo opened the front gate, and we walked through a well-kept garden into the white doorway of the little church. The inside was illuminated by candlelight, giving the chapel an amber glow. Kneeling at one of the two small altars, Paolo crossed himself and prayed silently. When he was finished, I followed him to the chapel's outdoor balcony, and we looked out at the Faraglioni.

"This old chapel is run by the Franciscan friars," Paolo explained.

"Don't they take a vow of chastity and silence?"

"Yes, so if you stop talking, you can enter their order," Paolo said with a wink.

"*You* couldn't."

"Ah, so my American cousin has a sense of humor." Paolo chased me around the balcony amid fits of laughter. Once I was trapped against the railing, he pressed his strong body against mine and said with a devilish grin, "We all break a vow here or there, cousin."

I wrapped my arms around his wide neck and returned the grin. "I wonder if any of the monks are cousins?"

His gaze searched mine, and we shared a deep, passionate kiss.

Paolo stepped away as if my lips were on fire. "We should get back. Mama will be serving lunch."

"Paolo."

He stopped without looking at me. "What is it?"

"Is it because we're cousins?"

"What?"

"Is that why you pull away from me every time we… whenever we become intimate?"

"Bobby, this is not an obstacle in my country. It is done by many couples."

"Then why do you push me away? Don't you like me? Are you still showing me around out of duty to your family?"

He looked at me with sad eyes. "If only it were that simple." Then he walked away.

We didn't speak during the walk back to the motor scooter or on the ride back to the villa.

Since Papa, Francesca, and Bruno were at work, Paolo and I ate lunch at the villa with Mama and Nonna.

The kitchen was a warm banana color and housed a huge oven, two large sinks, an industrial-size refrigerator, and a massive cutting station. Sitting at the head of the long marble table, Mama passed me a huge platter of pasta, chicken, and peas. "Did you enjoy your sightseeing, Bobby?"

"Everything on the island is so beautiful," I replied, serving my lunch on a china plate with a delicate rose and leaf pattern.

Mama poured wine into our crystal glasses. "Was Paolo a good guide?"

"The best," I said with a smile at Paolo.

Nonna asked, "Did you two meet any nice girls?"

Paolo paid attention to his lunch.

"They were sightseeing, Nonna," said Mama. Then she turned to Paolo. "What plans do you have for your cousin this afternoon, Paolo?"

I said, "Paolo doesn't have to—"

"I am going to the gym," Paolo replied. He looked me up and down. "Care to join me, cousin?"

After all the rich food I had eaten on my trip, I was happy to join Paolo at his gym. Watching my cousin work out in a tank top and shorts, I again was taken with his perfectly sculpted body and focused discipline. As he used hand weights to work his biceps and triceps, I sat on a universal gym machine pulling down a bar for a shoulder exercise.

Resting a moment between repetitions, Paolo placed the weights at his feet and turned to me. "You should use hand weights."

I turned to face him, and the bar hit me in the head. "What's wrong with machines?"

"Your muscles do not get the same intense workout."

I joined him at the weight rack.

"And use less weight with more repetitions at a slower pace."

I picked up the weights and began an exercise for my shoulders. "How do you know so much about working out?"

He winked at me. "I know about men's bodies."

After working out with the hand weights, Paolo and I headed for the locker room. As we changed into our bathing suits, I again marveled at his perfect V-shaped back, firm, round buttocks, and long, thick uncircumcised tool.

When we arrived at the swimming pool, I impressed Paolo with an acrobatic dive off the diving board. Paolo jumped into the water like a seal at an amusement park, and we met in the center of the pool.

"You continue to surprise me, cousin."

"Here's another surprise."

I dove under the water and tickled Paolo's thighs. He tickled my stomach. Laughing hysterically, he swam after me to the edge of the pool. Once I leaped out of the water, Paolo chased me back to the empty locker room. When we arrived at our lockers, Paolo pulled down my trunks and I pulled down his. As we stared at each other's naked bodies, our laughter faded and our eyes met.

Paolo threw a towel at me. "Dry off and get changed, cousin. It is time to go back home."

Again we didn't speak during the motor scooter ride back to the villa. When I returned to my room, I changed into a purple sweater and gray slacks and met Pablo in the villa's downstairs hallway. He was wearing a delectable ribbed white sweater and tight black pants.

"Do you have a dinner date tonight, Paolo?"

"Yes, cousin."

"With who?"

"With you."

"But what about dinner with the family?"

"They won't miss us."

After another speed-chaser ride on Paolo's motor scooter, we arrived at Ristorante Da Gioia, a beautiful restaurant over the sea. A waiter, who definitely noticed Paolo's assets, sat us at a corner table. Paying no attention to our server, Paolo ordered (again for both of us) white wine, Caprese salad, fisherman's risotto, Capri lobster, and tiramisu. Paolo was unusually quiet during dinner, deep in thought about something. When the bill came, he again insisted upon paying it, courtesy of Mama.

To walk off our delicious but filling dinner, Paolo led the way to the Piazzetta, the main walkway of Capri, which boasted festively lit stores, hotels, restaurants, bars, and nightclubs. When we arrived at Anema e Core (Soul and Heart), Paolo opened the large front door and escorted me inside. After ordering Limoncellos for us at the bar, Paolo walked me to a table in the back of the noisy, dark club.

"I'm surprised to see same-gender couples dancing alongside opposite-sex couples. Does this happen in every club in Italy?"

He shook his head no. "Anema e Core is a new and youth-oriented club on Capri."

As we sat at our table drinking and listening to the music, I was again amazed at how Paolo's focus and attention were solely on me.

During a lull in the music, a tall blond young man wearing a pink shirt and black blazer came over to our table. The handsome man winked at Paolo and said in Italian, "Hi, Paolo. It's nice to see you again."

Paolo looked up at the man and nodded.

"I haven't seen you lately. Where have you been?" the man asked with a flex of his broad shoulders.

Not looking at him, Paolo responded in Italian, "Busy."

Motioning toward me, the man said with a sneer, "So I see."

As the music resumed, the blond man said near Paolo's ear, "Let's dance."

Paolo took my hand, lifted me off my chair, and led me to the dance floor, calling out over his shoulder, "I have another partner."

Once on the dance floor, I said, "I don't know how to dance."

"I will teach you, cousin."

Paolo put his strong arms around me. Since it was a slow song and Paolo was such a confident dancer, it was relatively easy, even for me, to follow him. As the song continued, I rested my head on Paolo's large chest, and he squeezed his arms around me. I felt protected and peaceful.

The song ended and the next song began. I looked up and noticed Paolo's blond friend dancing with another man. "Was he your boyfriend?"

"Yes." Paolo placed my head back on his chest.

Looking up again, I asked, "Did you love him?"

"No."

"Now who's answering questions with only 'yes' and 'no'?"

He laughed.

Searching his handsome face, I asked, "Have you broken many hearts?"

Paolo put his strong hands on my shoulders. "The boys I... see are for fun. They do not love me. I do not love them. I do not even like most of them."

We stopped dancing. "Why would you want to be with someone you don't like?"

A tiny crease appeared between his thick eyebrows. "So nobody gets hurt."

We continued dancing. When the song ended, I looked up at Paolo. Just as our lips were about to touch, he said in my ear, "It is time to go."

While walking to Paolo's scooter, it suddenly dawned on me. "Whenever we become intimate, you push me away because you like me."

He stopped. "Of course I like you. You are my cousin."

I shook my head. "You *more* than like me. You have feelings for me. That's why you keep running away from me."

Rubbing his strong hand over his handsome face, Paolo said, "You do not understand."

"No, Paolo, I think I finally *do* understand. To avoid any… discomfort or possible hurt, you cut off your emotions. You push away anyone you care about… or anyone who cares about you, so there's no risk of rejection." I tried to stop talking, but my mouth was like a runaway train. "It's the same reason you don't show anyone your sketches… or admit your clothing designs are important to you."

He laughed it off. "I thought you wanted to be a lawyer, not a psychiatrist."

"I've been going crazy, Paolo, thinking it was me, but it's *you*!"

Messing my hair, he said, "Spoken by the virgin from America."

I grasped his shoulder. "I may not be experienced like you, Paolo, but I'm not afraid to care about somebody else. Even animals do it. But you won't let anyone else inside." My heart sank down into my chest. "And that is so sad for you… and for anyone who might love you."

He looked at me as if for the first time. "Nobody loves me, Bobby."

"I don't believe that."

"Believe it, cousin."

"Somebody could love you. You just have to be willing to risk it. It might end up with hurt and pain, but it might… not. It could be amazing. Don't you think it's time to give yourself the chance to find out?"

"Who would love me?"

I heard myself say, "I would. I do."

He laughed. "My American cousin is playing games with me again."

"No, I'm not, Paolo. I'm serious. And I think you are too."

We stared into each other's eyes. Suddenly Paolo drew my body to his.

"Do you know what I have been going through since you got here? The feelings I have had… emotions I have never experienced before? They scare the life out of me."

"I'm frightened too, Paolo. But don't you think we are worth the risk?" I held his hands in mine. "You said it on the dance floor. 'I will teach you.' Let me teach you how to love and be loved."

Tears brimmed in his beautiful eyes. "I don't know if I can."

"You've shown me so many beautiful things. Let me show you this."

Our lips met. Then they met again. We held on to each other, not wanting to let go. On the drive home, I wrapped my arms around Paolo's waist and kissed the back of his neck.

Upon arriving back at the villa, we continued kissing as we walked up the stairs, entered my bedroom, and closed the door.

Once inside the room, we tore off our clothes and jumped onto the bed. As we lay side by side, we looked into each other's eyes, as if gleaning the courage to embark on the new experience ahead. Paolo kissed my hands, eyes, and cheeks. I kissed his shoulders, pectoral muscles, and biceps. He moaned as I licked and nibbled at his nipples. After I kissed each of his abdominal muscles, I took him inside my mouth, kissing and caressing his foreskin and thick shaft while tickling them with my tongue. Then shifting positions and murmuring, "Fungo bello" (beautiful mushroom), Paolo licked and sucked the head of my penis, making his way down the long shaft. I pulled his face up to mine, and we kissed deeply and passionately.

Finally Paolo asked me softly, "Do you want me?"

I nodded.

After applying protection and lubricant, Paolo gently pulled back my legs, then slowly entered me while kissing and caressing me. Our gazes never broke contact as Paolo slowly and smoothly rocked his hips back and forth. I stroked the enormous muscles on his back as he took me in his hand, matching the rhythm of his thrusts. As we both exploded in ecstasy, Paolo shouted, "Ti adoro" (I adore you), and I whispered in his ear, "I am home."

We slept in each other's arms for a few hours, then woke for an encore lovemaking session even more powerful than the first.

Upon waking in the morning, alone, I washed, then dressed in a long-sleeved green-and-blue-striped polo shirt and jeans. I knocked on Paolo's bedroom door to see if he was ready to go down to breakfast. When I received no answer, noticing the door was slightly ajar, I slowly opened it. Finding the room empty, I spotted a large black portfolio perched next to Paolo's desk. I sat on Paolo's sleigh bed, rested the portfolio on my lap, and opened to the first page. Shocked, I turned from page to page, more delighted with each entry.

I was so engrossed in the portfolio that I barely noticed when Paolo entered the room and stood next to the bed.

Continuing to flip through the portfolio, I said, "These are amazing. They are really wonderful!"

He sat next to me on the bed. "They are just my sketches."

"No, Paolo, they are not just simple sketches. These are terrific men's clothing designs!"

Paolo shrugged his massive shoulders. "I have been doing them since I was a kid."

"I love the colors of the sweaters… and the lines of the shirts and slacks. The styles of the jackets are amazing. I'd buy every one of them." I clasped his arm. "Paolo, you have a real talent!"

"It is what I have always enjoyed doing."

"You should show these to somebody."

Paolo closed the portfolio, then put it next to his desk. "It is not as if Capri is the clothing design capital of the world."

I stood and put my arm around him. "No, but Rome and Paris are."

"I am not bringing my sketches to Rome or Paris, Bobby. The elite designers there will laugh me back to Capri."

As I looked at Paolo's open laptop on his desk, an enticing thought entered my mind. "Do you have these sketches on your laptop?"

"Some of them."

"Can you e-mail them to someone?"

"Sure. Why?"

"You remember I told you my father is a manager at the largest department store in Philly?"

He nodded.

"If he loves your drawings as much as I do, he might show them to some of his contacts."

Paolo nibbled my ear. "You only love my drawings because you love me."

I gently pushed him away. "No, I mean, yes, I love you, but that's not why I think your sketches are wonderful." I kissed the dimple in his chin. "And if my father loves them too, this could lead to a new clothing line. What can we call it…? *Paolo of Capri!*"

Kissing my neck, Paolo said, "You have quite an imagination. You will make a good lawyer."

I held his hands. "This could be a chance to use your amazing talent… while earning a good living."

"I have a job here with my family."

"Let me e-mail the designs to my father and see what he says?"

He thought a moment, then nodded. "All right, Bobby, e-mail them to your father, but I do not expect he will like my sketches."

As we opened Paolo's laptop, I replied, "I don't think he will like them either. I think he will *love* them."

After e-mailing the pictures, then eating breakfast, Paolo drove us on his scooter to the north part of the island to the port of Marina Grande, where he rented a boat to Grotta Azzurra (the Blue Grotto). As Paolo rowed our boat through the tiny portal of the expansive cave, my breath was taken away by the water's brilliant shades of iridescent sapphire and emerald from the sun's reflection on the water in the cove. When we reached a particularly low portion of the cave, we had to lie on our backs in order to pass through. To my surprise, Paolo unzipped his pants, and I quickly followed. As the boat rocked back and forth in the translucent water, shielded by the cave ceiling, we kissed and caressed each other until we both climaxed.

After Paolo drove us back and we had lunch with the family, I went upstairs to phone my father at work.

"Dad, it's me."

"Bobby, are you all right?"

"I'm fine, Dad."

"Thank God. I thought you were kidnapped and calling me for a ransom."

"Mom's relatives are taking good care of me, especially Paolo." I looked down the hallway and noticed Paolo's bedroom door was shut.

"Yeah, I got your e-mail."

"What do you think?"

"I think Paolo's sketches are terrific."

I leaped and punched the air. "Me too."

"He's got a lot of talent."

"Agreed. Can you show them to any of your buyers?"

"I did. Two of them want to meet him and see more sketches."

I did the happy dance in the hallway. "Thanks, Dad. I'll talk to Paolo about visiting us."

"Have you been studying?"

"Not too much."

"Good. Did you call your mother today?"

"I will."

Nonna came out of her bedroom.

"I better go, Dad."

"Bobby?"

"Yes?"

"You like Paolo?"

I felt my face flush. "Yes, Dad."

"I'm glad."

That evening the family gathered in the dining room, where we ate the traditional Christmas Eve dinner of seven fishes and sang Christmas carols.

While the rest of the family drank their cappuccino and liqueurs, Paolo and I raced up to his bedroom and made love on Paolo's bed. I lay on my stomach as Paolo's powerful chest pressed against my back. Kissing my neck and pushing deeper and deeper inside me with his thickness, he reached under my hips, bringing both of us to orgasm.

After our lovemaking session, Paolo and I rested in each other's arms, bathed in the Italian moonlight streaming into the room from Paolo's bedroom window. When the clock on the end table told us it was midnight, Paolo kissed my forehead. "Merry Christmas, Bobby."

I squeezed his strong body even closer to mine. "Merry Christmas, Paolo."

"This is the best Christmas for me."

Playing coy, I asked, "Why is that?"

He slapped my backside. "Because my cousin will be going back to America soon."

After we shared a laugh, I rested my head on his chest and said what my heart felt. "Being with you has made me feel… alive. I know we haven't known each other a long time, but it's as if I finally found the missing part of myself. I don't want to leave you, Paolo."

He kissed the top of my head. "You can visit me during your breaks from school. After you pass your tests, you can practice your law in Italy. You speak very good Italian. And you said that Capri is wonderful and magical."

Smiling from ear to ear, I replied, "Actually, it looks like *you* will be visiting *me*, Paolo. My father has two buyers who like your sketches and want to meet you."

Paolo looked at me pensively.

I kissed his neck. "Don't you want to be with me in America?" I smirked. "According to your sister, it's not too difficult for you to get off work."

Paolo sat up. His handsome face revealed he was lost in thought.

I joined him and rested my head on his shoulder. "What's wrong, Paolo?"

"This is a big change for me, Bobby."

Holding his hand, I said, "Come back with me for a visit. You don't have to make any commitments or plans for the future. Just bring your work—" I kissed his cheek. "—and yourself to Philly and meet my family and my father's clients."

After considering it, he responded, "All right, cousin."

I kissed his cheek. "I love you, Paolo."

"I think you only love my clothes."

"On *and* off." I laughed and lay on top of him. "And Paolo?"

"Yes?"

"When you come to Philly, *I* will show *you* the interesting sights."

Making his way down to the lower part of the bed, he said, "I am counting on that, cousin."

He took me inside his mouth, and we continued our lovemaking far into the night.

CHRISTMAS DAY brought a flurry of activity to the villa as we all hurried to get ready for mass. When I walked down the stairs, I nearly salivated at the sight of Paolo in his pinstriped dark blue three-piece suit, and his face lit up when he saw me in my gray suit and light green shirt. The other family members were equally dressed up, the men and Francesca in designer suits and the other women in fine dresses. As always, Nonno and Nonna wore black.

Mama and Papa herded us all into Papa's luxury black car, and we drove off.

Upon entering the domed church of Santo Stefano in the Piazzetta, I marveled at the baroque architecture, vaulted ceilings, and white marble interior. After we took our seats in a front pew, I listened to the choir sing their melodious hymns, accompanied by a grand pipe organ, while I scanned the beautiful stained glass windows in the church. Then the priest took the pulpit and spoke about the birth of a baby long ago and far away who brought new hope to his occupied land and to the entire world. I thought about that man, traveling with twelve other men, preaching against the judgmental religious and political leaders of his time, eating and socializing with those deemed outcasts as he dared people to love their neighbor as themselves. I couldn't help but wonder how that miraculous message had been transformed by some into a weapon of hate used to persecute so many people, including Paolo and me.

When we returned to the villa, Nonna and Mama went to the kitchen to help Lucia cook Christmas dinner. Nonno took a nap in his bedroom. Papa and Francesca talked business in Papa's study. Paolo went to his bedroom to gather more sketches for our trip to Philly.

Alone in the upstairs hallway, I phoned my family in Philadelphia. With my father ensconced in front of the television watching football and my sisters chasing after their children, I wasn't surprised when my mother answered the phone out of breath.

"Bobby! How's my favorite son?"

"I'm your only son, Mom."

"Are you taking a break from studying?"

I remembered my closed law books. "I'm afraid so."

"Good. How is Italy?"

"Like a dream come true." I meant it. "How are you, Mom?"

"Exhausted! Since nobody helps, I'm doing all the cooking, as usual."

I stifled a laugh.

"Your nieces and nephews will miss you at the kiddy table this year, Bobby."

I was happy not to be dodging food grenades.

"How are my Italian cousins?"

"They're really nice, Mom. Guiseppe's son, Paolo, has been taking me sightseeing all over this beautiful island."

"Are you and Paolo getting along well?"

I smiled. "Very well, Mom. Dad invited Paolo for a visit with us and to meet a couple of Dad's clients at work."

"So I heard. I'm anxious to meet him."

"You'll love Paolo, Mom."

I heard my sisters scream after their kids, "Don't climb up on that!" and "Don't put that fork there!"

Then I heard my father shout, "Touchdown!" He called out to me, "Bobby, I'm looking forward to meeting Paolo."

After I wished everyone a good Christmas, Mom said, "Merry Christmas, my son. Stay close to Paolo. He'll make sure you don't get lost and you come back to us safely."

I swallowed the lump in my throat and hung up the phone.

Christmas dinner at the villa was a bountiful feast, covering the beautifully decorated dining room table with platter after platter of meats, fish, pasta, breads, vegetables, fruit, and elaborate desserts. As usual Pino's head didn't leave my lap until Lucia offered him a ham bone in the kitchen.

When my stomach was about to explode, we all retired into the main sitting room and gathered around one of the three glowing fireplaces. As each member of the Mascobello family presented me with a beautifully wrapped gift, I silently thanked my mother for mailing me a gift for each of my relatives (as well as a green sweater with the price tag clearly visible on the collar for me).

Sitting next to Paolo under the tall tree with the gold ornaments and garland, I was surrounded by my opened gifts of two dress shirts, three dress slacks, a sweater, two pairs of shoes, a laptop, a wristwatch, and a book on renewable energy from the Mascobellos. Finally I anxiously opened my gift from Paolo and gasped with delight at the silver bracelet housing a moonstone gem.

Paolo said in Italian, "In Italy this is your birthstone, cousin." With a knowing smile, he added, "And the color of the water in the Blue Grotto."

"I love it!" I hugged him and whispered in his ear, "And I love you." Trying it on, I asked, "How did you know my size and my birthday?"

Mama smiled warmly from the sofa. "I phoned your mother. She said she will never forget your birthday, because she was in labor for twelve excruciating hours."

I was happy to see my mother's humor translated well into Italian.

After we all laughed, Paolo opened my gift, a plane ticket to Philadelphia. He smiled. "Thank you, Bobby."

Sharing the love seat with his wife, Nonno ran a hand through his gray hair. "Are you going somewhere, grandson?"

Paolo announced to his family, "Bobby has invited me to visit his family in Pennsylvania."

Perched on the window seat with Bruno, Francesca offered her brother a sarcastic smile. "When are you going, and when can I move into your room?"

I answered, "Paolo will leave with me in two days."

Sitting next to Mama on the sofa, Papa asked, "How long will you be gone, son?"

Squirming on the elaborate rug, Paolo responded, "I am not sure, Papa."

Nonna clutched a hand to her heart. "I hope I am alive when you come back home, grandson."

Bruno said to Paolo, "I can hook you up with a guy in the States who owns a chain of liquor stores. He needs someone to visit restaurants and… convince the owners to stock our brands."

"It is good for you to meet our American relatives, Paolo, but what about your job at the company?" Papa asked with a concerned look on his aging face.

Mama patted her husband's arm. "The business won't fold if Paolo takes some time off."

"He has been off all week," Papa responded.

I sat up on my knees, bursting with excitement. "My father thinks he can help Paolo."

"Help Paolo with what?" Papa asked with a side glance at Mama.

"Become a clothing designer in America," I responded, wishing that thought up to the universe.

Papa rose slowly from the sofa. "Paolo has a job here… with his family."

Sitting Papa back down, Mama said, "It is just a little visit, Papa."

"Is this about those pictures Paolo has been drawing since he was a kid?" Francesca asked with a smirk on her overly made up face.

Bruno said with disbelief, "You want to be an artist, Paolo?"

Then he and Francesca shared a laugh.

Nonna said, "The greatest artists in history were Italian. You don't need to go to America to draw pictures, Paolo!"

"Paolo's place is with his family," said Nonno with an arm around his wife.

"I want my grandson at my funeral," Nonna added with a squeeze of her rosary beads.

Trying to deflate the situation, I said, "Paolo has an amazing talent for design. My father has offered to introduce him to his clients at the department store in Philadelphia. They agree Paolo's sketches are quite good."

"And how did these *clients* see Paolo's sketches?" Papa asked.

"I e-mailed them to my father."

Papa's eyes doubled in size. "And what would these clients do for Paolo?"

"The buyers will introduce Paolo to the heads of their companies. This could be an incredible break for Paolo," I explained.

Nonna raised her rosary beads. "And Paolo will move to America. I never thought I would live to see the day when my grandson abandoned his family!" Nonna reached for a lace handkerchief in her bosom and wept into it.

"I forbid it!" shouted Nonno with a raise of his index finger.

Mama slid to the edge of the sofa. "Paolo isn't moving anywhere. He has been invited to visit Bobby and his family in Philadelphia. Bobby's mother is your cousin's daughter, Nonno. Paolo should meet her, and meet Bobby's sisters too. They are his family."

"Bobby's family should visit us *here*," said Papa with a no-nonsense look on his face. "Paolo's sketches are child's play. How can a pipe dream lead to a big job in America?"

Bruno said, like a coach talking to his losing player, "From what I hear, you need brains to make it big in the States."

Francesca asked her father, "With all that I have to do at the company, do I have to hire a replacement for Paolo in the warehouse too?"

"Enough!" With his Italian temper rising along with him, Paolo addressed his family. "I know being a clothing designer is nothing more than a fantasy. And I understand that I don't have the talent... or the brains to make it in America." He looked down at me with eyes brimming with tears. "I am sorry, Bobby." He handed me the plane ticket and walked out of the room.

I excused myself and followed Paolo up the stairs and into his bedroom, where I found him putting his portfolio in his closet.

"Hiding your assets in the closet won't make them disappear, Paolo."

"I do not understand your imagery, Bobby. I am just a stupid stock boy."

I reached for his shoulder. "Why did you let your family put those crazy thoughts into your head?"

He pulled away from me, and the plane ticket landed on the floor. "Nobody is putting thoughts into my head except you."

"Because I care about you."

"They care about me too."

"Paolo, I want what's best for you."

He shook his head. "No, you want what is best for *you*."

"And what's best for me is to be with *you*." I sat on his bed, feeling like a pouting child.

Paolo sat with his arm around me. "I want to be with you, Bobby. You can visit me here any time you like."

"And what about your dream to become a fashion designer?"

"It is just that... a dream," he said, looking out his bedroom window at the fluffy clouds hovering in the blue sky. Then Paolo stood up and reached for his jacket. "Come on, cousin. Let's go for a ride on my scooter to Positano. The views are really beautiful."

"No."

"What?"

I shook my head. "I don't want to do any more sightseeing."

"Fine. Then let's go to the gym."

"I don't want to go to the gym either."

"Then what do you want to do?"

"I want to talk about your future... our future."

"I am done talking, Bobby."

"You told me Italians tell it like they see it. So I'm going to be very Italian right now."

Smirking, he said, "A few days in Italy and you are Italian."

"You're afraid to come with me to Philly, because you think your family may be right about you not having the talent to succeed there." I rose and caressed his cheek. "Please let me help you get over this fear… like I helped you overcome your anxiety about being in a relationship."

He laughed bitterly. "Yes, you were the experienced one, teaching me how to make love."

"Making love and loving are two different things."

"Did you learn that from one of your law books?"

"No, I learned that by being who I am instead of living under the thumb of my family, frightened of my dreams, hiding in clubs with boys I detest!"

"Some people hide in bars. Some people hide in books."

"I'm not the one hiding, Paolo."

"Maybe it is time I hide from you." He started to leave the room.

I felt as if he had punched me in the stomach. "How can you say that?"

"You push me too far."

I came face to face with him. "But what about your family? What they said about you downstairs didn't 'push you too far'?"

"My family is my family."

"And what am *I*?"

Paolo glared at me. "A boy who is going back to America… alone."

I couldn't hold back the tears. "Paolo."

Pain filled his handsome face. "I tried to warn you about getting involved with me. The end result is always the same. Pain and rejection for anyone who loves."

I grabbed his muscular arm. "But it doesn't have to be that way!"

A tear brimmed in his eye. "You are right about *that*, cousin." Paolo left the room.

By the time I got to the end of the hallway, Paolo had gone out the front door. I closed my bedroom door and wept.

Later that night I knocked on Paolo's bedroom door, and there was no answer. After a sleepless night, the morning brought the same scenario. I ate breakfast alone in the kitchen, put on my jacket, and headed for the villa's gardens, where I found Mama under a winter coat and floppy hat, holding pruning shears.

Mama asked, "Did you eat breakfast?"

I nodded, though I hadn't tasted anything I'd eaten. "Thank you again for all the nice Christmas gifts. Christmas dinner was amazing. And the church service was really beautiful."

"Nonna asked the priest to light a candle and say a prayer for you after mass." She smiled. "It cost Nonno two hundred euros."

"Wow, thank you."

"Thank Nonno."

"I will."

Mama looked at me as if seeing me for the first time. "Your eyes match the color of my garden."

"And the feeling in my stomach," I replied, sitting on the stone ledge of a fountain.

"You and Paolo had an argument?" she asked.

"Did you hear us shouting last night?"

She cut a small branch off a lemon tree. "No. I heard Paolo storm down the stairs last night, then again early this morning."

I put the branch in her basket, then said through a tight throat, "I can't believe what I said to him."

She looked at me with narrow eyes, the same color as her son's. "We all say crazy things when the people we care for disappoint us, Bobby. I know all about *that*."

"But I basically called Paolo immature and afraid to succeed."

"Maybe the things you said weren't so crazy after all." She sat next to me on the ledge.

"What can I do to convince Paolo he deserves the chance to do what he loves?"

"Next to *someone* he loves… in America?"

My heart raced faster than Paolo's scooter. "Mama, Paolo and I are just—"

She put her finger over my lips. "Anyone who loves my son, I love too." She sighed. "Though like his father, Paolo can be difficult to love." She patted my knee. "I wonder if Mary had the same problem with Jesus."

Mama and I shared a warm smile.

I searched Mama's beautiful face. "Mama, do you think the Catholic Church leaders are right about…?"

"Boys like you and Paolo?"

I nodded.

"No. God created us all, Bobby, and God doesn't make mistakes. Jesus loved everyone. That's good enough for me." She shrugged. "So I go to mass on Sunday, then live my own life the rest of the week."

Leaning forward with my forearms on my knees, I asked, "When did you know about Paolo?"

"When he was a child. Maybe when he said his first words."

"What were they, 'This is fabulous'?"

She hit my cheek playfully. "There was always something different about Paolo, something special. Your mother says the same thing about you. And she is right."

"You spoke about Paolo and me with my mother?"

Mama nodded. "Quite a few times."

"Do you think it's okay for third cousins, like Paolo and me, to…?"

"I think it's just fine."

She rose and began pruning the brown spots on a green bush.

I followed her. "You are quite liberal on that count here in Italy."

Her eyes glistened in the sun. "Regardless of what is said by the church leadership, most Italians live their own lives and let their neighbors live theirs. We have enough to focus on in our own families." She stopped pruning. "I know all about each member of my family, including my son… and my husband. They are who they are, and I am who I am." She took my hand. "I know my son, Bobby. You are exactly what Paolo needs, and he is what you need. Don't give up on him." She smiled. "As your mother said to me on the telephone, 'What's meant to be is meant to be.'"

As if coming to the end of a mystery story, I asked, "Did you and my mother plan my visit here to meet Paolo, hoping we might—?"

"I'll never tell, Bobby." She winked, then walked to the other side of the garden.

The following day came and went with no word from Paolo. I tried studying and enjoying meals with the Mascobellos, but it was impossible to focus on anything except Paolo, as I played our last conversation over and over in my head.

Rising early the next morning, I dressed and packed, preparing for the journey home. I again knocked on Paolo's bedroom door, and this time the door opened. Paolo stood next to his bed, unshaven, wearing only sweat shorts. Even with his muscles rippling like a Greek god, he looked like a child woken from a nightmare.

"Are you all right?" I asked.

"I have not slept too well lately."

"Join the Sleepless in Capri Club."

Paolo sat on his bed. I sat next to him. "Where have you been? To the clubs?"

He shook his head no and patted down the hair sticking up at the back. "I went driving on my scooter… thinking."

"About what?"

"You know about what."

I couldn't resist taking his hands in mine. "Before I met you, the only thing that mattered to me were my law books. After this trip I realize there is so much more to life than being alone. There are amazingly beautiful places like Capri and passionate, outrageous people like my cousin in Italy. *You* showed me that. And I will always be grateful to you."

"I am not so wonderful, cousin."

"Yes, you are."

He turned away from me, and I moved his face close to mine. "You told me Italians never destroy anything but instead renovate their treasures. Don't you think what we have is worth saving? Don't you… don't *we* deserve a chance?"

He rose and stood at the window. "My place is with my family, Bobby. This is my home."

I wiped my tears with the back of my hand and joined him at the window. "I thought *I* had found a home too… with you."

"You will always live in my heart, Bobby."

He faced me and kissed me deeply. Our tears mixed on our cheeks.

"Paolo, please come with me."

"It is better this way, Bobby."

"Better for whom?"

"Bobby, please, go now."

"I don't want to leave you."

"Please, Bobby. Go… now!"

I backed away on shaky legs. "Good-bye, Paolo. I will never forget you."

When he didn't respond, I said, "Aren't you even going to say good-bye?"

Paolo looked out the window, and I left him.

As I stood in the hallway with my luggage at my feet, my relatives surrounded me.

I said, "Thank you for an amazing visit and for your hospitality."

Nonno kissed my cheeks with tears in his eyes. "My cousin's grandson."

Papa shook my hand. "Have a safe trip back, Bobby. You are always welcome in our home."

"I hope I will be alive the next time you visit," Nonna said, clutching her rosary beads.

Bruno handed me a package to deliver to a friend in Philly, and Francesca said, "Good luck on your bar exams, attorney."

At the doorway Mama kissed my cheeks, then whispered in my ear, "What's meant to be is meant to be, *caro*."

I waved, then walked through the orange double doors and past the gate crowned by the intertwined gold leaves. Closing the gate behind me, I looked back at the white stone villa and thought about Paolo.

During the bus ride, *funiculare*, and boat trip, I was like a spirit, watching myself from above but feeling nothing. In Naples Airport waiting for my flight, I fought back tears, trying to fathom how I would live my life without Paolo. Though we had known each other for a short time, I knew he would always be a part of me.

After boarding the plane, I took my seat and stared aimlessly at the pages of my law book. Feeling a presence in the adjoining seat, I assumed my companion would again be an obese passenger who snored.

"Are you still reading that law book?"

Nearly getting whiplash, I looked over to find Paolo sitting next to me. My heart could have taken the plane into flight. "Paolo!"

"Do you want some company on your trip, cousin?"

I nodded as the tears ran down my face.

"I think it is about time for me to meet my relatives in the States." He placed his laptop under the seat in front of him, then took my hand in his. "Will you introduce me to them?"

I swallowed hard, then said, "Just think of me as your guide, cousin."

We kissed deeply and passionately as the plane took off.

"I'm going home, Paolo."

He squeezed my hand. "Me too."

THE
PERFECT
GIFT

BOBBY
AND PAOLO'S
HOLIDAY
STORIES:
BOOK TWO

JOE COSENTINO

To Fred for everything over all these years, my Italian-American family,
the staff at Dreamspinner Press,
the readers who begged for another Bobby and Paolo novella,
and to everyone seeking the gift of love over the holidays.

Part I
December Grooms

"HI, MOM. What are you doing?"

"Sitting home alone like a dog."

That's Mom's logic. If their house isn't full of people eating and carrying on, she's alone. "Where's Dad?"

"In his den, watching the game on TV as usual."

I'm Bobby McGrath. Since this is my story, I should tell you more about myself. I have frizzy red hair, green eyes, and a swimmer's body, thanks to the pool at my gym. The swimmer's body is thanks to the pool. The red hair and green eyes are courtesy of my dad's side of the family, which my mom calls the Bad Seed. And I passed the bar. I don't mean I'm a recovering alcoholic. I aced my bar exam, and I've been a junior lawyer for nearly a year now.

"Bobby, are you listening to me or thinking about one of your cases?"

"I'm listening, Mom." I sat on the window seat in my Victorian apartment's turret and gazed out at the carolers appropriately dressed in Victorian garb as they sang in front of the department store across the street. That's the department store where my father is manager and plays Santa every December. "How did Dad's physical go with Dr. Sherman?"

"He said Dad's overweight. Like we didn't know. For that we shelled out a thirty-dollar co-pay."

"Did you mention how Dad's been forgetting a few things lately?"

"I told him how your father forgot to take out the garbage, sweep out the garage, and chase the squirrels out of our summerhouse in the backyard."

I couldn't help thinking Dad's memory lapses were intentional.

"Dr. Sherman asked Dad some questions, like Dad's birthdate and our anniversary."

"And?"

"Your father never remembers things like that, so I answered for him."

"Mom, you shouldn't have—"

"Your father's fine, except for an enlarged prostrate."

"That's prostate."

"Don't correct your mother, especially now."

"What's wrong?"

"You know I don't like to burden you with my problems."

"All right. I should get on my laptop to do some research for a—"

"I'm worried about your sister."

"Which one?"

"Both of them."

I took a sip of Lemon Zinger tea and braced myself for a long story.

"They work so hard at their jobs and taking care of the kids, they never see their husbands."

My sisters' know-it-all spouses? "Is that a bad thing?"

"Watch your mouth, mister. I'm your mother. In my day we never disrespected our parents, no matter how wrong they were about everything. And we never took drugs."

"I don't take drugs, Mom; neither does Paolo."

"But plenty of young people today are drug addicts, Bobby. They say they're nervous. If young people are nervous, they should do what I do, and take a Prozac."

As Mom rambled on about the sad state of our youth, I glanced over at the antique cherry coffee table to a framed picture of Paolo and me smiling in front of the Mascobello villa in Capri, Italy. That's where I met Paolo, when I visited my extended family. Don't freak out. Paolo is a very distant cousin. He has dreamy sapphire eyes, wavy chestnut hair, more muscles than a daytime television star, and a little-boy pout that makes me want to take care of him for the rest of his life. Which I do. Since Paolo was quite the playboy in Capri, I had my doubts about our relationship. But we've been living in boyfriend bliss here in Philadelphia, the City of Brotherly Love, for a year now.

"I just hope your sisters don't get divorces."

"Colleen and Roseann are getting divorces?"

"I wish I knew. They've always worked for the Secret Service."

That's Mom's code for people not telling her every detail of their lives.

"Unlike your sisters, you always told me every one of your problems. That's why I have that worry crease between my eyebrows." She whispered as if sharing international secrets, "I suspect Gavin is cheating on Roseann."

"Why do you think that?

"He's in finance."

"Everyone in finance doesn't cheat. You don't cheat on Dad, and you're a bookkeeper."

"For a very reputable sanitation engineering company."

"Yes, a garbage pickup company in Philly is the epitome of top business ethics."

"Will you stop being so smart and listen to me?" Mom paused for dramatic effect. "Gavin won't look me in the eye."

"Maybe he has a vision problem."

"Or maybe he's screwing around with an investor. I wanted to lock him in the basement, shine your father's flashlight on him, and interrogate him, but your father wouldn't let me. And Roseann talks about her personal trainer more than her husband." Mom sighed. "No wonder fifty percent of heterosexual couples get divorced."

"Where did you hear that?"

"At a PFLAG meeting and during the priest's sermon in church."

"Mom, you know when you donate to PFLAG and to the Catholic Church, your money is canceling itself out. PFLAG lobbies for equal rights for LGBT people, and church lobbyists fight for so-called religious freedom laws that take away our rights."

"Stop disrespecting the Pope, Bobby. He wears a beautiful gown. And he has an adorable wave. Plus, he loves Christmas time, just like you."

Dressed in a nightshirt and slippers, I felt the heat from the white marble fireplace. The dancing amber and vermillion flames, flanked by the gold lions on either side, complimented the sunset's radiant shafts of violet, scarlet, and marigold adorned by cottony snowflakes. In the department store windows were holiday scenes of sleigh-riders, children making a snowman, a family opening gifts at the tree. Did the husband and wife mannequins appear angry with each other? Were they happily married, or faking it for the sake of the smiling kids and expensive-looking home? "Thankfully Colleen and Roseann won't argue with the kids here. They learned that from your father and me."

"You and Dad argued when we were kids?"

"Never in front of you. But after you went to sleep, we had a few good ones."

It was difficult for me to imagine my mellow father arguing about anything.

As if reading my mind, Mom said, "I know you think I provoked him, but your father has a wild streak, Bobby." She giggled. "It's one of the things I like about him. But we don't argue too much. I don't understand all this talk about women's rights. Your father may put up a fuss from time to time, but in the end, he does everything I tell him to do."

"Are you doing all the cooking again this year for Christmas?"

"Of course. Who else is going to do it?"

"Roseann, Colleen, me—"

"Please. We wouldn't eat until Easter. I'll make everything as usual, from the antipasto to the stracciatella to the fettucine, manicotti, lasagna, eggplant parmigiana, mussels in clam sauce, chicken marsala, chicken cacciatore, chicken picatta—"

"Mom, you make too much."

"But everyone eats it. Still, it takes a toll on me. I may look like a young woman, but I'm not. One day you'll find me lying on the kitchen floor, dead." She sighed. "Then you'll all eat at my funeral. Remember I want to be buried in a mausoleum, not underground. I'm claustrophobic."

In order to avoid a lengthy story about how mom accidentally locked herself in a closet as a girl—therefore understanding first-hand the struggle of LGBT people everywhere—I focused the conversation back on Christmas day. "Mom, this year do Paolo and I have to sit at the kiddie table?"

"Of course. If you're not married, you're a kid."

"Speaking of that—"

"Are you and Paolo engaged!"

"No."

She groaned. "Oh."

"Not yet."

I peeked at the clock tower across the street and wondered when Paolo would get home from his fashion design firm. "Since we've both been working so hard, and we have some time off coming up for the holidays, I thought maybe… I'd ask him tonight."

Mom cooed. "What a wonderful holiday gift!" Her voice hardened. "Is your hair combed?"

"Yes, why?"

"What are you wearing?"

"My nightshirt."

"Ah! Put on your powder-blue shirt and tight jeans."

"Mom, Paolo and I have been living together for a year. We don't need to impress each other."

She sighed. "Only a year and the romance has gone?"

Our brushed nickel doorknob turned and the cherry front door separated from the swirled gold molding around it.

"Mom, I have to go."

"Call me tomorrow at work. Or afterward at the hairdresser's."

Images of Mom's teased-out, stiffly sprayed, dyed chocolate-brown hair had me wincing.

She said, "I'm getting a haircut, dye, and blow job."

"Enjoy!" I put down my phone.

Paolo hung up his coat and scarf. He looked good enough to eat in his apple-colored dress shirt and black dress slacks, both of which sculpted his muscles perfectly. The sapphire stone in his gold ring—handed down from his grandfather in Italy—matched his gorgeous eyes. Since he had run up the stairs, beads of sweat lined his olive-colored skin. He placed his laptop on our coffee table, walked by our white Christmas tree laden with gold ornaments, and sat next to me on the window seat. I felt as if in a lemon orchard as he rested his strong arm around me, kissed my cheek, and gently moved my head onto his shoulder.

"Rough day?" I asked.

"And evening. Edgar and his wife were in divorce court. As the junior designer, I had to finish all the new sketches for a client's summer sportswear line that is due tomorrow."

"Didn't your boss already get a divorce?"

"That was from his second wife. This is wife number three." He yawned. "And my sister called me from Italy. She and her boyfriend broke up."

"Francesca and Bruno are over?"

He nodded.

"Why?"

"She caught him in bed when he was in the hospital, getting knee surgery."

"Shouldn't he be in bed in the hospital?"

"Sure, but not with the anesthesiologist."

I sighed.

Paolo drew me in closer and buried his Roman nose in the fold of my neck. His Italian accent made the tiny hairs on my arms stand on end as he whispered in my ear, "What is it?"

"My mom and dad had a spat. And she's worried about my sisters' marriages because they never see their husbands, which I still contend isn't a bad thing."

His full lips parted, revealing a solid white smile. "That's why we do things differently in Italy."

I pulled away. "What do you mean?"

"Some men marry a woman to raise a family. While she feeds the babies, he goes out and feeds his passions. Then he confesses his sins to the priest, tosses some euros into the church collection plate, and the cycle begins again the following week."

"Is that the kind of marriage you want?"

"Of course not." His warm, thick hands enveloped mine, and I was home. "I want to spend my life with my distant cousin who wears a nightshirt and drinks strange tea."

That reminded me. "There's leftover dinner for you in the refrigerator."

"I know. I made it this morning while you were still sleeping."

I kissed his thick neck. "The chicken Florentine and Caesar salad were amazing."

"Like you." He brought me in for a long, wet kiss. As they say, there's no time like the present. With my heart racing about two hundred beats a minute, I said, "I have something to ask you."

We heard what sounded like a lion's roar inside a tunnel, and Paolo touched his stomach. "Ask me while I eat dinner."

A few minutes later, Paolo and I sat across from each other at our cherry dining room table. The scent of Italian cheeses, garlic, olive oil, mushrooms, spinach, and chicken filled the room. Between bites, Paolo asked, "What is it that you wanted to ask me?"

The candlelight from our antique brass candleholders made him look incredibly sexy. He didn't need much help. I took in a deep breath. Though I had rehearsed my speech a hundred times over the last few months, what came out was, "I bought lemon gelato for dessert."

He blew me a kiss. I caught it and placed it over my heart. Ready for take two, I took a sip of my herbal tea in a failed attempt at moistening my bone-dry throat. "Paolo, we've been living together for almost a year now."

"Are you tired of me already?" He winked at me.

I slid to the edge of my seat. "During that time, have you… did you ever think about…."

He swallowed his food. "Bobby, I told you before. I look at other men. But you are the only one I want."

"And you're the only one *I* want."

"Then it is a good thing we live together." He continued eating.

"Do you miss your life in the villa with your family in Capri?"

"Not when I am with you. Don't worry; we will never end up like Edgar and everyone else getting a divorce."

"Why not?"

"Because we do not need a piece of paper to validate our love."

The lawyer in me surfaced. "That piece of paper would enable us to make healthcare decisions for each other in emergency situations, and to protect our wills from a family member who might want to contest them."

"Bobby, what is this about?"

"Don't you want to stand in front of our family and friends and proclaim our love for each other?"

"Why would I want to do that?"

"Why *wouldn't* you want to do that?"

Finished with dinner, Paolo poured the limoncello and we drank. "Bobby, I do not have to prove my love for you."

"That's not what a wedding is about."

"Then what is it about?"

"The celebration of two people's love and commitment."

"Let straight people do that." Paolo rose, lifted our plates and glasses, kissed the top of my head, and headed into the kitchen.

I followed him. As he loaded our small dishwasher, I said, "You're suffering from internalized homophobia."

"Because I have little interest in an ancient ritual?"

"Because you aren't proud of our love." Tears filled my eyes. "Paolo, don't you want to proclaim our love, rejoice in finding each other, and take every legal step possible to bind us together?"

"*You're* the lawyer, Bobby." Paolo headed to our bedroom with me at his heals. At the closet, he stripped to his undershorts. With the moonlight reflecting on his broad back, he looked like an Italian statue at dusk.

I sat on the bed. "Is it because you want to go out with other guys, like you did before you met me?"

"No. I told you I am not interested in that."

"Are you embarrassed to be married to me?"

"No."

"Then why?"

"I do not want to end up like my father who has mistresses that my mother pretends not to know about."

"But we could end up like *my* parents instead."

"Who just had a spat." He sat next to me on the four-poster and our shoulders touched. "I have never loved anyone but you. I left my home and family to be by your side. And I intend on loving and living with you until the last beat of my heart. Because you *are* my heart. And you are my life." He kissed away the tears on my cheeks. Then Paolo eased me down onto my back, his body over me like a blanket. He kissed my forehead, eyes, nose, and lips. "Not loving you would be like not breathing."

"But—"

His warm, thick tongue explored my mouth as we kissed again and again.

Unable to stop myself, I wrapped my arms around his muscular back and slid them down to his firm, round buttocks. Paolo sighed, dropping his head against mine, and pressing our groins together. Clearly frustrated, he pulled off his undershorts, and I flung my nightshirt to the floor.

With the white comforter surrounding us like a fluffy cloud, Paolo kissed my neck and shoulders. I squeezed his pectoral muscles and then ran a finger around the eight compartments of his abdominals.

After he drew himself up, I nestled my nose in his thick black pubic hair and licked his scrotum. Saving the prize for last, I ran my tongue down the length of his long, thick, uncut shaft. I earned a shiver from Paolo, and a whisper of my name. When his head emerged, my dick shivered too, as if Paolo's breath had touched it. I sucked as he ran his thick fingers through my hair and then massaged my scalp. "*Ti adoro.*"

I wanted Paolo to fill every cell in my body. As if hearing my wish, he took a lubed condom from the night table, rolled it on, and gently slid inside me. I wrapped my legs around his thighs, pushing him in deeper. While I whispered my love for him, Paolo nibbled on my erect nipples. His thrusts were slow, smooth, and loving, but they grew in speed and intensity as I massaged the muscles in his back. In Paolo's arms, my fears and doubts were replaced with joy and fulfillment.

He grasped my long, thin dick and rubbed tenderly as we both released the result of our lovemaking. I looked up at the face I adored. Paolo's eyes were full of love. "*Sei tutto per me.*"

"You mean everything to me too, Paolo."

We nestled in each other's arms until pleasant dreams overtook us.

THE NEXT morning, after showering and dressing, we ate Paolo's delicious frittata, kissed goodbye, and headed to the gym, where Paolo hit the free weights and I broke my speed record for laps in the pool.

An hour later, I arrived at my law office a few blocks away to find my best friend, Jared, standing in my tiny office—previously a bathroom supply closet. He followed me to the coatrack. As I hung up my coat and scarf, his high nasal voice reverberated in my ears. "Weeeeeeeell?"

"Jared, we're both wearing blue pinstriped suits and red ties. People might talk."

He ran a delicate hand through his blond-tipped, layered hair. "Don't change the subject, pal."

"The subject of 'well'?"

"Stop playing coy. Did your hunky Italian say yes?"

I plopped down on the metal chair behind my oak desk. "Not exactly."

Jared sat on a white plastic chair that I had stolen from the conference room. "It's probably for the best, Bobby."

"What do you mean?"

"Paolo's too gorgeous to be faithful."

"But *I* have the looks of someone who would never stray?"

He mussed my hair, which wasn't difficult. "You're adorable. But Paolo is… Paolo. Besides, men are cheaters."

"I'm a man too! And my father never cheated on my mother." I perused my mail and messages.

"That's because your dad values his life. Your mom would kill him."

"True. But that's not the reason. They're really devoted to each other." I smiled. "Like Paolo and me."

"Nobody's too devoted not to cheat. I can personally attest to that. And I can also tell you, straight, married guys are incredibly hot."

"If they're dating *you*, they're not straight."

"They *are*—dating me. And they're incredibly frustrated and horny, which makes them wild men in bed, and out of bed. My latest, I call him Tarzan, swung from my chandelier in the dining room and ravaged me on the table." He put a finger in his ear. "I'm still finding roast beef in various orifices, which turns me on to no end. But I'd drop Tarzan like a hot potato if the guy I call Dracula calls me."

I gave up trying to figure out Jared's logic. "Paolo isn't cheating. He just doesn't see the importance of marriage."

"Did you throw the law book at him?"

I nodded. "I was gentle."

"Too bad. I like it rough, especially from the guy I call Wolf." Jared giggled. "Let me know if you finally penetrate Paolo. In one way or another."

Anxious to change the subject, I said, "Christmas is coming. Paolo and I will be at my parents' house. My mother's making enough food to conquer world hunger. I hope I remember the names of my distant relatives."

He smirked. "Sounds fun."

"What are you doing for Christmas?"

"Going to Maine, where my wimpy father secretly cheated on my dragon-lady stepmother. And since we're speaking of cheating—"

"*We* aren't. You are."

"Ever wonder at Christmastime why Joseph didn't have sex with Mary?"

"Excuse me?"

Undaunted, Jared said, "My guess is Joseph was more into his carpenter's apprentice. And the good book tells us Judas betrayed Jesus—with a kiss. Judas probably cheated with the other eleven disciples too. And I have some ideas on how Jesus rose Lazarus inside that tomb."

I couldn't help laughing. "Don't you have any work to do?"

Jared glanced at his gold and diamond wristwatch. "I have fifteen minutes to email my research on a case to one of the partners."

"Then shouldn't you get to work?"

He shrugged his narrow shoulders. "What I can't find out, I'll make up. It works for religion and government."

I rose and grabbed my laptop. "I have a client."

"Maybe *he'll* marry you."

"I already have a husband."

Jared said, like a knife in my back, "Somebody needs to tell Paolo."

"Let me know when Tarzan, Dracula, or Wolf propose to you."
I headed down the hall to the conference room, where a tall, thin, dark-skinned man with a closely-trimmed beard and short curly black hair stood waiting. Dressed in a black shirt, slacks, and blazer, he shook my hand and his long fingers felt cold to the touch. Then I motioned for him to sit. I took my seat at the other side of the glass table and opened my laptop. "Welcome, Mr. Dean."

"You're the first person here who did that."

"Did what?"

"Touch me." His eyes penetrated mine. "I don't have it."

"Have *it*?"

"My husband died of complications from AIDS."

I nodded. "I read that in your file."

"Is that why someone who looks old enough to be my younger brother was assigned my case?"

Having taken Jared's ribbing, I was fresh out of patience. "Mr. Dean—"

"Tyler."

"Tyler, I passed the bar. The state, and this law firm, find me qualified to represent you."

"Then I'm guessing you hit the jackpot with me because you're gay."

"Yes, I'm gay." I looked at him over my laptop. "Now can we prep your case?"

"Sorry. I'm a middle school teacher, and accustomed to battling for control of the room."

"My last client was a stand-up comic who said the same thing. I threatened screwing up his case."

He rested back in his chair. "I'll behave."

"Good." I scanned the screen. "Tell me about your case."

"Doesn't my file explain everything?"

"I thought you were going to behave."

He unleashed a warm smile. "Sorry again."

"Don't be sorry. Just tell me what's going on."

After taking a shallow breath, he replied, "Carl and I met five years ago through a mutual friend. We hit it off right away." He looked away as if reliving the moment. "It was like we had been waiting for each other our entire lives. We totally fit. On our first date, after dinner at my place, we didn't do anything. We just held each other, all night long. Like two lovers reunited. We were together every day after that." His face seemed to age ten years. "Four years later, the meds stopped working, and Carl got sick. His first concern, as always, was about me. Not whether or not he gave it to me, because he told me he was positive when we met, so we were always safe." Tears filled his dark eyes. "Six months later, when Carl was in the hospital, he worried if I was eating enough, getting enough rest, and if I was lonely when I'd leave him to go home at night." His voice cracked. "Though we had been together for years, we'd never gotten married. Carl wanted to. So we did. Right in his hospital room, with the chaplain marrying us. The hospital staff and our friends threw us a party. Carl looked so relieved, as if he had been holding out for that moment." He gasped as if witnessing it all over again. "He died that night… in my arms."

"I'm sorry." I handed him my handkerchief.

He nodded and wiped his eyes. "A week later, Carl's father called. I'd never spoken to him before."

"How come?"

"Carl's parents stopped talking to him when Carl told them he was positive. They're evangelical Christians."

I couldn't help thinking about the Bible stories where Jesus asks his followers not to judge others, and to love their neighbor as themselves. Never feeling luckier to have my supportive parents, I asked, "What did Carl's father say to you on the phone?"

"That he and Carl's mother wanted me to ship Carl's things, and his ashes, to them in Georgia. He also said they'd hired a lawyer, funded by their 'Christian organization,' who had started procedures to take the house, Carl's car, and his savings. Finally, he said he'd hoped we could settle this between us amicably before 'things got ugly.'"

"Things seem pretty ugly to me." I scrolled down on my screen. "Carl was a CPA?"

"Yes. Since he was smarter than me in money matters, he bought our house under his name."

"Did Carl have a will?"

"Yeah. He left everything to me." The lines in his forehead deepened. "I don't care about the car or the money. But I can't live without Carl's things around me in *our* house."

"No matter what Carl's father tells you, don't leave the house." I leaned my elbows on the table. "And as Carl's only beneficiary and legal spouse, you have sole access to his possessions."

"Carl's dad said their lawyer will prove that Carl signed the will and the marriage license under pressure from me—while Carl suffered from AIDS-induced dementia dying in the hospital." He looked away. "I wish we had done it sooner."

I asked, "*Did* Carl have dementia?"

"He forgot some things, but he remembered everything about us."

"Can anyone attest to that?"

"Carl's doctor, and our neighbor Maria."

"Did anyone else visit Carl in the hospital?"

"His brother, Kenny."

"He lives in Philly?"

Carl nodded. "Carl and Kenny were close until Kenny started doing drugs." Tyler's cheeks reddened. "I never trusted him."

"Does Kenny have a job?"

"He worked in a refrigerator warehouse, loading and unloading trucks… until he was fired." He slid to the edge of his seat. "My guess is Kenny's hit hard times and wants the house, hence his parents sudden interest in their deceased son's property."

"Where does Kenny live now?"

He shrugged. "Last we heard, his girlfriend threw him out."

I asked Carl for various names, descriptions, and contact information. Then I closed my laptop. "Let me do some research."

"Will we have to go to court?"

"Let's hope not."

Tyler grabbed my wrist. "If we do, what if we get an evangelical judge?"

"Let's take one step at a time. I'll answer their lawyer's letter and call you when I get a response."

After I walked him to the hallway, he gave me back my handkerchief. "Thank you for taking my case pro bono."

"Our firm is behind cases like yours."

"I wish I could pay you, but Carl's medical bills—"

"You're paying me by fighting the good fight."

"You're a good man. Carl would have liked you."

"I would have liked Carl too."

He squeezed my hand and was gone.

I finished some inquiries for two senior lawyers, did my research for Tyler's case, wrote the response, and then left. As I walked, I realized an afternoon snowfall had left a white blanket on the streets, sidewalks, cars, and trees. I dropped off the letter for Tyler's case at the lawyer's office.

When I arrived home, Paolo greeted me at the door with a kiss. The smell of cannellini beans, tomato, cheese, zucchini, and Tuscan bread filled the apartment. "You made ribollita?"

"With eggplant parmigiana, warm grilled vegetables over baby greens, and wild mushroom gnocchi." Looking gorgeous in a tight aqua shirt and black slacks, he hung up my coat and scarf and then led me into the dining room.

Once we were seated at the table, we devoured the delicious food as I told Paolo about my day.

After taking a sip of his red wine, Paolo filled me in on his day working on a new line of summer shorts—in December. Then he speared a piece of eggplant on his plate. "Your mother called. She asked the color of my mother's dress for the wedding. 'So we don't pick the same color.'"

I choked on a grilled asparagus tip. "I'm sorry, Paolo."

"Your mother means well."

"So do I."

"I know." Paolo finished his dinner, reached for our plates, and loaded them in the dishwasher. "Time to go."

"Where?"

"It is December. You and I are celebrating the holiday." He hurried me over to the hall closet and handed me my coat and scarf. Then he put on his and ushered me out the door.

We hurried down the steps, outside, and onto the bus at the corner.

"Where are we going?"

He winked at me. "You will see."

My lawyer-like interrogations were unsuccessful. Finally, the bus made a stop and Paolo held my arm and led me off the bus. As it drove off behind us, I looked up at a winter wonderland. "Are we still in Philly?"

Paolo nodded and then waved his arms like a magician. "Welcome to Blue Cross RiverRink Winterfest."

The winter garden was full of elaborately-lit holiday trees. "I was raised in Philly! Why haven't I ever come here before?"

"We do not always appreciate what is right under our own noses." He kissed my nose. "Come." Paolo put his arm around me and guided me into a rustic open-air lodge, where he rented ice skates for us. After leaving our shoes with the employee, Paolo and I sat on a thick wooden bench and put on the skates.

Then he led me to an Olympic-size skating rink with the inky Delaware River and lit-up Ben Franklin Bridge majestically serving as a backdrop. It was an incredibly romantic scene with the moonlight reflecting on the water, and the crisp night air caressing my cheeks and ruffling my hair. The twinkle in Paolo's eyes matched the bright stars in the onyx sky. He took my hand, led me onto the ice, and we glided along with the music, feeling like swans swimming in a tranquil lake. I gasped in awe as we approached a gigantic decorated holiday tree containing thousands of colored lights. When we grew tired, Paolo led me to rest against the ice rink boards, took me in his arms, and we shared a long kiss. "Our second of many more Christmases together, Bobby." Then he led me off the rink, back to the lodge to change into our shoes, and to an outdoor seating area next to a fire pit, where he bought us hot apple ciders.

The warm, sweet drink slid smoothly down my throat and the heat from the pit thawed my body. "This is such a beautiful place."

"You make it even more beautiful." He kissed my cheek.

When we finished our drinks, Paolo walked me through the forest and we admired the rows of trees laden with white lights. When we came to a wooden arch with a spring of mistletoe, he took me in his arms for a long kiss which warmed me to my toes.

"This is such a terrific surprise."

He grasped my hand. "And it is only the beginning of my tour."

"Where are we going next?"

A tree light reflected in his eyes. "Follow me."

Paolo took me out of Winterfest and onto another bus. This time I knew better than to ask our next destination. Instead, I nestled into Paolo's shoulder and watched the blur of street lights out the window.

When Paolo lifted me from my seat, I followed him off the bus, where he presented our next excursion. "Franklin Square Holiday Festival and Electrical Spectacle Holiday Light Show!"

My jaw dropped at the sight of a huge circular fountain leading upward to a large kite and adjacent key, lit up with various colors in sequence to the holiday music. "Paolo, this is amazing! Everything fits together perfectly."

"Like us."

I kissed the cleft in his chin. "I read somewhere that Benjamin Franklin was gay."

"You read somewhere that everyone is gay."

My eyes narrowed. "As gay people, we can't lose our place in history."

"I do not care who is gay, except for us."

We stood and listened to the music and watched the light show. After the dramatic finale where all the streamers lit a path to the kite, Paolo took my hand and I followed him onto a holiday-decorated train. Huddled together in a seat toward the back, we chortled in delight as Santa bellowed "ho ho ho" down the aisle and passed out candy canes to excited children— and to us!

After the short train ride, we arrived at a beautifully painted and lit carousel housing graceful horses, lions, and swans. Giggling like children, we each straddled a horse and waved to each other as the carousel escorted us around and around to the tune of Christmas carols.

When the carousel stopped, Paolo helped me off my horse, and we walked out of the park enjoying our candy canes. "On to our final destination for the evening."

This bus ride was a bit longer, so we sat at the rear and made out like teenagers on a first date. Paolo saw our stop coming and motioned for me to follow him off the bus. "A special evening tour of Christmas in Fairmount Park!" Paolo gestured grandly to six eighteenth-and-nineteenth-century mansions with stone fronts, quaint shutters, and wide porches. During the tour of the first house, we marveled at the home's long hallway, elaborate wreaths on the painted walls, and wide-beam wooden floors. As we walked through the home's front parlor and back parlor, Paolo pointed out the antique furnishings, fireplace mantels brimming with Christmas stockings, enormous chandeliers overhead, whittled miniature churches on side tables, and the tree decorated with hand-carved ornaments. In the dining room, I admired the long maple table beautifully set with white silk napkins and tablecloth, antique silverware, crystal glasses, and delicate china plates. Paolo, standing next to a window seat lined with elaborately wrapped gifts, whispered in my ear, "Someday we will have a house like this. But first—"

I ran to catch up with Paolo as he headed outside into a cozy lit garden. He stopped at a white gazebo with poinsettia plants lining its steps and railing. We met at the center, and I followed Paolo's gaze up to the mistletoe. After a long kiss, I said, "I love you more every day."

"Good. That will make this easier." Paolo bent down on one knee, took off his grandfather's ring, and said, "Bobby, I could never love anyone more than I love you. Would you be my husband?"

I fell back onto the bench as if I'd been hit in the stomach. "Did I pressure you last night? Are you doing this because my mother asked you about her dress?"

Paolo sat next to me and placed his finger over my lips. "Bobby, I thought about this all night and most of today. I said those things last evening because I was scared."

"Of what?"

"Finally finding happiness, but not feeling that I deserve it, given my lazy life in Capri."

"But you *do* deserve it. Everyone deserves to be happy."

"And if you are happy, then I am happy." He wrapped his arms around me and I felt warm and protected. "You are the only man for me, Bobby. I want to be your partner and your other half. And if that means making a legal contract, then I am happy to be marrying a lawyer."

"Don't do this just for me."

"I am doing it for both of us."

After another long kiss, Paolo said, "Well?"

"Well what?"

"Are you going to turn me down?"

I babbled like a fool, "Yes, yes, I'll marry you. Yes! I'll marry you, Paolo!"

He spun me in a circle. We kissed again and again, and embraced until our bodies felt as one. Then Paolo rested his forehead against mine. "Please do me a favor?"

"Of course?"

"I am still uncomfortable with pomp and circumstance in front of a lot of people. Can we have a small wedding?"

"How about our immediate families and best friends over the Christmas holiday when we are both off work?"

"I knew I loved you for a reason." We kissed again, and Paolo placed the ring on my finger.

"Your grandfather gave you that ring!"

"And now I am giving it to you. We will buy wedding bands soon."

I had never felt happier. "Let's go home, fiancé."

We took the bus home, stripped off our clothes, and climbed into bed. As we cuddled our way to peaceful sleep, I enjoyed sugarplum dreams of a perfect, simple wedding.

THE NEXT morning I woke ecstatic in Paolo's arms. "Are we really engaged, or did I dream it?"

"We are engaged." He ran his fingers through my hair. "And our life together will be full of wonderful dreams turned into reality."

After we showered, dressed, and had breakfast, we put on our coats at the front door. "Paolo, when do you want to get married?"

"How about Christmas Eve?"

"I like that."

"I like you."

We shared a long kiss, and I felt Paolo's erection against mine. As our lips parted, I asked, "When are you going to tell your family?"

"I will call them today from my desk."

"I'll stop off at my parents' after work to share the good news with my mom, and then I'll tell my dad at the department store." I giggled like a schoolgirl. "I can't believe we're engaged."

"Believe it."

We shared another kiss and left the apartment.

When I got to work and walked past Jared's office, his high nasal voice followed me down the hallway like a train whistle. I sat behind my desk and Jared dove into the opposite seat. "Your face is lit up like a Christmas tree. What gives?"

"Last night Paolo and I went to the Blue Cross RiverRink Winterfest, Franklin Square Holiday Festival, and Christmas in Fairmount Park."

Jared's eyes turned into slits. "Something happened bigger than holiday light shows. Don't make me punch your lights out. Spill it."

I enjoyed playing coy. "It was quite a memorable night."

"Why? Did you have a threesome in the winter garden? Dress as Tonya Harding and Nancy Kerrigan on the ice? Sing 'You're a Queer One, Julie Jordan' on the carousel? Get stoned in one of the mansions?"

I couldn't help smiling as I hummed the wedding march.

Jared slammed his hand down on my desk. "No!"

I nodded.

He hugged me. "That's amazing!" Then he pushed me away. "No, it isn't."

"Why not?"

"Because *I'm* not engaged yet."

"Your time will come... with Tarzan or Dracula or the Wolf."

He said matter-of-factly, "They've all asked me to marry them."

I did a double take. "They did?"

"Sure. But I turned them down. I wouldn't consider marrying any guy who would date me."

"Why not? You're cute, smart, funny, and a lawyer. You have a great apartment."

"I also haven't finished sowing my wild oats." He winked. "And are they ever wild. Just ask Superman."

I laughed. "How do you come up with these names?"

"Tarzan we already discussed. Dracula likes to suck. The Wolf ravages me in the park. Superman can go on for hours, including having his way with me in a phone booth."

"You made that up. There aren't phone booths anymore."

"I made one out of a refrigerator box. But why are we talking about me when you and the Italian stallion just got engaged? Tell me everything that happened. Why did Paolo change his mind? What did he say when you asked him?"

"*He* asked *me*?"

"Where's the ring? When's the wedding? What do I say as Best Man? What do I wear?"

I laughed. "Slow down."

"Is it true? Are you really engaged?"

I nodded.

We rose, held hands, and jumped up and down in our suits and dress shoes. One of the senior partners walked by my office. We resumed our seats, and Jared said loudly, "And after the girl played like that in the street, a car appeared from nowhere and hit her."

When we were alone again, Jared said, "Spill every bean in the jar!"

I said, "Paolo did some self-reflection and chose love over fear. As we sat in a gazebo under the mistletoe at Fairmount Park, he asked me to marry him."

"I love it! I'm totally jealous!"

I waved the sapphire ring. "I'm wearing his grandfather's ring until we get gold bands."

Jared tapped the screen of his phone and then aimed it at me. "You should get these rings. The leaf pattern around the band has a rainbow inlay!"

They were too gaudy for Paolo and me, but I didn't want to hurt Jared's feelings. "I'll speak to Paolo about it."

"When's the big day?"

"Since Paolo and I met at Christmas time, we're thinking about this Christmas Eve."

Jared was back on his phone. "Check out these tuxes." Gold lamé sequined tuxedos with red top hats and green canes filled the phone screen.

"Thanks, but I don't think Paolo would feel comfortable wearing that."

"Who's comfortable on their wedding day? A wedding is about looking perfect, no matter how much it hurts." Then he pointed at me. "Black pansy!"

"Excuse me?"

"Your wedding flower should be black pansies. Aren't they elegant?"

"Black flowers at a wedding?"

"Don't be racist."

"This has nothing to do with race."

"That's what every racist says."

"Jared, I don't want black flowers at my wedding."

"Sh!" He spun pictures on his phone like a silent movie. "I dated a wedding photographer, Overexposed. He'd be perfect for you. He can't see out of one eye, so the perspective on some of the pictures may be a bit off."

"Jared, Paolo and I—"

"I also dated a videographer, The Nightcrawler. His hands tremble from a nervous condition, so the movie of your wedding will have that hand-held camera, horror in the woods, organic feel to it, which makes me really hot."

"Everything makes you really hot."

"Especially a wedding. Here's a good site for gay honeymoon destinations."

"Jared, Paolo and I want to keep things really simple."

"Why? You'll want to remember this day for the rest of your lives. How can you do that without pictures and film of the big event?" He readied his phone. "Where do you want to get married?"

I hadn't thought about that. "Maybe our apartment."

"You're kidding, right?"

"No."

"Nobody gets married at home, except for shut-ins and billionaires."

"I have work to do." I ushered Jared out of my office as he shouted out his favorite wedding spots. As I did more research for cases, Jared emailed me what seemed like every wedding-related picture and link on the web. To my surprise, I heard back from Carl's parents' lawyer about Tyler's case. Generally, these types of negotiations take a long time. However, according to their lawyer, Carl's parents wanted no negotiation and were bent on going to trial. I phoned Tyler and made an appointment to meet with him again.

After work, I took the bus to my folks' house. My mother answered the door and hung up my coat and scarf in the closet. Then I followed her through the living room past their tree—filled with ornaments my sisters and I had made as kids. We reached the kitchen, and Mom served us dinner. As we ate, she complained about the ice dam on the roof, the stuck garage door, and the heating bill for the summerhouse in the backyard "that nobody uses now that you kids grew up and left us alone."

When I finally got in the big news, she dropped her plate on the kitchen floor and wept on my neck. As their dog ate the chicken *francese* and linguini in clam sauce on the floor, I shared my plans for a simple wedding at home. Mom wiped her hands on her apron, reached for her phone, and texted frantically.

"Mom, what are you doing?"

"Texting your sisters to come over."

"Why?"

"For an intervention."

"Mom, you've been asking me for months when Paolo and I would get married."

Her face was the same color as her raspberry dress. "Married. Yes. In a church. With the reception at a fancy hall of white marble and gold with a long staircase for me to descend as the disk jockey announces me as the mother of one of the grooms."

As if to highlight Mom's point, their pit bull, Bella, finished with her impromptu dinner, sat at my heels, and displayed her molars. I reached over to pet Bella and she growled. When I sneezed from my allergy to dogs, Bella seemed to take it personally and growled louder.

"See, even Bella agrees with me." As if speaking to a patient in a psychiatric ward, Mom said, "Bobby, your wedding should be a life-altering experience." She pulled up her sleeves. "More importantly, we need to show up your Aunt Crybaby Lou."

I should explain that the Italian side of my family name people after one of their attributes. Since Mom's youngest sister cried a lot as a girl, she had been nicknamed Crybaby Lou, and it stuck.

Mom waved her finger at me. "When Crybaby Lou's son, John the Earring, married Lumpy Lucy, they served a superb spread at that Italian catering hall." Her dark eyes were ablaze. "But we can beat them!"

"Mom, Paolo and I—"

"And remember when your cousin Lucky Lefty married Ginny the Giggler? The flowers they had on the church altar put the royal family to shame." She glared at me maniacally. "We need to do better—if it means importing flowers from Rome!"

"Mom, Paolo and I can't get married in the Catholic Church."

"Don't be so sure."

My pulse quickened.

"The Biatinis next door have a cousin who is a cardinal. I'll ask him to talk to the archbishop."

"Mom, please don't—"

"I'll go all the way to the Pope if I need to." Rubbing her hands together, she added, "Everyone has his price, Bobby, especially the higher-ups in Catholic Church."

As if agreeing with Mom, Bella's teeth grazed my ankle.

"Mom, Paolo and I want to get married in our open and affirming church."

"Bobby, that's a Protestant church. Jesus converted from Judaism to become a Roman *Catholic*."

"Jesus was a Jew crucified by the Romans! Besides, Paolo and I are members of *our* church."

"All right, we can make your church work. Some of my friends' kids from PFLAG got married there. But we'll need to dress up that plain altar with a marble statue of the Virgin Mary and some of the other popular saints. But not St. Christopher. I read he's no longer a saint. And that big wooden cross is too plain. Maybe we can spray-paint it gold, or dip it in chocolate. No, people might think we're trying to compete with Easter, and nobody can top rising from the dead. Wait a minute! I know someone who works at an elevator company. Maybe we can buy a lift for you and Paolo to rise up from the altar when you do your vows." She ran a hand through her teased hair. "The pipe organ and stained glass window at your church are nice. But we'll need to fancy them up with gold satin curtains and some artwork. Hm, I wonder how much it would cost to rent the *Pietà* from Rome."

"Mom, if you believe the Bible stories, Jesus spoke out against great wealth and greed, and about the importance of taking care of the poor and needy. Shouldn't we—"

"I certainly hope you don't mention that during the service. We don't want to depress anybody. *And* we need to encourage your rich relatives to give you a big gift at the reception." Mom rose and paced the kitchen with Bella following in support. "Maybe we should have the wedding on a cruise ship. Jon and John from PFLAG did that. Or at a luau in Hawaii. No, that's too commercial. I know, we'll have the wedding at a big hotel in Las Vegas!"

"We're getting married in Philly." I sat with my head in my hands. When I looked up, my sisters were sitting on either side of me, having let themselves into the house. Colleen flicked her long auburn hair over the shoulder of her white sweater. "What'd you do now, Bobby?"

Roseann rested her arms under her large bosom. "Leave him alone, Colleen."

"I just want to know what the arguing is about," Colleen said.

Mom explained, "Your brother is getting married."

My sisters each kissed one of my cheeks.

"Congrats, baby brother."

"Thanks, Roseann."

Colleen pushed up the sleeves of her sweater. A familiar gesture from my mother. "Mom, you'll need to paint the front of the house for the pictures. I can book the same makeup artist and hair stylist we used for my wedding. I'll call my videographer. And my vows writer. She's expensive, but she guarantees sobbing from the guests or your money back."

"Good." Mom added to Colleen, "And we'll use your artist for the invitations. Let's try to keep the list down to three hundred people, give or take a hundred." She collapsed into her chair, and Bella joined her on the floor. "This wedding will cost your father and me a fortune. I hope you appreciate it, Bobby."

"Mom, I think you and Colleen are overreacting."

Roseann adjusted the collar of her turquoise blouse. "I agree. Bobby and Paolo should be making these decisions, not you two."

Mom clutched at her heart. "They're men. What do they know about creating a wedding?" She snapped her fingers. "We'll also need to get our gowns designed. I'll call Mr. Josef in the morning."

Colleen asked me, "Am I going to be your matron of honor?"

"Excuse me?" Roseann said. "Bobby was closer to me growing up."

"But I'm helping him plan the wedding."

"Which he doesn't want."

I interrupted my sisters. "Thank you both for offering, but I don't think we'll be having a matron of honor or a best man."

"You have to!" Mom and Colleen said in unison.

"I don't blame you." Roseann said, "I'm not talking to *my* maid of honor."

"How come? Cheryl was your best friend," I said.

Roseann sighed. "Until she started dating Gavin."

I nearly fell off the chair. "Gavin is dating Cheryl?"

She nodded. "They think I don't know about it. I saw them having lunch together when I was out having lunch with Geraldo from my office."

"Cheryl's a financial investor. Maybe Gavin was having a business lunch, like you," I said.

"Mine wasn't a business lunch. Not totally." She sighed. "Geraldo came on to me. I was tempted, but I value my wedding vows."

"Is that why you're seeing your personal trainer?"

"Mom!" Roseann rested a hand on her hip. "Why did you tell him? And I'm not seeing my personal trainer. He's helping me stretch and tone."

I giggled. "I'll bet."

Mom waved Roseann away. "Bobby's your brother. He should know."

"Why should he know?"

"So he'll have somebody to console him if Paolo sneaks off with his friend Jared," Mom said.

I replied, "Paolo isn't sneaking off with anybody, including Jared."

"That's what you say now." Roseann patted my shoulder.

"Can we get back to the wedding?" Colleen asked.

Roseann groaned. "It doesn't matter to you that my husband is cheating on me?"

"Just like it doesn't matter to you that *my* husband is cheating on me with his coworker," Colleen said.

"Who?" Roseann asked.

Mom replied, "I told you. The woman who beat his sales figures. But she doesn't know for sure."

I asked, "Colleen doesn't know for sure if the woman beat Tom's sales figures, or if the woman is having an affair with him?"

"She isn't sure of either. We're interrogating the suspects," Mom said.

"The suspects?" I asked.

Mom nodded. "We're talking to the coworkers. Piecing the puzzle together. We should have an answer soon."

"Hopefully I'll be talking to my husband on your wedding day," Colleen said.

Roseann grimaced. "And I won't be headed for divorce court."

Mom clapped her hands together. "Nobody is getting a divorce. Not after what your father and I spent on your weddings. We'll pay for a marriage counselor, so your marriages will be healthy by the time the wedding rolls around."

"What date did you and Paolo set?" Roseann asked.

"Christmas Eve," I replied.

Six giant eyes surrounded me and Bella barked.

Mom stammered as if having a stroke, "We can't throw you a wedding in three weeks!"

"Paolo and I want a simple reception… maybe in our apartment."

"Oh, dear God! He's literally trying to kill me." Mom fanned herself with a napkin.

Colleen took my mother's hand. "Don't panic. My friend Cindy's father owns that new catering hall on the highway."

"The one with the ten gold swans and all the balconies in the front?" Mom asked out of breath.

Colleen nodded proudly. "The rooms inside are just as nice, and there's a gorgeous backyard with an adorable summerhouse. And, since Christmas Eve must not be a popular time for weddings—"

Mom nodded. "That's true. Nobody would be insane enough to get married on that day."

"—I bet I can book it." Colleen made a note on her phone. "I'll call from work tomorrow."

"But Paolo and I don't—"

"How's the food?" Mom asked.

"Cindy says it's terrific," Colleen answered.

"We'll need to go over there for the tastings."

Roseann pounded the table. "Bobby doesn't want to have his wedding there. He and Paolo decided on their apartment. They should have the perfect wedding for *them*."

"That's what we're giving them. At the catering hall on the highway." Mom added, "We'll have an appetizer room, salad room, ice sculptures room with fruit decorations, pasta room, fish room, and a dessert room with a chocolate fountain bigger than the one at my cousin Betty the Belcher's wedding."

Colleen rose to the sink, putting water in the tea kettle. "Zoe can be the flower girl, and Lucas the ring bearer."

Roseann stood and retrieved the cups from the cupboard. "Why can't Nicola and Franco do that?"

Mom said, "So they'll have two flower girls and two ring boys. And I'll need to buy a new ledger."

"Why?" I foolishly asked.

Mom got to her feet and uncovered the cake dish on the counter. "To keep a record of how much money each person gives you for the gift." She pointed to my sisters. "I keep the ledgers from their weddings in my safety deposit box at the bank. I take them out from time to time and say a prayer for the people who gave big, and make the Italian horn sign over the names of people who gave too little."

"Mom, Paolo and I want a *simple* wedding with just the immediate family and a few friends."

Mom and Colleen shared a laugh.

"I'm serious, Mom. That's what we want."

"Listen to your son, Mom," Roseann said. "You only get married once. At least I hope so."

My mother sliced the cake and put it on plates. "Bobby, after I spent all those hours giving birth to you, raising you, and running every PFLAG event in Philly since the day you came out to us—as if I didn't already know you were gay, by the way—how can you deprive me of doing this one last thing for you? The only thing I have ever asked of you?"

Under my mother's powers, I heard myself say, "All right."

"Good!" My mother gave me a plate brimming with cake and cheerily ushered me out of the kitchen to the front door, with Bella at my heels. "Tell Paolo not to worry about a thing. Colleen and I will take care of everything."

Roseann called out from the kitchen, "I'll try to talk some sense into them, Bobby."

"Talk some sense into yourself before your next personal training session, Roseann!" Mom handed me my coat and scarf. "Both you boys should meet me here tomorrow, right after work."

"Why?"

"To begin Operation Bobby and Paolo's Wedding!" The door closed behind me.

The cold night air stung my face. I tried to sort out what had just happened at my parents' house. On the bus ride back, as I ate my cake, I stared out the window at the ivory stars dotting the cobalt sky, and I thought about what I'd tell Paolo. After disembarking, I headed into my father's department store as a reprieve before going home.

I made my way past racks of clothes flanked by decorated Christmas trees, escalators layered with garlands, and a large plastic snowwoman pointing to the Homewares section at the other end of the store. As I walked by one of the many toy sections, I winced as children and parents argued over which expensive items to buy. Teenagers filled the electronics aisles, asking salespeople complicated technical questions that made me feel like a caveman.

When I arrived at the sign for Santaland, the white cottony North Pole was inhabited by eight plastic reindeer in front of a plastic sleigh, two dancing elves, and falling paper snow. Finding Santa's chair empty with a sign reading "Santa is on a break by order of Mrs. Claus," I made my way to a corner door marked Manager. After I knocked, a familiar voice called out, "Come in."

I entered and found my father sitting in his old leather chair with his black boots propped up on the enormous wooden desk. His rose-colored suit and hat matched the color of his cheeks and nose, which were barely visible through his long fake white beard. "Hi, Dad. Looks like even Santa needs a rest."

"Especially when three kids stepped on my toes, two yanked at my nose, and four buried gum in my beard."

"Why don't you hire a Santa, like all the other store managers?"

"I enjoy it. And it stops your mother from giving me chores to do at home." He imitated my mother, "Since you have nothing else to do, you can clean out your den. And while you're at it, do the same in the garage, shed, and summerhouse."

"Speaking of Mom." I rested the plate on his desk. "Can you take this home?"

"Sure." Dad's smile appeared at the space in his beard. "Congratulations on the engagement." He waved me to the chair next to his desk.

"Good news travels fast."

"As soon as your mother hears it." He took a bottle of scotch from his bottom desk drawer and poured himself a glass.

"Won't the kids smell that on your breath?"

"I'll only take a sip." He added like a wise old sage, "Nothing will ever hurt you, Bobby, if you take everything in moderation." He opened each drawer and winked at me. "So, I have a little scotch, a little whiskey, and a little vodka." After a sip, he said, "You don't look like a happily engaged man."

"I'm happy with Paolo, Dad."

"I picked that up watching you two guys make goo-goo eyes at each other every time you're together. Hey, how's Paolo's designer job going?"

"Great. Thank you for putting in a good word for him."

"I only said what was true. He's really talented."

"And he's also a private person. So, Paolo and I decided on a small, no-frills wedding."

Dad seemed like Santa as he laughed until his belly wobbled. "Not with your mother in charge."

I slid to the edge of the seat. "I appreciate Mom's help and interest, but shouldn't Paolo and I plan our own wedding?"

"Bobby, when your mother and I dated, we didn't have a pot to piss in. I was looking for a job in sales, and your mom was a secretary. Our parents were blue-collar people who couldn't offer us much help." He looked at the opposite wall as if watching a movie of his life. "So your mom and I pooled the little money we had for our wedding. My father's old suit hung off me, and your mother's hand-me-down wedding dress had a wine stain on the sleeve. After getting married at the church, we served ham and cheese sandwiches and potato salad in your grandparents' backyard."

Having heard Dad's stories before, I offered the moral. "But your wedding wouldn't have been better if you'd had it in a palace, because you and Mom were so much in love."

Dad did a double take. "No. I mean, we were nuts about each other. And we still are. But our wedding sucked a dead bear. And we both knew it." He sat up straight. "That's why your mother wants to do better for you and your sisters."

"But what if Paolo and I don't want a big fancy wedding?"

He seemed to ponder the question. "Then you have to follow your heart." Rising, he added, "Even if it breaks your mother's." Santa patted my shoulder. "Bobby, you have only one life, and it's yours. Live it to your heart's content. And know how much we love you." He left the office, and I followed.

As a long line of screaming children, pushy parents, and flashing phones entered Santaland, I waved goodbye to my father, ran across the street, and hurried up the stairs. When I opened the door of our apartment, I found Paolo on the sofa, rubbing his forehead. I hung up my coat and scarf and sat next to him. His apricot dress shirt barely contained his muscles, and thanks to his shampoo, he smelled of ripe lemons. I wanted to throw him down and make love. However, the look on his handsome face worried me. "What's wrong?"

Paolo rested his head on my shoulder. "I phoned my family today."

I held his hand. "Aren't they happy for us?"

He sighed. "Nonna kept asking when she will meet the bride."

I couldn't help giggling. Paolo's sober face stopped me midgiggle. "What did Nonno say?"

A tear stained his eyelid. "That I disgrace the family."

Wrapping my arms around him, I said, "They're from another world."

"A world in which I once belonged."

I leaned back on the sofa and rested his head on my chest. "And Mama and Papa?"

He said to my stomach, "Papa asked why we must make a spectacle of ourselves. And Mama and Francesa want us to have the wedding at the villa in Capri."

I considered the possibility. Capri was where Paolo and I had first met. It's the most beautiful, romantic, and magical place I've ever seen. Not to mention Paolo's family villa is stunning. Then I envisioned myself starring in *My Big Fat Italian Wedding*. "But our home, our jobs, and our lives are here."

"I told them."

I lifted Paolo's chin. "And?"

"And it started a big fight. Even Pino was barking."

"I'm sorry." We shared a long hug.

He broke first. "And how did *your* day go?"

"Not much better."

My phone rang. Paolo glanced down at the name on the screen. "Are you cheating on me with a florist?"

I sighed. "Mom is probably telling every business in town."

Paolo's sapphire eyes widened. "About our wedding?"

I nodded. "She and my sisters want to plan it." I added, "At a new catering hall on the highway."

His back stiffened.

"Paolo, I know we agreed to a small wedding, but it's really important to my mother that we do something more—"

"Gaudy? Ostentatious? Boastful?"

"That pretty much sums it up."

With his Italian temper alive and well, Paolo leaped to his feet and paced around the room flailing his arms. "I told you I am not the kind of person who likes to share my personal life with strangers."

"My family members aren't strangers."

"Really? Are you intimate with your Cousin Sal the Sniffer and Cousin Tony Tattoos?"

"Paolo, my father helped you get a job. My mother is an officer at PFLAG."

"You cannot out-guilt me, Bobby. I am one hundred percent Italian. You are only half Italian."

I rose and stepped into his path to stop him. "Paolo, would it be so terrible to please my parents by having a big wedding?"

"Yes. It would be absolutely terrible to say our vows in front of hundreds of people, dance with your Great Aunt Toni No Teeth, and flaunt ourselves in everyone's faces."

"You sound like the religious right."

"Bobby, I want to marry you. You. Not a horde of people I do not know well. And I want to marry you in a place that means something to us, not a faux palace on the highway."

"I want to marry you too… in our way, but—"

"There is no but."

"Actually, there is. My mother is expecting us tomorrow after work."

Paolo collapsed onto the chaise. "I cannot do this."

I sat at his side. "Let's just go and see what Mom has in mind."

"I know what she has in mind."

"We'll simply hear her out. If we don't like her plans, we'll tell her so." I brought him in for a long kiss. "Please? For me?"

Paolo cocked his head. "Are you sure we can say no?"

"Absolutely."

"I will hold you to that."

"And *I* will hold you to *this*." I dove on top of my husband-to-be, and our tongues danced in each other's mouths. In no time our clothes were off. With the tangerine, crimson, and saffron flames licking our fireplace, Paolo and I made love, and our wedding quandary seemed a million miles away.

PAOLO AND I rose early the next morning, showered, and ate blueberry buckwheat waffles on the way to our church a few blocks away. The sight of the stone structure with its tall steeple, stained glass windows, and rainbow flag always made me smile. Rev. Jillian, in a black suit, white blouse, and cross necklace, greeted us at the door and walked us into her office.

Walls full of brochures and flyers advertising marches and events to fight homelessness, hunger, global warming, and other social causes greeted us. Once we were seated on wooden chairs opposite her desk, she said, "What an exciting time for you both."

Paolo and I shared an anticipatory smile.

"Since on other occasions we've discussed your commitment as a couple, let's jump right into your expectations for the ceremony." She typed on her computer. "Our congregants will serve as musicians and singers. What kind of music are you thinking about?"

"Traditional hymns," I replied.

Paolo added, "But nothing too religious."

Rev. Jillian smiled. "I'll try to find some music that will make you both comfortable." She brought up another site on the computer. "Are you okay with our denomination's traditional wedding ceremony?"

"Yes."

"No," Paolo replied. When we both looked at him, he added, "Can we do something more personal?"

She nodded. "I'll come up with a few ideas and email them to you both. How about your vows?"

"I thought we'd write our own."

Paolo's face drained of color. "Can you write something, Reverend Jillian?" He wiped the sweat off his forehead. "And say it for us?"

Rev. Jillian typed on her computer. "I can talk about you as a couple, but I think it's important for you both to declare your love for each other."

Paolo nodded and I squeezed his hand.

"Would you like me to include some social issues in the service?" she said.

"Social issues?" I asked.

"How marriage equality is not possible in some places." Her young face seemed to age ten years. "And how LGBT people are imprisoned and even killed."

Striving for social justice at our wedding appealed to me. "I like that."

Paolo cringed. "You want our wedding to be about gay people being murdered in other countries?"

"Not only in other countries," I said. "And not only in the red states here."

"I do not want our wedding to be a political movement."

"I don't think it's a 'political movement' to mention that LGBT people in some places are less fortunate."

"We are not running for office. We are getting married."

"And some people, just like us, are unable to do that. Shouldn't we honor them in our ceremony?"

"You want us to hold up picket signs and chant 'Revolution!' at our wedding?"

Rev. Jillian stood and placed a hand on each of our shoulders. "Why don't you both take some time to think about this, and we'll meet after service on Sunday."

"I was hoping we could take care of it this morning," I said.

Paolo glanced at his watch and rose. "I have to get to work."

I sighed and joined him. "I guess we'll speak with you on Sunday. Thank you for your time, Reverend Jillian."

She shook our hands. "Always a pleasure, gentlemen." When we were at the front door, she said, "Think about the love you share. Let that guide your decisions, now and always."

Outside the church, the sunny morning lit up our faces, but our temperaments were as cold as the temperature. I turned to Paolo in an attempt to process our disagreements about our wedding ceremony. "We need to talk."

"We will. But I have to go." He kissed my cheek. "Have a good day." And he took off.

Feeling slighted and lonely, I headed over to my office. Upon arriving, I ignored the brochures on my desk advertising weddings on a nude beach in Kauai. "No, thanks, Jared." I took my laptop and hurried into the conference room. Tyler was already there, again dressed in black. I adjusted my tie and suit jacket and sat opposite him at the table. "Thank you for coming back in, Tyler."

His thin face looked drawn and tired. "I was relieved when you called. I can't focus on work or anything else. I keep thinking about the case."

"When did you eat last?"

"I don't remember."

"Tyler, it's important for you to eat, rest, and keep up your strength."

"I know."

"Is there someone you can talk to?"

"I haven't been able to talk to anyone, except Carl." He sighed. "I know he's gone. But I can't help seeing him in every corner of our house. It's hardest at night in bed when I reach out for him." He choked back a tear. "But all that's there is my bed, as empty as my heart."

I dreaded giving him the bad news. "Tyler, Carl's parents aren't backing down. I'm sorry to say it looks like we'll be going to trial."

The dark circles deepened under his eyes. "Will we win?"

"I think so."

"But you don't know for sure."

"A court system is only as fair as its judges."

"And our judge?"

I looked away. "They're filing their complaint with a judge appointed by a Republican."

His sad, dark eyes bore into me. "Can they take our house? My pictures of Carl?"

I had to admit the truth. "Only if they win the case and the appeal."

"Don't they have to justify their case, by the law? Carl and I were legally married!"

"His parents are saying your marriage violates their religious freedom."

"It's not *their* marriage, it's mine!" He swallowed hard. "It *was* mine."

"And they believe you coerced their son into marrying you, and into leaving you his belongings while he was in a state of AIDS-related dementia."

"But that's not true!"

"And that's what I plan to prove in court." I readied my fingers on the keyboard. "Give me the name and address of anyone who knew you and Carl as a couple."

When we were through, I asked, "Have Carl's parents been in touch with you directly?"

He shook his head. "But Kenny has."

"Kenny?"

"Carl's brother."

I remembered. "Has he come to your house?"

He nodded. "In a drugged-out stupor. To tell me to vacate *his* home."

"What did you do?"

"I threw him out. But he said he'll be back."

"I'll get a Protection from Abuse order today. Tell me if he comes back again."

He said through a tight throat, "Kenny had little use for Carl during the last few years. Until he heard Carl was dying and making a will."

"Did Kenny see his brother before he died?"

Pain wracked Tyler's face. "Kenny visited Carl only once in the hospital. He stood about ten feet away from Carl's bed and asked if Carl was sorry for turning his back on the Lord and being a sodomite. Then he asked if he could have the house."

"What did Carl say?"

"'Get him out of here.' And I obliged."

I closed my laptop. "I have everything I need. If anything else comes up, I'll give you a call."

We rose and I said, "Do me a favor?"

"What?"

I handed him a twenty-dollar bill. "Get something to eat, go home, call and talk to a friend, and then go to sleep. Promise me you'll do that?"

"Okay." He took a step and then stopped. "I don't know when I can pay you back."

"You'll pay me back by winning the case."

He nodded and left.

After work, I hopped on the bus and met Paolo at my parents' front door. I rang the bell, and Mom quickly escorted us into her car. I asked, "Are we picking up Dad at the department store?"

Mom snort-laughed. "Your father's job is to pay the wedding bills. I'll take care of the rest." She drove us to a catering hall that was a city block long. After Mom parked in the enormous lot, Paolo looked at me nervously as we passed a row of statues, walked through the wrought iron Tuscan gate, and opened the gold double doors. A heavy-set woman wearing a skintight burgundy dress with an enormous white pearl necklace greeted us next to a Christmas tree that rivaled the tree in New York City's Rockefeller Center. "You must be the McGrath Mascobello party."

Standing in our winter coats, we looked more like refugees.

"I'm Pierina Frescobaldi." She patted her raspberry hair. "I'll be your wedding warrior to help navigate you to the big day."

Paolo swallowed hard.

To nobody's surprise, Mom took control of the situation. "I'm Mrs. McGrath. Don't be fooled by the Irish last name. My maiden name is Mascobello. This is my son, Bobby, and his fiancé, Paolo. My daughter, Colleen, knows the owner, so we want the best package you have to offer."

Pierina offered a frozen smile. "That won't be a problem. Since we don't have a lot of time before the big event, let's get started." She gestured like a flight attendant. "Directly above me is the largest crystal chandelier in North America." Her spiked heel tapped the floor. "Beneath us is marble imported from Naples. Your guests will be quite impressed."

I couldn't help admiring the lobby full of marble statues and framed paintings of the Mediterranean shore.

"Follow me, please."

As if taking a historic house tour, we strode, mouths agape, through two gigantic sitting rooms appointed with expensive-looking chaises, sofas, and wide armchairs leading to numerous private balconies. She asked me, "Which of the two sitting rooms do you prefer, Bobby?"

I answered, "The first room is larger, but the second room seems more impressive with the three marble fireplaces, cushioned window seats, and gold columns."

Surprisingly, Paolo said, "But the double-story all-glass wall in the first room is quite beautiful. So are the exotic plants."

"Agreed, gentlemen. After the tour you can decide which room you prefer as your guest's sitting room."

Mom said, "We'll take them both."

"Good choice." Pierina next showed us a huge gallery painted in earth tones, which was filled with ten different food stations. Then she brought us into twelve dressing rooms and a private sitting room leading to a huge hall. I marveled at the room's ten crystal chandeliers, four french doors leading to a huge veranda, ten gold columns, a gigantic circular balcony above, and a winding marble staircase that made Tara's look like a miniature. Pierina said, "This room will easily accommodate your three hundred guests and our thirty waitstaff."

The three of us stood in wonder, making circles around ourselves. Once we were seated at a circular table with our coats on the backs of our chairs, a waiter brought out an array of tiny china plates filled with sumptuous appetizers. The handsome young man smiled and winked at Paolo with each delivery. Paolo, looking amazing in his tight cranberry shirt, whispered to me, "I thought we were just listening to your mother."

I whispered back, "We're listening and tasting."

He bit into a mini scallop in a creamy dill sauce. "This is delicious."

I swallowed a crab cake with sundried tomato and white lentils. "This is even better."

Paolo placed one in his mouth. "The scallop is my favorite."

"The butternut squash apple bruschetta is the best," Mom said.

Paolo and I each took a sample. "I like it," I said.

"Not me," he replied.

An hour later, after tasting main courses, side dishes, and desserts, there wasn't one dish both Paolo and I liked.

When we had finished the last tasting, Pierina hovered over us like a vulture at a picnic. "Well, what do you think?"

Mom pulled up the sleeves of her food-stained azure blouse. "Not as good as my cooking, but it'll do. We'll take them all."

During our tour of the outside photo shoot area, Paolo preferred the massive gazebo. I liked the white marble dock at the man-made lake. Mom ordered her favorite, the white sand mountain leading to the rainbow scaffolding.

Pierina next led us into her office, and sat us on a comfortable sofa opposite her gigantic white desk. Once she was perched behind her computer, she displayed gorgeous floral arrangements on her screen. Again, Paolo and I each selected a different arrangement as our favorite. Mom ordered bougainvillea, oleander, crocus, periwinkle, and jasmine imported from Italy.

"I can recommend orchestras, bands, or disk jockeys." Pierina's computer played snippets from classical to jazz to rock.

"Classical," Mom said.

"Jazz," I said.

"Rock," Paolo said.

"Do you have a band that can do all three?" Mom asked.

"If I don't, I'll find one." Pierina typed on her computer.

"Can you give us an estimated cost for the wedding?" I asked, sounding like a boy whose voice was changing.

Pierina typed again as Paolo and I looked at each other in frightened anticipation. Finally, she said, "I can guestimate that your big day will come in somewhere in the vicinity of a hundred and fifty thousand dollars. An incredible bargain!"

I steadied myself. "It's incredible all right."

Paolo sat dumbstruck, mumbling something in Italian.

Mom stood and shook Pierina's hand. "Mail me the contract."

Our visit to a graphic design company faired equally abysmally. I liked the invitations with the gold ribbon, curly font, and eggshell background. Paolo preferred the vermillion backdrop with the canary lettering. Mom made the decision on a three-dimensional silver invitation with corn-silk matting. The price quote for three hundred invitations was one thousand dollars.

At the tuxedo emporium, I liked a honeydew tuxedo. Paolo preferred to design our tuxes himself—in powder blue. Mom selected chestnut tuxedos with ivory ruffled shirts at two thousand dollars each.

Mom, Paolo, and I left with our heads spinning like wind tunnels. On the drive home, my mind was as dark and foggy as the charcoal sky. After Mom dropped us off in front of our apartment building, Paolo and I headed up the steps. He asked, "Did you really think the roasted chicken and shitake mushrooms with red wine demi-glace and four-cheese polenta tasted better than the marinated roast beef tenderloin with baby spinach in hollandaise sauce?"

"As a matter of fact, I did."

We entered our apartment and hung up our coats and scarves. Paolo headed for the study. "I thought you had a more sophisticated palate."

I followed. "It's amazing to me that you could taste anything since you seemed so preoccupied, flirting with the waiter."

"He was flirting with *me*!"

"So I noticed."

"How? You barely looked at me the entire time we were at the catering house. I thought you and Pierina were getting married."

"Funny, I was thinking the same thing about you and the waiter. Maybe he would like the boring invitations you selected."

"Your invitations were fine—for a tea party at a nursing home." Paolo sat behind the oak rolltop desk. "And I thought you had better taste in music."

"My taste in music is fine—for someone over sixteen."

Paolo turned on his laptop.

I stood at the doorway with my hand on my hip. "What are you doing?"

"Working on my design for our tuxes. I hate what your mother selected. They were almost as hideous as your honeydew tuxes."

My Irish temper surfaced. "And your baby-blue idea would be fine if we were five years old."

Paolo's Italian temper exploded. "If we were children, we would not be getting married."

"There's a lot to be said for being a child!"

He came Roman nose to Irish nose with me. "*You* started all this."

"*My mother* invited us to the catering hall!"

"That is not what I mean."

I took a step back. "Getting married?"

"I was perfectly fine with the way things were."

I choked out, "You don't want to marry me?"

"I did not say that."

"Then what are you saying, Paolo?"

"I am saying this. I am getting married in a church because it is what *you* want. And now we are having a huge reception because it is what your mother wants. Nobody seems to care what *I* want!"

"What do you want?"

"None of it!"

Cursing myself for starting the conversation and resenting Paolo for finishing it, I ran to the hall closet, grabbed my winter things, and stormed out of the apartment.

Once outside in front of our building, the cold air froze the moisture on my cheeks. I sat on the steps not knowing where to go or what to do next.

"Do you know McGrath, the lawyer?"

I looked up at a tall, thin young man with frizzy blond hair and cold blue eyes. He had his hands in the pockets of his bomber jacket. "You're speaking to him."

He took a wrinkled piece of paper out of one pocket and waved it in my direction. "A restraining order? Are you for real, dude?"

Putting the pieces together, I stood on shaky legs. "Kenny? How did you get my address?"

"I told your receptionist I was your brother from out of town. Speaking of brothers—" He threw the paper at me. "—you can't keep me away from my brother's house."

Frightened by his agitated state, I tried to speak calmly. "Come to my office tomorrow morning, and we'll talk about this."

His eyes were wild and in constant motion. "There's nothing to talk about, man. My brother's dead. His house is mine, not some sick pervert's."

I took a step toward the door. "I have someone waiting for me upstairs."

"Is that 'someone waiting for you upstairs' a faggot, like Tyler, and like you?"

I reached for the door and felt a jab in my side, followed by a wet sensation. White dots danced in front of my eyes. Then I saw two Paolo's standing next to me, punching Kenny again and again. A buzzing sound filled my ears, and everything turned to darkness.

"Bobby? Wake up now. Bobby?"

Paolo's warm hand covered mine. His smiling face looked down lovingly at me. "Welcome back."

"Paolo."

I heard Velcro tear as a nurse wrapped a blood pressure cuff around my arm. At the same time, a doctor pressed a cold stethoscope against the front of my hospital gown. Then he shined a light in my eyes and told me to follow his finger. Finally, he asked me incredibly obvious questions. I couldn't figure out why I was in the hospital. "Ow!" My side was sore. "Is that a bandage?"

Paolo nodded. "You should see Kenny. He has many more bandages."

I remembered. "Is Tyler all right?"

Paolo squeezed my hand. "The police got the details from Kenny's side of the story and checked on him. Tyler is fine. And you will be too."

After the doctor confirmed Paolo's diagnosis, he explained that the cut in my side was clean and not close to any organ. I thanked him, and he was gone. The nurse typed on her laptop and then disappeared after him.

Paolo sat on the side of my bed and kissed my hand. "I do not know what I would have done if I had lost you."

"Paolo, I'm sorry about our fight. It was all my fault. You were right. The wedding plans were out of control. We don't have to get married."

Paolo kissed my cheek. "No, but we have to stand up for ourselves, and for our lives as a couple. Because it is *our* lives, and nobody else's. We will always be together, Bobby, in our union, in *our* own way."

I heard other people enter the room.

"This nearly killed your father!"

I gazed up at Mom looming over me with Colleen and Roseann at her shoulders.

"You look terrible!"

"I'm okay, Mom."

"The doctor told us," she said. "Thank God."

"Where's Dad?"

"He's on his way from the store." Mom collapsed into a chair on the other side of my bed and pulled her long chestnut-colored coat around her. "Where's the mugger?"

Paolo replied, "In critical care, but the doctor believes he will make a full recovery."

Colleen handed Paolo a can of apple juice and then sat on the other chair next to Mom. "Are you going to get arrested, Paolo?"

He shook his head. "The police officer understood my actions to be in defense of Bobby."

Roseann sat on the other side of my bed. "If that guy ever comes near you again, I'll kill him."

Colleen giggled. "So will Gavin, Geraldo, and her personal trainer."

Roseann groaned at our sister.

"What's the criminal's name?" Mom removed a pad and pen from inside her purse.

"Why?" I asked.

"I know people at my sanitation company."

"Mom, let the police handle this! Promise? Please?"

"All right." Mom asked, "How could you go and get yourself mugged, Bobby?"

"Bobby's the victim here, Mom," Roseann said.

"That's obvious," Mom replied.

Feeling my blood pressure rise, I explained, "He was the recipient of a restraining order."

"Well, he obviously didn't read it!"

"I issued the Protection from Abuse order for a client."

Mom rocked herself back and forth in her chair. "Why did you have to become a lawyer?"

"Because you paid for my law school."

Roseann unbuttoned her magenta coat. "You should have been a teacher, Bobby. They have it easy with all their days off. I'm going broke paying for day care."

"Tell me about it," Colleen said.

Mom snickered. "If Bobby was a teacher, he'd get himself taken out by some nutty teenager with a bazooka."

Colleen said, "You could have followed the stereotype and become a hairdresser."

"The chemicals in the hair dyes would have given him cancer—on my birthday, no doubt." Mom fanned her hand over her face. "With all I have to worry about, the last thing I need is you nearly getting stabbed to death and lying in a hospital." She gasped for air. "I think I'm having a heart attack."

"You're in the right place." Colleen flicked her hair over the collar of her burgundy coat and then handed Mom the cup of water on my food tray.

"And only a few weeks before your wedding!" Mom sipped the water and seemed revived.

I asked, "Are you all right?"

"I better be." Mom stood and paced the room like a general. "I'll have to take over all wedding plans. Bobby, you concentrate on getting better. Paolo, you watch over him and make sure he doesn't get a flesh-eating hospital disease. He needs both hands to hold the bouquet."

Colleen nibbled on the fruit in my food tray. "What can I do?"

Mom took the plastic plate away from her. "Stop eating so you can fit into your gown for the wedding. Get a personal trainer like your sister." She sighed. "Never mind."

"Not funny, Mom." Roseann ran a hand through my hair. "How are you doing with all this wedding chatter?"

"How's *he* doing? *I'm* planning everything."

"So I see, Mom," Roseann replied with a wink to me.

"I should go on a diet." Mom turned to Paolo. "Why does your mother have to be so svelte and fashionable? I'll pale in comparison." She looked at me. "And I hope we can find a tuxedo that fits your father."

Colleen giggled. "Maybe Dad can wear his Santa suit."

"Bobby and Paolo aren't getting married at the North Pole."

"No, we aren't, Mom." After a glance at Paolo and a deep breath that hurt my side, I added, "And we aren't getting married on Christmas Eve."

"Thank goodness you've come to your senses." Mom clapped her hands. "Tell me the new date, so I can text Pierina, the tuxedo house, and the invitations company."

My side pinched as I sat up taller. Paolo rested an arm around me for support. "Mom, Paolo and I aren't getting married. At least not in that catering hall."

"What!" Mom shouted.

Colleen looked on in terror, as if watching a horror movie. Roseann smiled.

Mom gasped. "Did you two have a fight?"

"Yes." I smiled at Paolo. "But it helped us realize something."

"Don't you love each other anymore?"

Paolo squeezed my shoulder. "Bobby and I love each other very much."

"Then what's the problem?" Mom ticked off on her fingers. "Is it the sitting rooms at the catering hall, the menu, band, tuxedos, invitations?"

"Yes."

"Which one?"

"All of it," I said.

"I told you, Mom," Roseann said with her arms folded over her chest.

After shushing Roseann, Mom said, "Tell me what you want changed and I'll change it."

I reached for my mother's hand. "Mom, you, Dad, Colleen, and Roseann are the best family I could ever want. But everything with the wedding is out of control. It's causing arguments and bad feelings, not to mention wasting a ton of money."

"It's *my* money," Mom said.

"But it's my *life*. Mom, my marriage to Paolo, when that happens, has to be the way Paolo and I want it. Just like your wedding was for you and Dad."

Dad entered.

Mom groaned. "My wedding was a low-class affair."

Dad put his arm around Mom. "But it was *our* low-class affair. And we loved every minute of it."

She smiled at him. "I guess we did."

"And just like you and Dad did all those years ago, Paolo and I need to decide when, where, and how we get married."

Dad winked at me. "I'm relieved you're feeling okay, Bobby. And I agree with everything you said, except for one thing. I had no say in the when, where, and how of my marriage."

We all shared a laugh. I leaned over and took my mother's hand. "I'm lucky to have a family that loves me."

"We love you like crazy. And Paolo too."

Paolo blew a kiss at Mom.

"Here, here," Roseann said.

"Amen, brothers," Colleen added.

Mom forced a smile. "That's why we want you both to have the perfect wedding."

"Then love us a little bit more, Mom. Just enough to let us make our own decisions about our future."

Mom searched for a tissue in her purse. "Don't you want any help from me?"

Dad kissed her cheek. "If they do, they'll ask."

"So you want me to cancel all the wedding plans?"

Paolo and I nodded.

"Are you sure?"

"We're sure." I nestled my head into Paolo's chest.

"Do it, Mom," Roseann said.

Dad and Colleen nodded.

Mom raised her hands in defeat, took the contracts out of her purse, and ripped them in two. "All right." She added quickly, "But let me know if you change your minds."

"We won't," Paolo and I said in unison.

Dad came over to my bedside and took my hand. "The most important thing is that our boy is fine."

Mom nodded. "Bobby, when Paolo called to tell me what had happened to you, I got down on my knees in the bedroom and begged God to take *me* instead of you. I did that because you are my only son. The answer to my prayers. And the joy of my life." She wiped a tear from her cheek. "I thank God for sparing us both. And I think he did that so I could dance at your wedding. Think about that." Mom led Dad and my sisters out of the room.

I WAS released from the hospital a few days later. Paolo, Mom, and Jared fussed over me as if I were a wounded war hero. I went back to work the following week. Tyler was apologetic over what Kenny had done to me. After convincing Tyler that I didn't blame him, I pressed him for the names and contact information of more character witnesses. After he had gone, I wrote my brief asking the judge for dismissal based on lack of grounds and standing.

Paolo and I spent a quiet Christmas Eve at home. He cooked the traditional Italian dinner of seven fish dishes, and we opened our gifts at the tree: gold rings inscribed with our initials.

Christmas at my parents' house was the usual overblown affair featuring relatives, dressed in red and green, who I hadn't seen since last Christmas. Thanks to Mom, they all relayed their concerns about "a street gang chasing you for blocks and crucifying you like Jesus on the cross." Paolo was the hero of the day for "single-handedly taking out ten gang members" to save me. Everyone shook his hand, patted him on the back, and some of the kids asked for his autograph.

When it was time for dinner, my mother filled the dining room table with enough food to feed a third-world country. Sitting at the kiddie table with Paolo, I heard my father's grace in the other room. "Thanks, God, for all this good food. Please tell my wife to let me eat as much as I want." With a tight throat, he added, "And thanks for saving my son. I owe you one."

Paolo and I ate with my nieces, nephews, and cousin's children who lobbed meatballs, spun eggplant rollatini, and ricocheted manicotti at each other. I looked wounded with large red tomato stains on my kelly-green sweater. Bella sat at my feet and showed me her teeth whenever I tried to leave my chair.

Looking incredibly sexy in an amaranth sweater, Paolo took my hand. "Are you sorry we didn't get married on Christmas Eve?"

I squeezed his hand. "We'll know when the time and place are right."

He kissed me.

"Ewwwww. It's soooo corny when adults kiss. My parents used to kiss. Now they just argue." My nephew, Lucas, asked his cousin, Franco, "You want to play in the basement?"

Franco nodded and screamed, "Mom! Can Lucas and I play in the basement?"

Permission was granted from the dining room, and the boys disappeared.

My niece, Zoe, turned to her cousin, Nicola. "I know somewhere we can play that's even better."

"Where?" Nicola asked with bulging emerald eyes.

"The summerhouse in the backyard."

"Won't it be cold out there?" Nicola asked.

"It's heated in the winter." Zoe led Nicola out the kitchen door.

Paolo and I looked at each other and smiled.

I asked, "Are you thinking what I'm thinking?"

He nodded and we embraced.

ON NEW Year's Eve at 7:00 p.m., Paolo and I stood at the far end of my parents' summerhouse. We wore white tuxedos designed by Paolo, as did Rev. Jillian, at our side. The large, rectangular, all-glass structure was decorated with white lanterns, ribbons, bows, and candles. We looked out at our immediate families, best friends, and a few relatives—invited by my mother—who wore white suits and gowns and sat at circular tables covered with white silk cloths and red roses. Rev. Jillian said, "On this special evening, we celebrate the dawn of a new year, and the creation of a new marriage. Robert and Paolo follow in the pathway of our spiritual ancestors Jonathan and his adored King David, soulmates Ruth and Esther, the centurion and the cherished member of his household, and our Lord Jesus and his most beloved discipline John. Robert McGrath and Paolo Mascobello, this evening you form a new union before God, family, and friends. Two hearts are joined as one. And two families, already linked, forge a firmer and everlasting bond."

She motioned to our parents. At their table, Dad held a tall white candle for Mom to light. Paolo's parents did the same at their table. Then the four of them brought the lit candles to Rev. Jillian who placed them together on a small table with a picture of Paolo and me on a beach in Capri.

"Bobby and Paolo, this is your day." Rev. Jillian nodded to us.

Paolo took my hands in his and looked deeply into my eyes. "I lived as a selfish child, constantly seeking gratification. But fulfillment did not come until I met you. Bobby, you are my heart, soul, and reason for living. You are my home, my life, and my joy. I am honored to be your best friend, partner in love and life, and husband."

I squeezed his hands. "I took a trip to Capri to meet my extended relatives and came home with the love of my life. You are my today, tomorrow, and always. Paolo, you are my protector, my hope, and my everything. I fell in love with you the first moment I met you. And I will always love you, my companion and my spouse."

Rev. Jillian handed us the rings. "Bobby and Paolo, do you take each other as lawfully wedded husbands in good times and bad, sickness and health, challenge and celebration, to love and cherish each other more each day, as you share adventures, create memories, and live your lives together?"

After placing the rings on our fingers, we both said, "I do."

"Family and friends, do you pledge to support this couple on each wonderful twist and turn in the journey of their lives?"

"We do!"

"By the power vested in me by the state of Pennsylvania, the holy spirit of love, and this glorious summerhouse, I pronounce you husbands for life. You may kiss now and often."

As Paolo and I kissed, everyone cheered and threw white confetti. Mom nudged Dad. "Robert, give a toast!"

At their table, Dad raised a glass for the toast, and everyone joined him. "I always thought I was lucky having the best son a guy could ever want. Now I have two terrific sons. To Bobby and Paolo, the best sons in the world. And I'm Santa Claus, so I should know. Drink up, everybody." Paolo and I walked over and hugged my father, and everyone drank.

A chamber orchestra, consisting of a flute, violin, and harp, played elegantly at the far end of the summerhouse as our guests congratulated us.

"Congrats, pal." Jared hugged me and whispered in my ear, "Maybe someday I'll join you."

"With Tarzan, Wolf, Superman, Dracula, Nightcrawler, or Overexposed?" We shared a laugh.

Tyler appeared on my other side. "Congratulations, and thank you again."

I shook his hand. "Right back at you. The judge did the right thing by accepting my motion to dismiss your case due to Tyler's parents' lack of grounds and standing."

"Whatever that means."

"It means, you won. And you deserve it."

He replied, "And you deserve a happy marriage."

Jared took one look at Tyler and gasped. "Bobby, you never told me your client was a male model."

"Thanks for the compliment." Tyler offered Jared a shy smile.

"Jared, this is Tyler, my pro bono client."

He offered his hand. "I'm Jared, Bobby's pro lawyer and pro friend."

"Hi, Jared."

They shook hands. Then Jared put his arm around Tyler. "Let's go over to the buffet and whet our appetites."

"Sure. I'm really hungry. I'll probably have seconds."

"Good. We'll call you Oliver Twist." Jared walked him to the food tables.

My sisters congratulated me next.

"Thanks. How are things with the hubbies?"

Roseann gestured toward Gavin. "We talked things over, and we're working on it. If all continues to go well, we may renew our wedding vows." She looked around. "This might be a nice place to do it."

Colleen flicked back her hair. "Tom and I were thinking of doing that!"

"Well all three of us can't have our weddings here!"

"Why not?"

As my sisters argued, I joined Mama, Papa, and Francesca speaking with Paolo. Papa looked regal and handsome in his tuxedo, and Mama and Francesca were radiant, their dark hair contrasting with the white gowns. After kissing their cheeks, I said, "Thank you for coming all the way from Italy."

Francesca pinched his buttcheek. "I'd go anywhere to see my brother finally tie the noose, I mean the knot."

Paolo made a funny face at his sister, and she offered one in return.

"Bobby is the perfect husband for you, brother." Francesca pinched my bottom.

I felt like part of the family. "How's Pino?"

"Still insulted that you're allergic to him." Francesca offered me a dazzling smile.

Paolo took in Papa. "I know this was difficult for you, Papa."

Papa rested a hand on Paolo's shoulder. "Are you happy with Bobby?"

"I am happy, Papa."

"And you?" Papa asked me.

"I'm happy too, Papa."

"Then that makes three of us." Papa embraced us.

Then Mama grabbed my arm, her sapphire eyes sparkling. "As I told you in the villa's garden, Bobby, everything will be all right."

I kissed her cheek.

Mom placed her arm through Mama's other arm. "Yes, you did well, Caterina. And you handled Giuseppe beautifully." She smiled. "And we handled our sons beautifully, by bringing them together."

"That we did, Carmella. That we did."

As they walked off, Mom patted her teased hair. "Wait until you taste the food. I made it all myself. And I'm not a young woman. It's a miracle that I'm still standing up."

Paolo and I looked after our mothers and we shared a smile. The quartet played our favorite song. Paolo offered a slight bow. "Will you have this dance with me, Bobby?"

"Always." I joined hands with Paolo and placed my other hand on his wide back. When I rested my head on his shoulder, I was home.

My mother's cousin Betty the Belcher tapped my arm, her buck teeth nearly grazing my face. "Bobby, this was the most beautiful wedding I have ever attended, and with three kids married three times each, I've been to many."

Mom appeared next to her. "You see, Bobby, I told you a small, simple wedding was the way to go." Mom and cousin Betty disappeared in the crowd.

Paolo and I laughed. Then he whispered in my ear, "We are married, *amore mio*."

"Now and forever."

We shared a long kiss. Paolo and I danced as the moon cast a radiant glow over the summerhouse.

Part II
An Unexpected Present... a year later

"HI, MOM."

"Bobby! You haven't called me in a week."

"I called you yesterday."

"I was watching my game show on TV. I wasn't paying attention."

At twenty-five you'd think I'd be accustomed to this. But talking to my mother is always a surprising adventure.

"Have you forgotten about me, Bobby? It's rude to watch TV and ignore your mother."

Back to Mom. I sat on the bay window seat in the turret of our living room, gazing out at the department store laden with winter holiday scenes in the display windows: falling snowflakes, Scrooge and the three ghosts, and dancing nutcrackers. "How's Dad?"

"Working too much, like you."

"Is he playing Santa again at the department store?"

"Of course. He starts at eight in the morning, sitting on that big red and gold chair in Santaland next to the plastic North Pole house filled with dancing elves and never-ending paper snowfall. Kids sit on his lap and tell him all about their greedy little desires while their parents blind him with light from their phones. He 'ho ho hos' straight through until ten o'clock at night. Then he catches up on his office work and gets home at midnight."

"How are *you* feeling?"

"Don't ask."

Meaning 'ask.' "Did you go to see Dr. Sherman?"

"He said my sugar, yeast, water, and fat levels are high. I could be a cake."

"You should do a cleanse."

"Are you calling your mother dirty?"

"You should eat more fruits and vegetables."

"Bobby, do you think I *like* eating meat?"

"I guess so. You eat a lot of it."

"Well I don't. I eat meat for strong bones to take care of the family, including you."

"So it's *my* fault you have high cholesterol?"

"Of course. I'd be svelte and healthy if I never had kids."

Mom and I have a secret understanding about her occasional 'stretching of the truth.'

"What are you wearing, Bobby?"

"Am I talking to my mother or having phone sex?"

"Don't be smart with me, mister."

I sipped my hot cocoa as the snow created a white blanket over the city and the mountains in the distance. "I still have on my dark blue pinstriped suit from work, minus the tie and jacket."

"Both of which I got you for Christmas last year."

"And you bought each of my sisters a house. You sure I wasn't adopted?"

"Believe me you weren't adopted, Bobby. You have my temperament, and red hair from 'his' side. You had so much hair all over your face and neck when you were born, the nurses in the hospital thought I had given birth to a monkey. I was mortified. I've never gone back to that hospital since. I still don't understand how you could have embarrassed me like that."

"Sorry."

"And I didn't buy your sisters a house. Colleen got a pool, and Roseann, a new patio."

"My heart runneth over, but my scale cometh up empty."

"It's a beautiful suit! Besides, you don't have kids, so you don't need a pool or a patio. Speaking of kids, the sons of our friends at PFLAG are adopting, hiring surrogates, or placing their sperm into test tubes like high school kids at a science class experiment gone wild. Millie's son Butch and his husband Blake got an adorable baby from France who hums 'Frère Jacques'."

"Mom, Paolo and I can barely take care of ourselves."

"Like Dad and me when we had you kids."

"Were we unwanted?"

"Not unwanted. Unexpected. Your father was a young salesman, and we needed my income as a bookkeeper to make ends meet."

"What did you do?"

"We borrowed from our parents, shopped at thrift stores, and had the time of our lives making it all work. We didn't realize we couldn't afford shoes and that the floor was cold from having no heat. The love we had for you kids kept us warm."

"Thanks, Mom."

"Don't ever thank a mother. It's our job to love our kids. How's Paolo?"

"Still at work."

"Bobby, it's nearly nine o'clock!"

"Paolo's been working practically around the clock."

"What is he designing?"

"Men's summer wear."

"In December?"

"He has to design far in advance, except I've hardly noticed since I've been busy at the firm trying to fit in my research for the senior lawyers, and working on my pro bono cases."

"You both work too hard."

"We have no choice. I'm a junior lawyer and he's a junior designer." Paolo and I were ready to get out of the junior league. "Paolo's the new guy at his design firm, and he's gay, and married to his cousin."

"Paolo is your third or maybe your sixth cousin, depending how you do the math. You're barely related. Besides, it's no big deal in Italy."

"We aren't in Italy. We're in the US."

"Where it's legal to marry your *first* cousin. And probably your sibling in the red states."

Laughing, I glanced over at the bookcase and focused on the framed picture of Paolo and me in our bathing suits at a white stone beach in Capri. Paolo's wavy chestnut hair, sapphire eyes, Roman nose, and rippling muscles made me wish he would come home. "How's it going doctoring the books at the garbage company?"

Mom sounded like the matriarch on a BBC historical costume drama. "As you know, I'm a bookkeeper for a sanitation engineer. I don't make as much money as you, but I have a lot more time off."

"Once I become an associate attorney, I can hang back a bit." Even I didn't believe me.

"Hm. And Paolo?"

"He'll take a breather after he finishes the summer line."

"I doubt it."

I doubted it too. The evergreen wreaths on the lampposts outside reminded me. "We're looking forward to seeing everyone at Christmas. Do Paolo and I have to sit at the kiddie table again this year?"

"If you don't have kids, you're a kid."

I giggled at a tipsy Santa leaving the bar outside. "What are you making?"

"Not too much. Just antipasti, stracciatella soup, minestrone, eggplant rollatini, manicotti with meatballs, shrimp scampi, chicken marsala, chicken francese, chicken cacciatore, veal piccata, Italian cheesecake, cannoli, struffoli, and panettone."

The sky suddenly seemed like an artist's pallet of indigo, vermillion, and persimmon swirls. Our antique cherry grandfather clock, a gift from Paolo's parents, reminded me of the time. "What did you get Dad for Christmas?"

"A PFLAG sweatshirt, hat, water bottle, and duffel bag."

"Will he use them?"

"No. But it's for a good cause. See what I do for you? Your own father doesn't get a nice gift because of you. What did you get Paolo?"

"I haven't had the time to buy him something yet."

"Bobby, Christmas is in two days."

A group of young carolers serenaded shoppers entering the department store.

"I'll get him something nice."

"Why don't you both come over on Christmas Eve? I'm making twelve different kinds of fish in honor of the disciples."

I thought about the twelve single men traveling together, preaching to love your neighbor as yourself, take care of the outcasts, and not judge others. So many who call themselves conservative Christians nowadays have moved far away from that beautiful message. "I want to take Paolo to see the holiday markets."

The door rattled. "Mom, I have to go. We'll see you on Christmas." I hung up the phone and placed a log on our fireplace, admiring the white marble mantel and the gold lions guarding each side.

Paolo came through the door. Even after living together for two years, every time I see Paolo, my heart skips a beat. Not only do I still find him incredibly good-looking, Paolo oozes sex appeal and a lost-boy quality that always makes me smile. After Paolo hung his coat in the closet, his tight azure dress shirt, designer black slacks and blazer, and European-style black shoes emerged. As he placed his white silk scarf and black leather gloves inside the closet, I wanted to throw him onto the cerise satin chaise, tear off his clothes, and kiss every inch of him. Instead, I settled for, "How was work today?"

He rested his laptop and blazer on the coffee table next to our white Christmas tree laden with gold ornaments. Then he kissed my cheek, and I smelled lemons. As his shoulder rubbed against mine, my pants tightened. "Edgar wants me to redo the designs."

I did a double take. "The summer wear?"

He nodded.

"But your sketches were fantastic!"

Paolo ran a strong hand through his hair and his bicep pressed against his shirt. "Not according to Edgar."

"What doesn't he like about them?"

He plopped down on the sofa and rubbed his eyes. "The line, the color, the texture. I need to do new ones by next week."

"Paolo, your polo shirt designs were terrific. And your shorts and slacks were totally hot." I paced around the room, flailing my arms like a lunatic.

Paolo craned his thick neck to follow me. "Edgar is the boss. There is nothing I can do."

"You can quit."

"And be jobless on Christmas?"

"Why continue to work so hard for someone who doesn't appreciate your talents?"

"Because it is a good company, and my name will be on the designs when they are approved." Paolo giggled. "But when Edgar wasn't looking, I lifted my two fingers and gave him the Italian horns to curse his life forever."

I collapsed onto the sofa next to him, and Paolo and I burst out laughing.

After we sobered up, Paolo said, "I will have to work at night."

My phone buzzed. I read the message and groaned.

"What is it?"

I talked as I texted a reply. "Harvey assigned me another pro bono case. An associate attorney gave it up because his caseload is too heavy. I have to meet with the client tomorrow. So I need to do some research tonight." Feeling like a modern-day gay Bob Cratchit, I said, "Some Christmas for us, huh?"

Paolo's firm, round knee pressed against mine, feeling warm and inviting. He looked at me with his teddy bear eyes. "Are you sorry you married me?"

"No way!" My hand disappeared in his. "Do you miss your life as a playboy on Capri?"

"Never." He kissed me, his breath warm on my neck. "I was a spoiled child living in a fantasy." Paolo ran his thick fingers through my hair. "Your hair is so beautiful. Just like you."

At peace and at home in Paolo's arms, our lips met with a burst of passion as our tongues explored each other's warm mouths. He nibbled on my neck and began unbuttoning my shirt. I caught my breath and massaged his mountainous back muscles. "Shouldn't we eat dinner first?"

His eyes sparkled. "I am hungry—for *you*."

We quickly tossed off our clothes. Paolo kissed me hard and deep. "*Bellissimo*, Bobby." As we continued kissing, Paolo walked me near the fireplace and then lowered me onto my back. The gold throw rug cradled our bodies as Paolo lay on top of me. I glanced over at the dancing vermillion and coral flames. We didn't need them to warm our bodies. Our desire for each other was as explosive as a volcano.

I rubbed my cheek against Paolo's smooth neck. He lifted my chin and we kissed again and again.

"You mean everything to me, Bobby."

"Everything is *you*, Paolo."

I slid my hands downward and squeezed his firm bubble butt as he pressed his erection firmly against mine. Then I turned him over. Feeling the effects of the warm fire on my back, I kissed his wide pecs and sucked on his firm nipples. Paolo let out a shriek of delight, which told me to continue down to his six-pack abs. Kissing each crevice, I bathed in the firelight, and in Paolo's soft words of love. Paolo massaged my hair and scalp as he lowered my head to his navel, and then to his curly jet-black pubic hair. As he moaned in delight, I kissed his scrotum, and took each of his sizable balls into my mouth. Finally, I kissed down the length of Paolo's long, thick, uncircumcised manhood from the base. Then I sucked softly on his foreskin, and more forcefully on the head. Possessing Paolo was more than a desire. It was a hunger—and a need for my survival.

Paolo flipped me over onto my back. With him still inside my mouth, he thrust his hips back and forth in a gentle, yet deliberate, rhythm, possessing me deeper and deeper. I rubbed his muscular thighs and happily became a receptacle for Paolo's love. My jaw ached from stretching it to accommodate Paolo's girth, but it was sweet pain. I continued sucking until Paolo pulled out of my mouth, and then leaned over to blow into my ear and squeeze my nipples—causing me to writhe in ecstasy. Moments later, Paolo's warm mouth devoured my long, thin dick.

Before I could explode, Paolo gently pressed my knees toward my chest, and guided himself inside me. I cried out at first. Paolo slid out a bit, waiting for me to adjust to him. When I nodded, he continued until I released to his love, and every inch of him was inside me. Feeling as if we were one person, I mirrored Paolo's tempo as he thrust inside me again and again. Our lips met with joyous surrender.

"*Ti amo*, Bobby."

"I love you too, Paolo."

Paolo reached out for my dick and stroked softly and then more forcefully. Our gazes connected as we both screamed out our orgasms, the thick, warm expression of our love covering my chest and filling my innermost recesses.

Out of breath, we lay in each other's arms with the flames illuminating us. I nuzzled my head into Paolo's neck. "What if I had never taken that trip to Capri to meet my distant Italian relatives?"

He kissed the top of my head. "I would be miserable in Capri, and you would be unhappy in Philadelphia."

I kissed his firm jaw, turned on by his five o'clock shadow. "Are you really happy living in the US?"

"I miss the beauty of my home." Paolo seemed to watch it all before him. "I also miss living in the villa, and the enormous white stone cliffs towering over the white sandy beaches with sparkling turquoise water." He kissed my cheek. "But you are more beautiful."

"And my family adores you."

He winked. "I think you adore me more."

"I think you're right."

We kissed again.

"Do you miss your family?"

"You are my family now."

I kissed his Roman nose. "But we hardly see each other. Doesn't that bother you?"

He sat up. I could tell he was struggling with expressing himself correctly. "You are so busy at your law firm. I am busy with my designs. We look at our laptops. We groan at bills. We see friends and family members." He seemed old beyond his years. "I feel as if we are slipping away from each other."

I couldn't disagree.

"Our time in Capri was exciting. Getting married in your parents' backyard and declaring our love and commitment in front of family and friends made my heart sing."

I headed to the bathroom, turned on the faucet, placed a wash towel underneath it, and called out over the running water, trying to convince myself as much as Paolo. "Things will get better once we're more advanced at work."

He called back, "I wonder."

I wiped my chest with the wash cloth and then leaned out of the bathroom doorway. "What do you mean?"

"I feel as if… there is something missing."

After throwing the wash cloth into the sink and shutting off the faucet, I came back into the living room and sat next to him. "Do you want to do volunteer work for a gay charity? They need all the help they can get nowadays."

"PFLAME is for your parents, not for me." Paolo stood and put on his clothes.

"That's PFLAG. And there are other organizations."

"You know I am a private person."

I got dressed. "Would you like to get involved more in our church?"

"Not really."

"See our friends more frequently?"

His eyes were full of sadness. "I love you, Bobby, but I think we need more than work, family, and friends."

I had to admit I shared his feelings. "What should we do?"

"For now, let's eat."

While Paolo cooked, I headed to the study to do a bit of research on my new case.

A half hour later, Paolo and I sat at our table opposite our matching sideboard in the dining room. As usual, Paolo and I talked about our work. Looking down at my pasta, pinto beans, and rapini in garlic, lemon, and olive oil, I heard Paolo say, "What is your new case?"

"You know I can't talk about my cases."

"Give me the gist, without mentioning names or specifics."

I popped a piece of broccoli rapini into my mouth and said between bites, "A gay man was refused medical service in an emergency clinic because the intern on duty cited her religious beliefs."

A knot formed between Paolo's bushy eyebrows. "She cannot practice medicine because of her religion?"

I shook my head and felt the hair graze my forehead like windshield wipers. "She quoted one line in the Bible supposedly against homosexuality, conveniently leaving out the rest of the chapter that, if followed, would forbid her to treat just about anyone. Not to mention the line about a woman not having a position over a man, which would mean she couldn't be a doctor."

"But in the stories, Jesus served everyone, including a lot of people others looked down upon."

"Good point."

Paolo twirled his angel hair pasta with his fork. "There are no laws in America prohibiting things like that?"

"Not federally."

"In our state?"

"Yes, but the other side—funded by tax-exempt 'religions,' Republican groups, and 'family organizations'—are quoting laws from red states and federal claims they feel support *their* case."

"And the US Constitution?"

My cheeks burned. "Says we have the freedom to practice whatever religion we want, not the freedom to force others to believe what we believe. But it is interpreted differently by judges, depending upon whether the judge leans more liberal or more conservative, meaning whether or not they were appointed by a Democrat or a Republican."

"Who is the judge?"

"Someone appointed by a Republican." I took a sip of limoncello, discovered on my trip to Capri, and let the sweet and sour liquid permeate my mouth and throat. "So while you work on your designs in the living room, I'll clean up in the kitchen, and then get back to work in the study." I rose, kissed the top of his head, and exited to the kitchen and then the study.

Once at my oak rolltop desk, I turned on my laptop and researched antidiscrimination laws and statutes in Pennsylvania. I also did a bit of research on the intern who had coincidentally treated Jewish, Muslim, and divorced patients. When my head dropped to my keyboard, I headed into our bedroom, stripped off my clothes, and fell into our oak four-poster bed.

Shortly afterward, Paolo joined me. I spooned with the man I love, feeling safe and secure in his strong arms. However, I didn't get much sleep that night, tossing, turning, cuddling, and staring out into the dark, thinking about the case—and about what was missing in my marriage.

EARLY THE next morning, having left Paolo in bed and snoring softly, I managed to get in some research and eat breakfast before going to the gym. My hair still wet from the swimming pool as I headed into the street in my gray suit and cashmere coat, I realized that today was the last day to buy a gift for Paolo. The snow had stopped. I walked along the busy streets to the City Hall courtyard with its towering white and blue historic building and clock tower accompanied for the season by an elaborately trimmed Christmas tree, giant candy cane, and LOVE sign welcoming tourists and residents. Nearby, at Christmas Village, I joined other last-minute shoppers as we strolled past a woodwind orchestra, evergreens laden with twinkling lights, and an old-fashioned carousel filled with children giggling and waving on rising and falling horses. I smiled at the proud and thrilled faces of the parents waving back to their children.

Next, I perused the open wooden houses inhabited by eager but exhausted-looking merchants selling their holiday wares. As the scent of hot mulled apple cider, gingerbread, and bratwurst filled my nose, I admired the colored glass ornaments, bejeweled music boxes playing holiday classics, and the designer scarves and hats. While I found a number of possible gifts for Paolo, none were just right.

Walking on, I made my way through the crowds, traffic, and tall buildings to Holiday Market at Dilworth Park. I stopped to enjoy the children on skates whizzing or flailing along the ice while "White Christmas" appropriately played from the loudspeakers above them. Then I moved on to the white open tents stocked with masterful creations by local artisans. After watching artists paint portraits of delighted children, I sat in carved-wood furniture, ran my hands along handmade quilts and pillows, sniffed locally made soaps, held organic candles, and tasted five different kinds of caramel. In the booth all the way at the end of the row was a stunning jewelry box in the shape of a house. The chimney, windows, and door opened to Persian red velvet receptacles for rings, necklaces, and watches. I asked the middle-aged, bleary-eyed merchant, "Did you make this?"

The woman, all in blue, rubbed her gloved hands together. "My husband carved it out of cherry. The window shutters are made from amethyst, the doorknob is sapphire, and the chimney top is blue topaz. Isn't it beautiful?"

"I've never seen anything more beautiful. How much is it?" I held my breath.

"Two hundred and fifty dollars."

My chin dropped to my chest. Then my hand reached for my credit card. When the transaction was complete, the merchant wrapped my gift. I thanked her, exchanged a "Happy Holidays," and went on my way, hoping the extravagant gift would make Paolo happy and help fill the void in our marriage.

After arriving at my office, I met with my new client at the long table in the firm's glass-enclosed conference room. Matias Cardona stared at me like a puppy who had lost his master. "What happened to Mr. Cheng?"

"He's busy with other cases."

He ran a hand through his dark hair. "Are you going to tell me to 'act straight' in court?"

"Why would I do that?"

"Because straight guys, like you and Mr. Cheng, are uncomfortable around gay guys like me."

"Let's back up a minute. First, I'm not straight."

Matias's thin shoulders dropped and he seemed to breathe.

"Second, I agree that discrimination based on sexual orientation is not acceptable."

Matias smiled. "Thank you."

"You're welcome. I read Mr. Cheng's notes, and I did some research on my own." I opened my laptop. "The firm took on your case because we believe it has national implications, and I think we can eventually win."

"Eventually?"

"We have a few hurdles to jump over first." I opened his file on my laptop. "How long have you been married?"

He wiped his forehead with a handkerchief. "Four years."

"Are you and your husband monogamous?"

"Yes."

"Either of you have a criminal record?"

"No."

"Are either of you HIV positive?"

"No."

"What do you do for a living?"

"I'm an EMT."

As I typed my notes, I smirked at the irony of an emergency medical technician being denied medical service. "Why did your husband take you to the emergency medical clinic that night?"

Matias took in a shallow breath. "I woke up in the middle of the night feeling weak, dizzy, freezing cold, and nauseous. My body ached, and my pulse was racing. I started panting. I thought I was going to black out."

"What happened at the clinic?"

"The reception nurse asked me to fill out a form, which my husband did for me. After waiting for about an hour, a nurse led me back to lie on a gurney in a cubicle. She took my vitals and told me my blood pressure was low and my heart rate was high, which I had already suspected. About fifteen minutes later, Dr. Johnson arrived and asked me how I was feeling. My mouth was really dry, so I asked my husband to get me some water. Dr. Johnson asked me about our relationship. I said Tomas is my husband. As Tomas returned with a cup of water, Dr. Johnson told us she couldn't treat me because she's a Christian. Tomas went off on her, but she wouldn't back down. I asked her if another doctor could treat me. Dr. Johnson replied that she was the only doctor on duty, and she advised me to go to the hospital. Tomas explained the hospital is a half-hour drive away. She left the cubicle. Tomas chased her and called her a bad name. She replied that we are guilty of discrimination."

I typed and spoke at the same time. "What did you do then?"

"I vomited. Then Tomas complained about Dr. Johnson to the reception nurse, telling her I'm an EMT. She sympathized, but told him there was nothing she could do. So he helped me back into a taxi, and we went to the hospital. After an hour wait there and more vomiting, an intern saw me, gave me intravenous fluids and some medicine. I was released the next morning with a diagnosis of probable food poisoning."

"Lucky for you it wasn't more serious."

"I don't feel lucky. People have died from untreated food poisoning."

I rose. "I'll call you if I need anything further. Did Mr. Cheng give you the court date and the name of the judge?"

He stood. "It's next week with Judge Miguel Ortega."

"Right."

His dimples appeared. "The judge is a Latino, like me."

"But unlike you, he's a Republican conservative married to a woman."

He frowned. Then he touched my wrist. "Can I ask you something?"

"Yes?"

"How can so many people hate Tomas and me when they don't even know us? Haven't they ever heard of the Sermon on the Mount?"

"I don't know, Matias. But *I* have, and I'll do everything I can to help you win this case."

His dark eyes looked into mine. "I'm glad you're my lawyer."

"Me too."

I spent the rest of the day in my office doing research on senior lawyers' cases. It didn't take long for Jared's high nasal voice to fill the small room. "Wanna come over and watch *It's a Wonderful Life* tonight and mock Donna Reed's hairstyle?"

"I'm going out with Paolo."

"A date with the hubby! How unusual."

"Tell me about it."

He sat on my desk, careful not to crease his new dark suit or mess his layered and tipped blond hair. "Is there a problem between you and Paolo?"

"No."

"I don't believe you." He patted my head. "I'll chant for you both."

"*Chant* for us?"

"I'm attending a Buddhist monastery."

"Finding spirituality are you?"

"And lots of hot guys." He rose and reenacted his experience. "When I first entered, a really muscular, tall, dark-skinned guy asked me to take off my shoes. I said, 'I'll take off anything you'd like.' And boy did he like—in the back room on a meditation mat. We 'meditated' together and he made me chant, 'Ah! Ooow! Ah!' Afterward, in the main meditation room, there were so many hot guys, I didn't know where to look first during the meditations. When it was all over, another amazing looking guy with long blond hair and striking blue eyes invited me to his hot nude yoga session."

"Of course you went along."

"Did I ever!" He fanned his face with his hand. "All those sweaty naked hunks with lean cut bodies bending over, raising their legs up in the air, and saluting the sun. I was more hot than two celibate monks meeting in the bell tower. When this tall guy next to me went into warrior pose, I surrendered into downward dog."

I couldn't help laughing.

He sat in the chair. "Feel better?"

"Not really. But thanks for trying to cheer me up." I closed my laptop.

He placed a hand on his hip. "Stop acting like a drama queen and tell me what's wrong."

I sighed. "There's something missing in our lives, Paolo's and mine."

Jared laughed, sounding like the Wicked Witch of the West. "You're both gorgeous, smart, successful, have adorable parents, an apartment out of a BBC historical miniseries, and me as your best friend. What more do you want?"

"Good question." I glanced up at the clock on the wall and realized it was time to go home. I stood and put on my coat, scarf, and gloves.

Jared rose. "You know you can always call me to talk. Lord knows nobody else will be talking around *my* Christmas table with my wimp of a father and dragon-lady stepmother."

"Thanks, pal." I opened my large lower desk drawer and took out the wrapped gift I had bought for Paolo.

Jared feigned surprise. "For moi? Thank you!"

We shared a smile. "It's for Paolo. A hand-carved jewelry box. I bought it at the open market."

"I'm sure he'll love it." Jared giggled in anticipation. "I wonder what he got *you*."

I shrugged.

"Don't look so excited about it."

I realized I was being a bit of a diva. "I'm sorry, Jared. I'm just not feeling the holiday spirit this year."

"Maybe you should go volunteer at a soup kitchen or something."

"I've got enough volunteer work to do." I looked at the clock again. "I better go."

"Give your sexy hubby a big Italian kiss for me. Actually, make that a french kiss." When I didn't laugh, he put a manicured hand on my shoulder. "Bobby, I hope you figure things out."

"Me too." I gave him a hug. "Merry Christmas, Jared."

He returned it. "You too, pal."

I hurried through the busy city streets and then ran up the three flights of stairs to our apartment.

I entered to the smell of fish. Rather than the traditional seven for Christmas Eve, Paolo had Americanized and economized down to one. I hid Paolo's gift under my coat, kissed him hello, placed the gift behind one of the wingback chairs at the fireplace, and then hung up my winter things in the closet. After I changed into a red and green hoody and jeans in the bedroom, we sat down in the dining room.

Over the delicious dinner of lemon sole, asparagus, and bucatini pasta in marinara sauce, I filled Paolo in on my day. "And you?"

In his sapphire sweatshirt and jeans, Paolo grabbed his laptop from the sofa, and displayed his work on the dining room table.

"Paolo, they're beautiful! The beige summer suits are so light and stylish. And I love the shorts and colorful V-neck shirts. Edgar better love them too."

"I have more work to do on them."

"Not tonight. It's Christmas Eve. We are going to finish this amazing dinner, and then it's my turn to take you on a holiday adventure."

He smiled. "I can never say no to you."

"And that's the way I like it."

Finished with dinner and doing the dishes in the kitchen, I said, "Before we go—" Racing behind the wingback chair, I scooped up Paolo's gift. "—Merry Christmas, Paolo."

He wrapped his arms around me. "I have been so busy. I did not buy you a gift. Please forgive me."

"We can fix that tonight. In the meantime." I handed him the present.

Paolo tore open the wrapping paper.

"Isn't it beautiful? The windows and door of the house open up to compartments for your jewelry." I revealed the red velvet receptacles. "You can put your wedding band here, the watch from Nonno and Nonna in this one, the gold chain from Mama and Papa in here, and your pinky ring from Francesca in there."

He kissed me hard on the mouth. "It is beautiful, like you. Thank you."

Though Paolo clearly liked the gift, the joy in his face quickly faded. He placed the jewelry box on his bureau in our bedroom. Then we put on our winter outer garments, and headed out into the cold to wait for the bus. Thankfully it came quickly. As we rode, I enjoyed the view of the star-laden cobalt sky creating a backdrop for the buildings, trees, and wreaths lit up in gold, red, and green. The bus was quiet since the other passengers were texting on their phones or typing on their laptops. We were silent as well, as Paolo no doubt thought about his designs, and I created various arguments for my new legal case.

A half hour later, we arrived at Germantown Avenue in Chestnut Hill. Paolo and I quickly blended into the crowd on the street. We marveled at the Winter Wonderland scene with Victorian-costumed carolers and bell ringers singing and playing in front of elaborately lit, gold-trimmed trees. I led Paolo to the bright store windows featuring elves scurrying around their workshop, Mrs. Claus baking holiday cookies, Rudolf heading to the front of the reindeer line, and Santa sitting on his sleigh, which was overflowing with beautifully wrapped gifts.

Paolo stopped in front of a store window. "Come with me."

I followed Paolo inside as he gaped at a coat on display. It was auburn with a thick collar and deep pockets.

"It is so beautiful. And it matches your hair perfectly! Do you like it?" I nodded.

"Merry Christmas, Bobby."

I reached over and glanced at the tag hanging from a sleeve. "One hundred percent wool." Then I flipped it over. "Two hundred and sixty-nine dollars! Paolo."

"You should have this coat. And you will." Paolo paid for the coat with his credit card and arranged for delivery to our apartment.

While I really liked the coat, I again had the feeling that there was something lacking in our Christmas together. As we strolled down the street, I could tell that Paolo felt it too.

A bus ride later, we took in Dickensian Street, where people dressed as characters from Dickens' novels stood in front of Victorian-style, bay-windowed shops lit up for the holidays. We nodded hello to Scrooge, Marley's ghost, Bob Cratchit, Mrs. Cratchit, and Tiny Tim. Then Paolo led me over to a snowman as tall as us. He wore a black brim hat and had cherries for eyes, a carrot nose, and a red pepper mouth. Paolo took off his scarf and wrapped it around the snowman's neck.

"Paolo, your scarf!"

"It looks better on him."

Since my hands were cold inside my gloves, I bought us some hot mulled cider in Styrofoam cups and roasted chestnuts in a paper bag from a street vendor. We sat on a bench under a tree and ate the warm, nutty wonders chased down by the sweet nectar.

A little boy of about seven years old appeared out of nowhere, reached into the bag, took a chestnut, and ran away. Paolo handed me the bag, threw our empty cups into a trash can, and then chased the boy with me following along. Paolo caught up to him and grabbed the back of the boy's worn, plum-colored jacket. "What are you doing?"

"I want a chestnut," the boy replied looking down at his closed fist.

"Give it back."

The boy shook his head.

"Paolo, let the kid have it."

Paolo glared at the boy and tightened the grip on his neck. "I said give it back."

The boy opened his fist and Paolo took back the chestnut.

"Didn't anybody ever teach you not to steal?" Paolo asked.

"I didn't steal it. I taked it."

"You *took* it," I said.

"Right."

Paolo and I shared a smile.

"Let's start this again." Paolo held out the chestnut. "Would you like a chestnut?"

The boy nodded.

"Say 'please'." Paolo winked at me.

"Please!"

Paolo handed the boy a chestnut and he ate it quickly.

"How about a thank you?" Paolo asked.

"Thank you. I want more."

"Then you need to say 'please' again," Paolo replied.

"Please?"

Paolo reached into my bag and gave him another chestnut, which he ate rapidly.

I noticed a clump of blond hair sticking out of a hole in the boy's ski cap. As he shivered, I asked him, "Are you cold?"

The boy nodded.

"Who brought you here?" Paolo asked.

"Carol," he replied with deepening dimples.

"Where is Carol?" I asked.

"At work." The boy pointed to a restaurant. "She told me to get out from underfeet."

I handed Paolo the bag and kneeled next to the boy. "That's 'underfoot'."

He nodded.

Paolo kneeled on his other side. "Is Carol your mommy?"

"I ain't got a mommy."

"You *don't have* a mommy," I said.

"That's what I said. You two guys don't listen too good."

"We don't listen too *well*," I said.

"You said it!"

Paolo and I laughed.

The boy joined us. "You're funny. Can I hang out with you guys?"

Paolo smiled. "Are you trying to get more chestnuts?"

The kid nodded. "I'm Geoffrey."

"I'm Bobby, and this is Paolo."

We shook his hand.

"See my empty hands?" Geoffrey asked with a twinkle in his eyes.

"I didn't hear it," Paolo said.

"Please?"

Paolo gave him another chestnut and waited for it.

"Thank you."

When Geoffrey shivered again, I asked, "Don't you have a scarf and mittens?"

Geoffrey shook his head.

I assumed his caretaker probably didn't have enough money to buy them.

Paolo must have been thinking the same thing. He handed me the bag, excused himself, and hurried into a clothing store. While we waited, Geoffrey coughed.

I rose. "Are you sick?"

He nodded. "Another chestnut might help." He added, "Please?"

I gave him one.

"Thank you."

"You're welcome. Where do you live?"

He pointed to an alley behind one of the stores. When he coughed again, I removed my scarf and put it around his neck.

Paolo appeared with a pair of mittens. He put them on the boy and then gave him the bag of chestnuts. "Merry Christmas, Geoffrey."

Geoffrey's face lit up. "Now you're talking!"

"What do you say?"

"Wanna buy me another bag?"

Paolo shot dagger eyes at him.

"Thank you."

Geoffrey coughed again.

"We should get you back to the restaurant."

Geoffrey looked up at us. "Can I stay with you guys?"

"I'm afraid not," I said.

"You could buy me marshmallows in there." Geoffrey pointed to a nearby store.

"Carol may be looking for you."

Paolo and I led the way back.

As we walked, Geoffrey slipped his hands in ours.

At the entrance to the restaurant, Paolo smiled at him. "It was nice meeting you, Geoffrey."

"Happy holidays to you."

Geoffrey pouted.

Paolo folded his arms over his chest. "Don't you want to say anything to us?"

The boy shook his head and moped to the side alley door of the restaurant. As we started to walk away, he turned around, ran back, gave us a hug, and then disappeared.

"What a charming kid… with such terrible manners."

"And such an adorable smile covering such a sad soul," I replied. "I hope he's okay."

"I am sure Carol will look after him."

I wasn't so sure.

As Paolo and I entered the Byers' Choice shop, we pointed and gawked at the endless displays of miniature gingerbread houses, singing reindeer, comical merchants selling their wares in front of quaint shops, and shoppers merrily greeting each other on snow-filled streets.

When we came to the many nativity scenes, I gazed at the Magi and their expensive gifts, and remembered the jewelry box and coat. As I stared at that special baby of hope, I thought of Geoffrey: poor, wanting, and so in need of love. I also wondered what that enchanted baby, who grew to preach a message of welcoming, hospitality, and servitude to all, would have thought about my upcoming court case.

The bus ride home wasn't very crowded. We sat in the back in silence until Paolo nudged my shoulder. "Thinking about your case?"

I nodded.

"People in Italy do not care about what other people do in their bedrooms."

"That's why the Catholic Church has fought us tooth and nail on marriage equality."

"I am not talking about religion or politics. I am talking about people."

"Without people there would be no religion or politics."

"In Italy we keep our personal lives separate from our church and our politicians. Everybody has secrets and nobody asks about them. Here everybody is in each other's business, trying to tell the next person how to live and how not to live. Your case. That man was sick. He went to a clinic, and he was turned away because he is gay. That would never happen in Italy."

"Nobody is turned away for medical help in Europe because you have socialized medicine."

"And a little boy would not be left to fend for himself on the street. Someone would take him in."

I was surprised that, like me, Paolo was thinking about Geoffrey. "There are laws in the US. People can't just take in a child without being charged with abduction."

He took in a deep breath that filled his wide chest. "Bobby, in Italy people are not ruled by their work and their social status. A very few people do not own everything while the rest of the country works around the clock to simply exist. Things make sense to me there."

My eyes became clouded. "Paolo, are you saying you want to go back to Italy?"

"No, Bobby. No." Paolo took me in his arms. As I rested on his chest, he hugged me in closer. "My home is where you are. I don't want to be anywhere else."

I pulled away. With watery eyes, I looked up at Paolo. "Then why aren't you happy? Why aren't *we* happy?"

Paolo seemed to ponder my question.

When the bus let us off on our street, I pulled Paolo by the arm and led him inside the department store.

We walked past stairways decorated with green holly and adorned Christmas trees of various shapes and sizes in every store nook. When we arrived in Santaland, I spotted my father in front of the North Pole house, wearing his red-and-white hat and suit. I smiled, since Dad no longer needed padding for Santa's stomach as he did when my sisters and I were kids. Though the white beard covered much of his face, I could tell he was as exhausted as the dancing elves around him. When the line of wanting children and persistent parents ebbed, Dad promised the little boy on his lap a space station to his parents' chagrin, and then he announced, "Ho ho ho! It's time for a ho ho ho-holiday break!"

Paolo and I greeted Dad, and he looked happy to see us. A few minutes later, with Paolo studying the small stock left of men's clothing, I followed my father into his office. Dad sank into his leather chair behind the huge desk. I took the seat opposite. "The kids seem to be having fun."

"Their parents like it more." He giggled. "Until I promise the kids gifts their folks haven't bought yet."

"I can't believe you're still doing this."

"It's tiring, but I enjoy seeing the faces of the kids light up when they see Santa." He pushed away a stack of print-outs. "And it helps with the store budget."

"It doesn't seem fair for you to work day and night. Why don't you hire a Santa, like the other department store managers do?"

He sat back in the chair. "I've been doing it since you and your sisters were kids."

I remembered feeling special because Santa looked like my dad.

He checked his watch. "Soon I'll be off—for this year. What are you two guys up to?"

I filled Dad in on my Christmas Eve excursion with Paolo.

Then Dad rubbed his red nose. "What's wrong, Bobby?"

Even as Santa, I didn't recall my father having psychic ability. "How do you know something's wrong?"

"You never come in here to talk to me unless you're upset about something. What is it, son?"

I told my father everything that had happened over the last two days, except for the specifics on my lovemaking session with Paolo by the fireplace.

When I had finished, he smiled. "When your mom and I were first married, we worked different shifts and hardly saw each other. It was a tough time. But the moments we had together, we'd giggle and coo with each other, hugging and necking every chance we got. And when you kids came along, we were in seventh heaven. I know you and Paolo are going through a rough spot, but at the end of every sharp curve is a wide road full of beautiful scenery. Hang in there."

I rose and kissed the top of his hat. "Thanks, Dad."

As we walked to the door, Dad put his arm around me. "Merry Christmas, son."

I smiled. "Merry Christmas, Santa."

Dad made his way back to Santaland, and I found Paolo reading the label of a gray cashmere sweater.

"Have a good chat with your father?"

I nodded. "Did you enjoy checking out the competition?"

He replaced the sweater on the shelf. "There are some nice things."

"Your designs are better." I meant it.

His dimples appeared. "Let's go home."

As we weaved our way to the door, a woman screamed. I followed the commotion to Santaland. Assuming one of the kids had thrown up on Santa, I motioned for Paolo to follow me over there.

People stood in clusters. Some, like me, were confused and looking around for the source of the commotion. Others seemed to know what was wrong. One teen tugged out a phone, nudging his friend and smiling, no doubt at the thought of his next YouTube upload. I pushed him out the way.

"Shit!" My father lay on the ground, clutching his chest. Moving like a zombie, I pushed confused children away and kneeled at his side. "Dad, what's wrong?"

He looked up at me with fear in his emerald eyes. He panted, "My chest. And my arm."

"Don't talk, Dad."

The assistant manager quieted the crowd and asked everyone to disperse from the area. A few minutes later, two EMT workers arrived. One of them was Matias Cardona. I hurried over to him. "My Dad collapsed. He said something about his chest and arm." Sweat dripped down my back. Paolo took my hand.

Concern filled Matias' face. "Does he have a history of heart disease?"

"No."

"Is he allergic to any medications?"

I couldn't think clearly.

Paolo replied, "Penicillin."

Matias kneeled next to Dad, opened his bag, put on a stethoscope, and listened to Dad's heart. He motioned for his partner to get the stretcher.

Frightened and in shock, I couldn't help crying. A man dressed as Santa appeared and put his hand on my shoulder. "Everything will turn out fine."

The EMTs carried Dad to the ambulance, with Paolo and me behind them. We rode next to Dad as Matias put the oxygen mask on his face and connected an IV drip to Dad's arm. He looked so helpless and weak.

I somehow stopped my hand from shaking and held Dad's hand. "You're going to be okay, Dad."

As Dad closed his eyes, the ambulance sped through the city streets with my heart pounding in my ears.

When we got to the hospital, Matias and the other EMT delivered Dad to the emergency room. As he was leaving, I heard myself say, "Thank you, Matias."

He smiled sadly. "Unlike me at the clinic, your father will get good care here."

As I sat on a sofa in the emergency room waiting area, I was too scared to fill out the forms. Paolo took the clipboard and finished while I phoned my mother and sisters. I stopped breathing when an East Indian man in a white coat approached me. "Are you Bobby McGrath?"

Paolo held me up. All I could do was nod.

The man said, "I am Dr. Sami. We ran some initial tests. Your father had a cardiac episode. It seems to be a mild one. We will not know what damage has been done until we do more tests."

Paolo asked him, "What do you think?"

"We will know more in about an hour. Your father should be in his room at that time."

After the doctor left us, my mother and sisters arrived. We wept, kissed, and hugged in hysteria. Coming from Italy, Paolo took it all in stride and relayed to them what the doctor had told us.

An hour later, my nails were bitten to the quick. The tests completed, the orderly wheeled Dad into his room. We all quickly surrounded his hospital bed.

Mom shouted at Dad, "I told you to stop working day and night at the store!"

Colleen glared at Mom. "This probably isn't the best time to scold him, Mom."

"He nearly gave *me* a heart attack." Crying, Mom took Dad's hand. "I was so worried."

Roseann patted Mom's shoulder. "Dad's going to be fine."

"Thanks to my boys." Dad smiled up at Paolo and me.

I kissed Dad's bald head.

As my mother and sisters fussed over my father, I whispered to Paolo, "I need some air."

He whispered back, "Should I come too?"

I shook my head. "Please make sure Mom doesn't strangle Dad with his IV tube."

I made my way out to the hallway, and took in some deep breaths, begging the cosmos for good news about Dad. The second Santa from the department store appeared next to me. It seemed perfect casting, given the man's long white beard and red nose. "How nice of you to come after closing to see Dad! I'll tell him you're here."

He waved a white glove. "I'm sure he'd rather be with his family right now."

"You're a good employee."

"You're a good son."

"Thanks. And thank you for what you said to me back at the store when you came in to replace Dad. How are things there?"

"Fine." His blue eyes twinkled. "More importantly, how are things here?"

"We're waiting for the report on Dad from the cardiologist. Would you like to see him?"

The man glanced into Dad's room and laughed at the commotion. "I'd better be going. It's a busy night for me."

"Ah, another Santa job for tonight. I'll tell Dad you were here." I was about to ask his name when a young Latina woman with long dark hair approached me.

"You are Robert McGrath's son?"

I nodded.

The woman in the white coat added, "I saw you in his room earlier." She offered a smooth, manicured hand. "I'm the cardiologist, Dr. Ortega. I'm headed to your dad's room."

My heart pounded out of my chest. As the hallway grew hazy around me, I was glad when Paolo appeared at my side. "Paolo, this is Dr. Ortega." I turned to her. "What did the tests show?"

"Your father suffered a mild heart attack, but we can't find any permanent damage to his heart."

I breathed a sigh of relief.

"If he continues to improve, he can go home for Christmas with instructions to rest, eat well, stay hydrated, and take his medication. I'll phone Dr. Sherman about all this as well as a rehab exercise regime."

I couldn't stop myself from hugging her. "Thank you!"

Paolo joined me.

When Paolo and I released the doctor from our embrace, I felt my cheeks burn. "I apologize, Doctor."

She smiled. "No need. It isn't often that I get a hug from two handsome young men."

He returned the smile. "I am Paolo."

"Paolo's my husband."

She held my arm. "How nice. I hope my son meets a nice man someday too. Excuse me. I need to speak to your father."

Before she left, I checked the nametag on her white coat. "Dr. Miriam Ortega." It sounded familiar, but I couldn't place it. Then it hit me. "Paolo, Dr. Miriam Ortega has a gay son!"

"I did not think she would want her *straight* son to marry a nice man," Paolo replied.

I couldn't believe my good fortune. "I did research. Judge Ortega, who is trying Matias's case, is married to a cardiologist!"

Paolo grinned. "What a nice holiday present."

Hearing the word "holiday," I was reminded of the man dressed as Santa. I looked around and spotted him at the end of the corridor, turning a corner. I wanted to get his name and thank him again for coming. "Paolo, come with me."

I followed the man around another corner and another until I lost him. Paolo caught up with me. "Why are we running?"

"The Santa replacement from the store was here, but he's gone." I realized we were no longer in the cardiac wing, but in the children's wing. I looked into the room opposite us and noticed a familiar-looking child lying in bed with an oxygen tube in his nose. "Geoffrey?"

I entered the room with Paolo at my heels. When he saw us, Geoffrey used the remote to turn off the children's show on the television screen opposite him.

"Hello, Geoffrey? It's Bobby and Paolo."

He nodded, adjusting his hospital gown.

Paolo smiled at him. "Did you finish all the chestnuts?"

Geoffrey cocked his head. "Did you bring more?"

"I'm afraid not. We were visiting my father in the cardiac wing," I said.

The boy's blue eyes widened. "Is he sick too?"

"Yeah, but he's going to be okay."

"Do you have a father?" Paolo asked him.

He shrugged.

"Why are you here?" I asked.

Geoffrey's round cheeks reddened. "I couldn't breathe so good."

"Well."

"Well what?" he asked.

Paolo smiled. "Is that why you were coughing in front of the restaurant?"

"Uh-huh."

"Were you scared?"

He nodded.

After my father's incident, I could relate. "Are you scared now?"

"Not so much."

"Are you feeling better?" Paolo sat in the chair.

"Yeah."

"Where's Carol?" I sat in the other chair.

Geoffrey shrugged.

Paolo glanced at me. "Do you go to school?"

"Sometimes."

That accounted for Geoffrey's bad grammar. I asked him, "Do you have a little friend or a teacher we can call to come visit you?"

He shook his head again.

A tall dark-skinned woman wearing a cranberry-colored coat stepped into the room with a clicking of her heels on the orange tile floor. "Why are you two gentlemen in here?"

"They're with me," Geoffrey explained.

A look of horror filled her young face. I wondered if there would ever be a time when a man and a boy could be together without instilling fear in some people's minds. "We met Geoffrey in front of the restaurant earlier tonight. Are you Carol?"

She caught her breath. "Cynthia Hamilton. I'm a social worker. And you are?"

I made the introduction. "Bobby McGrath and Paolo Mascobello. We're visiting my father in the cardiac wing."

"This is the *children's* wing," she said.

"A man in a Santa suit led us here." I knew it sounded ridiculous.

She sighed. "Children shouldn't be left alone in a hospital."

Geoffrey said, "I ain't alone. I'm with Bobby and Paolo."

"I'm *not* alone," I said.

"Right. You're with me."

I winked at him, and he returned the wink.

Cynthia made her way to the side of Geoffrey's bed. "Are you doing okay, Geoffrey?"

"Um-hm."

"I was talking on the phone to Carol. She needs to work a second job. She's really sorry, but she can't keep you with her any longer."

Geoffrey nodded, looking as if he had heard that story before.

"Who's Carol?" I asked.

"She's Geoffrey's foster mother." Cynthia looked down at her dark shoes. "Rather, she was." Then she said, "Can I speak to you both in the hallway?"

"Sure," I replied.

Cynthia turned to Geoffrey. "I have another child to look in on. The nurse said she'll watch over you. Will you be okay here tonight?"

"Can Bobby and Paolo stay with me?"

"I need to speak to them outside."

Paolo mussed Geoffrey's hair. "After that, we will come back and say good night to you. Okay?"

Geoffrey nodded.

"I'll be back tomorrow, Geoffrey." Cynthia led Paolo and me into the hallway, out of sound's reach from Geoffrey's room. "What is your interest in this child?"

I explained, "We met Geoffrey today and shared some chestnuts."

"That wasn't wise. He could have been allergic to chestnuts."

"Is he?" Paolo seemed concerned.

"No." She continued her interrogation. "Did you give him the scarf and gloves?"

Paolo and I nodded.

A crease formed across Paolo's forehead. "Is there something wrong with them?"

"Hardly." She smiled. "He wouldn't take them off. I had to pry them out of his hands when he was admitted."

"Is it a problem that Paolo and I visited him tonight?"

"No." She sighed. "Geoffrey has been through a rough time."

"How rough?"

"Pretty rough." She sat on a chair.

Paolo and I sat opposite her on a sofa. "I know this is none of our business, but I'm a lawyer. Perhaps I can help."

"I doubt it." Cynthia seemed to be at odds with herself over how much to tell us. Finally she said, "Geoffrey's mother was a prostitute and a drug addict. He needed a great deal of medical attention when he was a baby.

Since then he's lived in a different foster home each year of his life. Some of the foster parents weren't exactly… model parents."

"Was Geoffrey molested?" I asked, feeling the bile rise up my esophagus.

"I'm not at liberty to divulge sensitive information about Geoffrey."

Paolo offered her a no-nonsense look. "Can you at least tell us if the boy was violated?"

She rubbed her forehead. "Not in the way you are imagining."

The lawyer in me interrogated. "But he was mistreated by some of his foster parents?"

She nodded.

"And you allowed that?" Paolo's eyes widened.

"I took him out of the abusive situation."

"And put him into another one?" Paolo smirked.

"Not if I could help it."

Paolo rubbed his hands together. "He is an adorable, smart little boy."

"With a big appetite," I added.

"Why hasn't someone adopted him?" Paolo took the words of out my mouth.

Cynthia replied, "Geoffrey has severe asthma which flares up a great deal. Most adoptive parents want heathy children."

"What about this Carol?" I wondered.

"She dropped him off at the hospital and then terminated her foster parentage," Cynthia replied.

I knew the answer before asking. "What happens to Geoffrey now?"

"After he's released from the hospital, he goes into another foster home."

Paolo clenched his fists. "Moving around so much cannot be good for his asthma."

"No, but I have no other choice."

"Can we stay and visit with Geoffrey a while longer?"

"We'll be here for my father anyway," I added.

"It certainly seems all right with Geoffrey. So, I'll agree." She started to leave.

Paolo stood in her path. "When is Geoffrey's bedtime?"

She walked around him and said over her shoulder, "He doesn't have one. But the children's ward likes all lights out about now."

Paolo and I checked in on my father. I was happy to see Dad's color had returned and he was feeling better. Since my family was still with him, we headed back into Geoffrey's room. "How are you doing?" I asked him.

"Breathing okay?" Paolo asked.

Geoffrey nodded.

"Good." I sat on the chair.

Paolo sat at the edge of the bed. "Did you eat dinner?"

Geoffrey nodded and his blond hair wisped around his face. "Turkey, potatoes, and peas."

"Sounds good. I should check in here."

Geoffrey giggled at Paolo's joke. "But no chestnuts."

I laughed at Geoffrey's relentlessness. "Are you feeling tired?"

"No." Geoffrey yawned.

"Did the doctor say when you can go home?" Paolo rubbed his palms against his knees.

Geoffrey shrugged. "It don't matter."

I couldn't resist. "It *doesn't* matter. Do you miss Carol?"

"Not really."

I silently thanked my parents for wanting me.

"Would you like Bobby and me to stay and visit a while longer?"

Geoffrey nodded so forcefully he dislodged his oxygen. Paolo leaned over and placed it back inside his nostrils. "Do you guys live near here?"

I replied, "Not too far away."

"Where?"

"In an apartment across the street from a big department store that my dad manages."

"Are there toys in it?"

"Lots of them."

"Can I have one?"

"Maybe another time."

"Do you work there?"

"No. I'm a lawyer."

"What does a lawyer do?" He winked at me. "Besides eating chestnuts."

I wanted to reply, "Research older lawyer's cases and make half their salaries." I thought better of it and said, "I help people in trouble."

Seeming satisfied, Geoffrey turned to Paolo. "What do you do, besides make kids say 'please' and 'thank you'?"

"I make drawings."

"Are you a artist?"

Paolo laughed. "I like to think so, though my boss might disagree."

I explained, "Paolo is *an* artist who designs men's clothing. His drawings are really beautiful."

"Can I see them?"

"Maybe at another visit." Paolo smiled.

Geoffrey yawned again. "Do you live in that apartment with Bobby?"

"Bobby and I are married."

Geoffrey cocked his head. "Two boys can get married?"

Paolo nodded.

I asked, "Does that bother you, Geoffrey?"

He shook his head. "Can I see your apartment?" Geoffrey yawned.

Paolo gently lifted Geoffrey and placed him onto his back. "I think you should go to sleep instead. It's lights-out time."

"Will you visit me tomorrow? And bring me a gift?"

"We'll see," I said.

Geoffrey seemed to struggle to stay awake. "Don't leave until I fall asleep. Okay?"

"Okay." Paolo placed the blanket over him.

Geoffrey opened one eye to see if we were still there. A minute later he drifted off.

We tiptoed out of the room, passing a nurse who was entering to shut off the light and check up on Geoffrey.

After finding my family gone and my dad asleep in his room, we left the hospital. Despite the Christmas trees, garlands, and wreaths, a hospital was not a fun place for a little boy to be on Christmas Eve.

Paolo and I took the bus home, and then huddled together against the wind, walking toward our apartment. The evening had been a drain on us, physically and emotionally. The moment we entered our apartment, we stripped off our clothes, dove into bed, and cuddled in each other's arms. My dreams were full of images of Matias, Dad, and Geoffrey in pain—with me powerless to help them.

I WOKE Christmas morning to the sound of Paolo moving around the kitchen. I washed and dressed. Then sitting at our dining room table, we giggled at our attire: green shirt, red sweater, and black slacks. We ate whole-wheat blueberry pancakes for breakfast and looked out our window at the people below carrying presents on foot or in cars. The sight of children sledding and making snow people caused me to think about Geoffrey stuck in the hospital on Christmas Day.

"It's time to go." Paolo scooped up his laptop from the sofa.

"Are you planning to work on your designs during Christmas dinner?" I feared the answer.

"I thought we could stop off to see Geoffrey after church and show him my designs."

Paolo and I thought alike. We bundled up at the closet. Then I grabbed the shopping bag of gifts for my nieces and nephews, and we headed out the door. It was a sunny, clear, cold day, and the streets didn't seem as crowded as usual.

When we arrived at our local church, we sat at our usual pew, toward the middle. Unlike regular Sunday services, the church was full. I took in the stained glass windows stationed all around the church, highlighting Jesus of Nazareth's birth, ministry, crucifixion, and resurrection. The sound of the giant pipe organ up front filled my ears. And I took in the pleasing scents of the vanilla white candles and bright red poinsettia plants on the altar as they permeated the historic building.

We sang carols, prayed, and listened attentively to Rev. Jillian's sermon on how, as Christians, we should be Christ-like by striving for social justice, working to protect the outcasts, and helping the impoverished and destitute. I couldn't help thinking of my legal case and the irony of wealthy "Christian" organizations supporting a campaign to not serve gay people and to deny us basic human rights.

When the service ended, we filed out of the church, shook Rev. Jillian's hand, and took the bus to the hospital.

Paolo and I stopped off at the hospital's gift shop. Then we made our way through the corridors, thankful for the carolers and hard-working staff who worked through the day. We found Geoffrey sitting in a nook with other children, listening to a story read by a hospital volunteer. When he saw us, he hurried our way, looking adorable in his blue and red striped pajamas.

"Hi, Bobby and Paolo."

I kneeled next to him and whispered, "Don't you want to hear the rest of the story?"

He shrugged. "I heard it before." Geoffrey took our hands and led us to a sofa nearby.

When we were seated with Geoffrey between us, Paolo asked, "Where is your oxygen tube?"

"Callie took it out," Geoffrey said.

"Is Callie your nurse?" I asked.

Geoffrey nodded.

"Then you must be getting better." Paolo smiled.

Geoffrey explained, "I gotta use the machine with Callie."

I assumed he meant a nebulizer.

Paolo handed Geoffrey our gift. "Merry Christmas, Geoffrey."

Geoffrey's face lit up.

"Say 'thank you.'"

"Thank you." Geoffrey hugged the stuffed giraffe to his tiny chest. "I'll call him Bopalo."

Paolo and I shared a smile.

"And we brought you something else." Paolo beamed.

"More chestnuts?"

I sounded like my mother. "Didn't you eat breakfast?"

"Eggs and fruit. But I'm a growing boy."

I giggled.

Paolo placed his laptop on the end table and turned it on. "These are my drawings."

Geoffrey kneeled next to it in fascination. As Paolo displayed his designs, Geoffrey stared in wonderment. "The blue ones are cool!"

"Good choice, Geoffrey," I commented.

"But I like them all!"

"You should be my boss." Paolo winked at him.

"You're a great drawer!" Geoffrey shook Paolo's hand.

"You *definitely* should be my boss."

"Sold!"

The three of us laughed.

I checked my watch and realized it was later than I had thought. "Geoffrey, has Ms. Hamilton visited you today?"

"Nope," Geoffrey replied.

"I'm sure she'll be here soon. Paolo and I enjoyed our visit with you, but we need to get to my family and give them their gifts."

Geoffrey looked at me with sad eyes. "Can you take me with you?"

"I'm afraid not." I swallowed the lump in my throat. "You need to stay here and continue to get better."

Paolo intercepted with, "And you do not want to miss Ms. Hamilton when she comes to see you."

"And my family will be upset if we don't come," I added.

Geoffrey asked me, "Do you got a mommy?"

I nodded. "And I also *have* a father, and two sisters who each have two kids. And I have lots of aunts, uncles, and cousins."

Geoffrey rested his little hand on my knee. "You're lucky."

I bit my lip. Paolo came to my rescue. "I am sure Ms. Hamilton will bring you to a nice family with children for you to play with."

Geoffrey nodded but looked doubtful.

To my surprise, I heard myself say, "And maybe they'll let Paolo and me come visit you."

Geoffrey perked up.

"Back again?" Cynthia Hamilton stood behind the sofa, with her cranberry coat open revealing a wine-colored dress and heels.

Paolo and I rose.

"We dropped off a little gift for Geoffrey," I said.

Geoffrey sat on the sofa and displayed his stuffed giraffe.

"That was nice of you." She turned toward Geoffrey. "How are you feeling, Geoffrey?"

"Okay," he replied.

"That's what Nurse Callie told me."

"She works the machine good."

Cynthia looked to us for help.

I explained, "I think he means the nebulizer."

"Ah." She turned to Geoffrey. "And the doctor on duty said that if you keep getting better, you can leave here tomorrow."

"Can I go home with Bobby and Paolo?"

Paolo and I did a double take.

Cynthia smiled. "I'm afraid not."

Paolo caught his breath. "We are flattered, but it is not possible, Geoffrey."

Geoffrey asked Cynthia, "Where do I go?"

"For now, let's get you back in your room."

After we had settled Geoffrey in bed with the television on, Paolo and I said goodbye.

When Gregory pouted, Cynthia asked him, "Don't you want to thank Bobby and Paolo for visiting you?"

"Thank you for visiting me."

"And for the gift?"

"That too." Geoffrey pouted. "Have a good Christmas with your family."

"Thank you, Geoffrey." Paolo and I left the room.

When the three of us were back in the hallway, I asked Cynthia, "Are you spending Christmas with your family?"

She nodded. "I have to leave in a few minutes." Cynthia motioned for us to sit on the sofa. She joined us on the chair opposite. Staring at Paolo, she asked, "What do you do for a living?"

"I'm a clothing designer." Paolo closed his laptop and rested it on his knees.

"How long have you two been married?"

"A year," I said.

"Where do you live?"

I gave her our address.

"Do either of you have a record?"

"No." I asked, "Is there a problem with us visiting Geoffrey?"

She shook her head. "I've known Geoffrey since he was born. It pains me to see him tossed around the foster care system."

"You could adopt him," Paolo asked.

She chuckled ironically. "If I adopted every kid I saw coming through the system, I'd need a stadium for an apartment."

Cynthia slid to the edge of her seat. "I can see you like Geoffrey, and he's obviously quite taken with both of you." She handed me her card. "Visit him as much as you like."

We all stood, and I asked, "Where will Geoffrey go now?"

Cynthia sighed. "I've found parents with three children of their own. They're struggling financially, but they're willing to take Geoffrey on a temporary basis. He'll be safe there."

"But?" I asked.

Cynthia nodded. "He won't get the full care and attention he needs."

"Then why place him there?" Paolo scratched his head.

"Because I have no other options."

"What do you think will happen to him?" I asked, concerned.

"I think he'll wind up back here. Merry Christmas, gentlemen."

As we left the hospital, I turned to Paolo. "No kid should have to spend Christmas in a hospital. Or live with parents who are tolerating him on a temporary basis."

On the bus ride to my parents' house, I gazed out the window at the blur of buildings, people, and trees. "Why do people bring children into the world if they can't take care of them?"

Paolo took my hand and we sat quietly. Geoffrey obviously wasn't our problem, but the thought of him moving into another dysfunctional foster home bothered me.

When we arrived at my parents' house, we took off our winter things, hugged and kissed everyone hello, and put our gifts with the others under the tree in the living room. I smiled at the tree decorations that my sisters and I had made in school as kids, wondering if Geoffrey had made any holiday decorations.

While Paolo played with my nieces and nephews in the basement, I walked through the dining room, where my sisters were sitting at the table, complaining. "I feel like a chauffeur," said Colleen with a flick back of her auburn hair brushing against the shoulders of her red blouse adorned with Santa himself. "Driving Zoe to daycare before I go to work, and carting Lucas to gymnastics after school is killing me."

Roseann clutched at the Christmas tree covering the ample chest of her green dress. "I know! And when Isabella can't come in, I'm stuck having to make dinner, do laundry, clean up after the kids, and get Franco to his sporting events and Nicola to ballet."

Colleen gazed up at me. "You're so lucky you don't have kids, Bobby."

Roseann kissed by cheek. "You lead a charmed life, brother."

I smiled and moved on to the kitchen, where I found my mother standing in the center of the room with makeup caked on her face and her dark hair teased like an old movie star's. Her bright red dress was covered with a white apron.

"How's Dad doing?" I asked.

"I'm supposed to think he's resting in bed. I know he's watching the ballgame in his study with your brothers-in-law." Mom whizzed around me, removing platters of food from the refrigerator, oven, and microwave.

I shouted over the noise, "Mom, can I help?"

"Don't be ridiculous. What could you do?"

I looked around the kitchen. "I can carve the roast."

"You don't eat red meat. How can you carve it?"

"Can I set the table?"

"I did that at six this morning before I picked up your father at the hospital." She pushed me into a chair.

Bella sat at my feet, growled, and displayed her large teeth.

"What's wrong with Bella?"

"That's her chair."

"The dog has a chair?"

"Not anymore," Mom said, looking down disdainfully at me.

I rose and Bella jumped onto the chair in my place, continuing to growl and bark until I was out of her personal zone.

As Mom brought platters of chicken and veal dishes, pasta concoctions, and vegetable medleys to the dining room, I followed her.

"Did you call your Great Aunt Sofia for Christmas?" she asked.

"I think I lost her number."

"That's terrible, Bobby. She's my mother's sister. With your grandparents dead, Aunt Sofia is your oldest relative in this country."

"Dad's parents are still alive."

"Your father's side doesn't count. They're Irish." She turned up her Roman nose. "And they live in California."

I reached for my phone. "Okay. Give me Great Aunt Sofia's number in Florida and I'll call her."

"Too late. She died this morning. You happy now?"

"Are you joking?"

"Of course. But she could be dead for all you'd know." Mom pushed me out of her way to bring more food out to the dining room.

When she returned to the kitchen, I asked, "Mom, how did you and Dad know when you were ready to have kids?"

"When I skipped my period."

"I'm serious, Mom."

"So am I." She stopped working and wiped her hands on her apron. "I believe children are a gift from God, who gives us the wisdom and patience to take care of them."

"How about all the unwanted kids in the world?"

"They need people to want them."

"How does a couple know if they want them?"

"You'll know." She kissed my cheek and checked on the desserts in the refrigerator.

My aunts, uncles, and cousins arrived to screams, hugs, and kisses. Paolo, coming from Italy, was still a celebrity to them. Sitting in the living room, they interrogated him as usual about the old country. As every Christmas since I was eighteen, they asked me if I was still working at "your secretary job downtown," a temporary job I had one summer while in college. Before I could respond, they reminisced about our "small" wedding, and asked if any more of my cases ended up with me getting assaulted and Paolo having to save me. I was thankful when Mom called everyone to their respective tables for dinner.

While I couldn't see my parents from my seat at the kiddie table in the kitchen, I heard them saying grace in the dining room. Mom was first. "Today we thank God for Jesus coming to America and starting the Catholic Church. We are especially thankful my husband is alive after he nearly gave *me* a heart attack and—"

Dad cut her off with, "*Salute*! Let's eat!"

The house was noisier than a war zone. With Bella growling at my feet, I dodged flying meatballs courtesy of my nieces, nephews, and my cousins' children. Paolo enjoyed eating the Italian dishes.

When all the food was either in our stomachs, in Bella's mouth, or smeared on the kitchen appliances, I took the kids' napkins and wiped their faces. My nephew Franco, who was at our wedding, turned to Paolo and me as I dug marinara sauce out of his ear. "Do you guys have kids?"

Before I could answer, my niece Zoe said, "Two boys can't have kids, stupid!"

My niece Nicola lifted her cup of juice and spilled it all over her red velvet dress. "Tisha and Talia in my class have two dads."

Paolo pressed his napkin against the stain in her dress. My nephew Lucas stuffed my piece of cheesecake into his mouth.

"Say please, Lucas."

"Please!" Lucas spit the cake in my face. I missed Geoffrey's manners.

After I wiped my face, we were all herded into the living room to watch the children open their gifts. As Paolo and I took our seats on the floor in a corner of the room, each child ripped open elaborately wrapped boxes of stylish dresses, suits, train sets, computers, gold jewelry, bicycles, furniture, and even a stage with a microphone. After a while the children seemed to go through the paces with little excitement over their gifts. I thought of Geoffrey's elation when we gave him the stuffed giraffe.

My father's television played in his study. While Zoe opened a vanity that would make a princess envious, I snuck away and knocked on his door.

"I'll be right out, Mom."

I opened it and spotted my father on his easy chair, watching a ballgame on the large screen. "It's me, Dad."

"Bobby. Come in."

I sat on the ottoman next to Dad's chair. Since he wore his favorite old flannel shirt and jeans, I was transported back to my childhood.

"Don't tell your mother I changed clothes."

"My lips are sealed."

We shared a smile.

Though his belly protruded over his belt, my father was still a handsome man. "You look good, Dad. How are you feeling?"

"Much better." He picked up the remote from the armrest and lowered the volume of the television. "Thanks again for what you did yesterday."

"Are you taking your medicine?"

He held up a vial of pills. "My blood is getting thinner by the minute."

"Obey your doctor's orders."

He saluted. "I will."

"And take some time off work."

"No more Santa for me"—his eyes sparkled—"until next year." Dad asked, "Are the kids still opening their gifts?"

"With no end to the lavishing in sight."

"And they wonder why kids are so spoiled nowadays." He pointed at me like Exhibit A. "We never did that with you and your sisters. Back then nobody had a lot."

"Dad, how did you feel when Mom told you Roseann was on the way?"

"I nearly hit the roof." He laughed. "Good thing I didn't, because the plaster and the snow outside would have come tumbling down on top of us."

"You said you were living in a small apartment and just starting out in your career. Weren't you scared about having kids to raise?"

"No. We were terrified! Neither of us knew anything about taking care of kids. We worried about how we'd get by on only my measly salary. And how we'd pay for diapers, baby food, a crib, stroller, baby clothes."

"Didn't you use your store discount?"

"Even with ten percent off, we were about fifty percent short."

"How did you do it?"

"Laughing all the way." He leaned back. "Don't get me wrong. There were some tough times when we didn't know if we'd make it. But we asked our parents for help, made some personal sacrifices—like not always eating ourselves—and most of all we focused on how much we loved you kids." He winked. "And look at what a good job we did!"

I hugged him. "Thanks, Dad." Standing up, I said, "I better get back inside."

He looked at me covertly. "Don't tell anyone where I am."

I nodded and left the den. When I got back into the living room, I found Paolo sitting on the floor, next to Bella, who was adorned in a new diamond-studded collar.

After hugging and kissing everyone goodbye, Paolo and I put on our winter things and took the bus back to our apartment. The sky enveloped us in hues of gold, peach, and violet.

When we got home, Paolo and I undressed and slid under the white comforter covering our bed. As we rested our backs against the headboard and worked on our laptops, I noticed him staring out the window at the snow—making mosaics as it fell past the streetlamps.

"Did you have a nice Christmas?" I asked him.

"I always have a nice time when I am with you." He squeezed me in closer and nestled his nose in my hair. "*Ti adoro.*"

"I love you too, Paolo."

We closed our laptops and left them on our night tables. I rested my head on his chest and he put his arm around me. "My dad looked good."

"So did your brothers-in-law."

I bit his pec.

"Ouch!"

"You deserved it."

We shared a laugh.

"I'm glad my sisters made up with them. And it's great how you played with the kids."

"The way Papa played with Francesca and me," Paolo said.

"Have you thought about having a child of our own one day?"

"Of course. As we discussed, in a few years, after we are established in our jobs."

"Do you want to go to a clinic or adopt?"

"We have plenty of time to make plans, Bobby."

"Have you ever thought about a trial run as foster parents?"

As if reading my mind, Paolo replied, "Bobby, Geoffrey is a little boy. A little *sick* boy."

I sat up cross-legged. "So?"

"So"—Paolo counted off on his thick thumbs—"if we became his foster parents, we would need to take him to regular doctor visits."

"Dr. Sherman's office is within walking distance from here. He takes children."

"We would have to feed him three meals a day."

"*We* eat three meals a day."

"Buy him clothes."

"You're a clothing designer."

"Register him for school."

"There's a school within walking distance from here."

"Which gets out at three o'clock."

"And many of the kids stay later for after-school programs."

Paolo sat up. "Bobby, I don't think this would be right for us now, or for Geoffrey."

"Geoffrey was sure open to the idea. And don't pretend you weren't considering it, because I know you were. We can convert the study into a bedroom and—"

"I am taken with Geoffrey too, but raising a child takes money."

"The agency gives foster parents money."

"Not very much." He tented his fingers. "And we are so busy with work."

"My parents can help."

"Your father just had a mild heart attack. And they are busy at their jobs."

"Jared can pitch in."

He laughed. "He avoids children like the plague. Geoffrey has wants and needs to be met."

"Will his wants and needs be met living with a poor family where he'll be one of four children?" I pressed my knees into my chest and wrapped my hands around them. "Foster parenting is a temporary situation. Maybe we can try it and see if it's a good fit."

"And if it is not? Is our little experiment fair to Geoffrey?" He took my hand. "I think it is very sweet that you are considering this. But we need to be practical. Geoffrey is not a doll or a puppy. He is a human being. This is not the time in our lives for this."

I was all out of objections and arguments, including a closing one. And I had to admit that everything Paolo had said made sense. But I wasn't in the mood for sense. We spooned with Paolo behind me, my favorite position. "Since we're both off work tomorrow, let's visit Geoffrey in the morning to say goodbye."

"I would like that."

"Me too."

I fell asleep in Paolo's arms, wondering if Geoffrey was sleeping too.

WE BOTH woke the next morning, put on chinos and rugby shirts, and ate buckwheat waffles and strawberries in the dining room. Paolo called his mama, papa, nonna, nonno, and Francesca in Italy, wished them a *Buon Natale*, and thanked them for our gift: a crate of limoncello. I phoned my grandparents in California to wish them a Merry Christmas and thank them for the gift they had sent—a crate of oranges. Then as Paolo worked on his designs in the study, I checked my phone for messages, and then returned a call from Jared. Sitting on the living room sofa, I asked, "Have a good Christmas?"

Jared's twang filled my ear. "It's about time you called back."

"What's wrong?"

"My father and stepmother had a huge fight."

"At least they were talking to each other."

"I wish they weren't. It seems dear old Dad has been having a dear old affair with someone from work."

"A man?"

"I wish." He sighed. "Alas, it was a coworker of the female species. It's been a war zone around here."

"When are you coming back from Maine?"

"As soon as I can escape unscathed. What have you and the hunky Italian been up to?"

I sat back on the sofa. "We went to church yesterday morning."

"Bad move."

"Why?"

"Because being a Protestant doesn't work."

"What do you mean?"

"A lot of cute guys looking for husbands go to your church."

"So?"

"I prayed for an hour that one of them would ask me out, and it never happened. So much for the power of prayer. That's why I've become a pagan."

I put my feet up on the ottoman. "Worked your way up to Paganism, have you?"

"As you know, I tried Catholicism, but having sex with a priest in a confessional was too confining."

"How about Judaism?"

"The Jewish guy with the long beard and ringlets was hot, but it was too complicated keeping a kosher kitchen."

"And the Mormon?"

"He was so busy with his wives, he had no time for me. And the evangelical screamed 'Hallelujah' so loud when we came, I nearly went deaf."

"Weren't you going to a Buddhist monastery?"

"Yes, until I meditated to get the cute guy next to me, and he took off with a monk."

"And now Paganism."

"Think how much fun I'll have running through the woods with some nature-loving, hairy bear worshiping the sun, moon, earth, sky, and me!"

I couldn't help laughing out loud.

"But this isn't about me, though it should be. What else did you do for Christmas?"

I filled Jared in on my father's heart attack and dinner at my parents'. "And Paolo and I visited Geoffrey."

"Geoffrey? You two decided to open up your relationship, and you didn't ask *moi*?"

When I was through talking about Geoffrey, Jared said, "When I was a New Ager, I learned that kids pick their parents."

"I think that refers to a spiritual connection before birth."

"Clearly not with you and Geoffrey. Listen, pal, I'd ask the social worker about becoming the kid's foster parents before you lose him, or before Geoffrey gets lost in the system."

I couldn't believe my ears. "I thought you didn't like kids."

"I *love* kids! Other people's kids."

"Last night in bed, Paolo ticked off a number of reasons why we shouldn't be foster parents right now."

"Whatever floats your boat in bed, pal. But I'll give you one reason to do it. You're smitten with this kid. And it sounds like he's pretty crazy about you guys too. Besides, I want to be an uncle."

Paolo entered the living room. "Do you want to visit Geoffrey before he is released?"

"I rest my case," Jared said in my ear.

I said goodbye to Jared. Then Paolo and I put on our winter things and left the apartment.

The bus ride was interminably slow. I could tell Paolo was as anxious as I was to check on Geoffrey. When we finally arrived at the hospital, we found him asleep in bed. He wasn't hooked up to oxygen, so we didn't panic. When we spotted Geoffrey's nurse in the hallway, Paolo asked her, "Is Geoffrey all right?"

Nurse Callie nodded. "The poor little guy had a rough night."

I felt my heart racing. "Was he coughing?"

"Nightmares." Her eyes softened and her cheeks reddened. "He was up a good deal of the night."

After she left, Paolo and I looked around in vain for Cynthia. Hearing a scream, Paolo and I raced into Geoffrey's room and found him sitting up in bed crying. Geoffrey threw his tiny arms around me and wept on my shoulder. Like my mother did when I was a child having nightmares, I sat on the bed rocking him back and forth. Paolo sat on the other side and rubbed Geoffrey's back.

A few minutes later, Geoffrey stopped crying, wiped his face with the sleeve of his pajamas, and sat back in bed. "I had a bad dream."

"What about?" Paolo and I asked in unison.

Geoffrey shrugged.

"You can tell us, Geoffrey," I said.

He took in a deep breath. "Jack pushed me down the stairs."

"Who is Jack?" Paolo gave me a worried glance.

"A boy I lived with."

I took over. "What else happened in your dream?"

"Carl said I didn't clean the toilets good."

"Carl?"

"Carol's friend."

"What did Carl do?" I feared the answer.

"He pushed my face in the water. And Carol hit my behind with the mop." Geoffrey reached for Bopalo and hugged him to his chest.

Cynthia appeared at the doorway holding Geoffrey's nebulizer, inhalers, medicines, and clothes. "Callie told me you had a bad night." She came to the edge of Geoffrey's bed. "Are you okay?"

Geoffrey looked at Paolo and me. "I am now."

"I signed the release papers." She handed Geoffrey his clothes. "Put these on in the bathroom."

Geoffrey did as he was told, no doubt from years of fearing the consequences if he disobeyed orders.

Paolo and I stood as I asked Cynthia, "Are you taking Geoffrey to his new foster home?"

She sighed. "Looks like it."

"Will they hurt Geoffrey there?" Paolo asked.

"No."

"But they will not give Geoffrey the full attention he needs," Paolo said.

"Geoffrey doesn't belong there." I couldn't stop myself.

After looking from Paolo to me, she said, "Can I be honest with you guys?"

She had seemed pretty honest so far. "Sure."

"I can see that Geoffrey has grown attached to you. I work for the government rather than a private religious organization, so same-sex couples are eligible. Have you thought about applying to become foster parents?"

I took in a deep breath. "Cynthia, Paolo is a junior designer, and I'm a junior lawyer. We're at crucial and very time-consuming places in our careers."

"Everyone's busy," Cynthia said, "including me."

Paolo nodded. "But a little boy needs two devoted parents around the clock."

"In an ideal world. Which this isn't." She smiled hopefully. "If you're interested, I can push your paperwork through quickly."

Geoffrey came out of the bathroom in his street clothes. Obviously having overheard our conversation, he stood between Paolo and me. "Can I go home with you guys?"

I kneeled down next to him. "We'd like you to stay with us. But it's not that simple."

"I'll say 'please', 'thank you', or whatever you want," Geoffrey said.

Paolo kneeled on Geoffrey's other side. "Bobby and I are both very busy. We cannot take care of you."

"I'll be good, I mean, *well*, and do whatever you tell me to."

Paolo and I shared sad glances.

"It is just not possible now, Geoffrey."

I smiled. "Maybe we can visit you at your new home."

Cynthia gave Geoffrey his hat, scarf, and gloves. "We'd better get going." She said to Paolo and me, "You've got my card. Let me know if you change your mind."

After Geoffrey put on his winter things, Cynthia took his hand and walked him to the door. He looked back sadly at Paolo and me. And they were gone.

As Paolo and I sat on the bed, he rested his head in his hands. "This is not the right time."

"I understand." I felt numb.

"And we do not have all the proper resources."

"I know. Let's go home." Rising from the bed, I noticed the department store Santa in the hallway, visiting children in the wing. Between children, he nodded to me and pointed to the stuffed animal on the bed that Geoffrey had left behind. I nodded back, grabbed the giraffe, and headed out the door with Paolo at my heels.

By the time we reached the front desk and asked the receptionist, Cynthia and Geoffrey had left. Paolo and I ran out to the lobby and looked around. When we didn't find them, we headed out the revolving door and looked both ways. They were nowhere to be found. Paolo spotted a bus across the street with passengers making their way onboard. I saw Cynthia and Geoffrey at the end of the line. I shouted to them and held up Bopalo. Geoffrey saw us and ran into the street. Spotting a car heading straight for

Geoffrey, Paolo and I sped into the street, each grabbed one of Geoffrey's hands, and ran him to safety on the curb.

As the bus took off, we bent down to Geoffrey.

"Are you all right?" I asked.

Geoffrey nodded.

I kissed his forehead. "I was so frightened."

Paolo added, "Never run across the street like that again. Do you promise?"

Geoffrey nodded.

Paolo hugged Geoffrey into his chest.

Cynthia stood over us with her hand on her hip. "Since we missed the bus and have some time to kill, care to fill out that application now?"

Paolo and I looked at each other, our breath making fog in front of us. "Yes!"

Geoffrey's face lit up. "Yeah!" He threw his arms around the both of us.

As we shielded Geoffrey from the cold with our bodies, Paolo said, "I do not know how we will manage, but we will try."

"Will you help us?" I asked Cynthia.

She smiled. "I thought you'd never ask."

THE NEXT week brought some good news. Paolo's boss loved his new designs and green-lighted "The Paolo Line" of men's summer wear. Matias won his case, which the religious right organization appealed with the support of the local Republican Party leadership. I was ready for the fight. I visited Dad at home when I could, and I was thankful when he was well enough to go back to work—taking the day shift only.

It hurt us to think about Geoffrey living with a foster family who didn't really want him. Cynthia fast-tracked our medical exams, interview, home assessment, and fingerprinting. However, it takes months to receive the foster parent certification. So, with the approval of Geoffrey's current foster mother, Cynthia pulled some strings and arranged for Paolo and me to be temporary custodians of Geoffrey under her supervision until the final certification arrived.

Though it was just over a week later, it seemed like a month before Cynthia finally dropped Geoffrey off at our door. Paolo and I called out a thank you to Cynthia's back, and we welcomed Geoffrey to our home. After putting his winter things in the closet, Geoffrey followed us with mouth agape as we showed him the living room. "What's that?" he asked.

"A chaise. A place to rest," Paolo said.

Geoffrey pointed to the fireplace. "What's that?"

"A fireplace," I said. "To keep us warm in the wintertime."

He sat on the window seat in the turret and stared out the window. "Are them toy cars?"

"*Those* cars are the real thing," Paolo replied.

Geoffrey did a double take. "They look so small."

"That's because we're so high up." I tweaked his nose.

When we reached the kitchen, Geoffrey said, "Should I clean here first, or in the bathroom?"

Paolo bent down and rested his knees around Geoffrey. "You do not have to clean anything, Geoffrey."

"Except behind your ears." I smiled.

Geoffrey seemed in shock. As we arrived at the next doorway, he asked, "Who sleeps in here?"

"You do," I replied.

Geoffrey's eyes seemed to double in size as he slowly entered and gazed around our study converted into his bedroom.

"Do you like the furniture?" I asked.

Geoffrey took in the colonial-style sleigh bed, desk, bookcase, and chest.

"It's a gift from my mom and dad."

"Will they sleep in here with me?"

Paolo and I shared a smile.

"My parents sleep in their own house, which you'll visit someday soon."

After we placed Geoffrey's medicines, inhalers, and new nebulizer on top of his bureau, Geoffrey added the final touch of Bopalo. "He can watch over everything."

Paolo opened the closet door to reveal Geoffrey's new wardrobe.

Wearing an old flannel shirt and jeans, Geoffrey examined his new clothes. "Who wears these?"

"You do," I said. "They're a gift from my sisters."

"How do I know what to wear?"

"We'll help you. And I'll design you something special one day." Paolo opened the chest, brimming with toys from Dad's store. "And these are from us."

Geoffrey picked up each toy, gazed at it, and then put it back inside the chest. Then he turned to us with wet cheeks.

We rushed to his sides. "What's wrong, Geoffrey?"

Paolo placed a hand on his shoulder. "Do you like your new bedroom?"

Geoffrey found his voice. "I like it really good. I mean well."

We shared a three-way hug.

Since it was time for lunch, after showing Geoffrey our bedroom and bathroom, we sat him at the dining room table. He seemed confused when we served him. "What do I do?"

"Eat your lunch," I said.

While enjoying his tuna sandwich on eight-grain bread and green salad, Geoffrey said, "How long can I stay?"

Paolo pinched his cheek. "You can stay here as long as you like."

"I like!" Geoffrey smiled from ear to ear. When he talked with his mouth full, Paolo asked him to swallow first. Then Geoffrey asked, "Should I still call you guys Bobby and Paolo?"

"What would you like to call us?" Paolo asked.

"My dads."

Paolo and I shared a smile.

"Call me Papa," Paolo said with a lump in his throat.

"And I'll be Dad." I thought of my father and blinked back tears.

Geoffrey grinned. "I like it!"

Paolo and I held hands under the table.

After Geoffrey changed into a rugby shirt and jeans like mine and Paolo's, we put on our winter things—including a new coat for Geoffrey—and spent the rest of the day showing Geoffrey around the neighborhood.

When we entered the department store, Dad hurried of out his office. "Here's my three guys!"

"I'm Geoffrey," he said with a handshake.

"It's a pleasure to meet you, Geoffrey. Do you like my store?"

Geoffrey nodded. "Who makes the steps move?"

"Let's find out." Dad and Geoffrey went up and down the escalator as if it were a ride at a theme park. Then Dad lavished Geoffrey with various electronic gifts that Paolo and I knew would take us days to figure out how to use.

Back at home, Geoffrey ate a vegetarian lasagna dinner, played his first computer game, used his nebulizer, and took a shower. Then he snuggled in his new giraffe pajamas under the giraffe comforter with Bopalo under his arm. Paolo and I sat on opposite sides of his bed.

I adjusted the comforter. "Did you have a good time today?"

"The best!"

Paolo moved the hair off his forehead. "Tomorrow we register you for school and after-school daycare."

"What are your favorite subjects?" I wondered.

"I do good in English."

I realized we'd need to make some time for tutoring.

Paolo brought up the inevitable. "Geoffrey, some of your friends at school may not like it that you have two dads. How do you feel about that?"

"Too bad for them. I'm keeping you guys."

"Sounds like a good plan." I smiled.

We kissed Geoffrey good night.

He gazed up at us. "Thanks."

"For what?" Paolo asked.

"Nobody ever kissed me good night before."

Too choked up to speak, I turned out the light, and Paolo and I went into our bedroom. After taking off our clothes, we met in the center of the bed under the comforter. We cuddled together for a while. Then Paolo lay on top of me and began kissing my neck.

"How are we going to work this with Geoffrey in the next room?"

Paolo ran his fingers through my hair. "Very quietly, and very intimately."

"Definitely sounds like a good plan."

We embraced with the moonlight filling our room and love filling our hearts.

A piercing scream woke us in the middle of the night. Paolo and I threw on our robes and raced into Geoffrey's room.

Paolo sat on the side of the bed. "Another bad dream?"

Geoffrey nodded.

I sat on the other side and held Geoffrey's trembling hand. "Geoffrey, I know a lot of people hurt you, or maybe even worse, ignored you. But that part of your life is over."

Paolo took his other hand. "You are a part of our family now. We will protect you and take care of you. We will not let anyone hurt you again."

Geoffrey threw his arms around us, and the three of us shared a long hug.

THE NEXT day, I borrowed Dad's car and drove Paolo and Geoffrey to Peddler's Village in Bucks County. Geoffrey gazed at the colonial style buildings and colorful holiday lights. When we arrived at the village gazebo, we walked through the rows of decorative gingerbread houses. Paolo whistled. "These are magnificent."

Geoffrey took my hand. "Yeah, but our house is better."

When we strolled through the landscaped gardens, Geoffrey picked a bit of holly for Paolo and me. "This is my wellest Christmas ever!"

"Ours too," Paolo and I said in unison, accepting our gift.

Tired from walking, we stopped at a local restaurant for lunch. Geoffrey sat between us. When the server asked Geoffrey what he'd like to eat, he turned to Paolo and me. "I'll have whatever my dads are having."

Paolo glanced at Geoffrey.

"Please." He added to the server, "I found these two guys in front of a restaurant. But it wasn't as well as this one."

After lunch, we drove on to Morris Arboretum's Holiday Garden Railway with its quarter mile of track. Geoffrey giggled as the toy train made its way through seven loops and tunnels. He gasped at the fifteen rail lines, two cable cars, and nine bridges made of all-natural materials.

On the drive home, Geoffrey fell asleep in the back seat. As I drove, I said to Paolo, "Are you upset that you haven't been able to do any new designs lately?"

"Are *you* concerned that you were not able to work on your cases recently?"

We both shook our heads and giggled like teenagers.

"Remember when we first met at your family's villa in Capri?"

"Of course. You wanted to study your law books, but Mama made me take you on a tour of the island instead."

"And I'm really glad she did."

We kissed at a red light, and then laughed as I drove on.

OUR TWELFTH Night party was catered by Jared's new boyfriend, a macrobiotic chef he met at his Unitarian church. Sitting on the living room chaise between Mom and Dad, Geoffrey asked them, "Are you my grandparents now?"

"Yes we are!" Mom kissed every inch of his face.

Dad squeezed him into his flabby chest for a tight hug. "And we couldn't ask for a better new grandson."

Colleen joined them. "Looking pretty sharp in your new outfit there, Geoffrey."

Roseann tucked his emerald dress shirt into his gray slacks. "You're adorable."

"What do you say, Geoffrey?" I asked.

"Thank you Aunt Roseann and Aunt Colleen."

My sisters each kissed one of Geoffrey's cheeks.

Jared leaped out of the wingback chair and shielded Geoffrey from them. "Careful of his hair!" Then he bent down toward Geoffrey. "Give your Uncle Jared a high five?"

"Okay. But don't ruin my manicure."

"The kid's a chip off the old block," Jared said as he and Geoffrey gave each other gentle high fives.

My nieces and nephews circled around Geoffrey to meet their new cousin.

Matias stood in front of our Christmas tree at the window. The lights on the tree joined the silver stars in the sky twinkling behind him. Raising a glass of organic punch, he got our attention and then said, "A toast to the new family!"

Everyone cheered, clinked glasses, and drank.

Cynthia Peterson, in a fire-engine-red dress, lifted her glass to Paolo and me. "I knew you would make terrific parents for Geoffrey."

"Thanks to your help." I kissed her cheek, which turned the color of her dress.

Dad rubbed his stomach, which protruded through his red dress shirt atop his green pants. "*Salute!* Let's eat!"

As our guests herded into the dining room for the buffet, my parents pulled me over toward the roaring fireplace. In her red and green dress with Happy New Year sprawled across her chest in gold, Mom patted her large, sprayed hairdo. "Bobby, I told you things get better when you have kids."

"Yeah, now Paolo and I won't have to sit at the kiddie table next Christmas." I added, "And we owe it all to you, Dad."

"*Me?*"

I nodded. "We met Geoffrey briefly while out shopping, but we saw him again when we visited you in the hospital. Your replacement Santa led us to Geoffrey's room."

Dad did a double take. "After I went down for the count, they didn't book a replacement Santa at the store. You must have seen a Santa from the hospital."

"But—"

"Come on, let's eat."

As I followed Mom and Dad, Paolo took my arm, looking handsome as always in his olive dress shirt and gray slacks. "*Buone vacanze, amore mio.*"

I wanted to ponder the identity of the Santa in the department store and later in the hospital, but thought better of it. Santa had brought Paolo and me the perfect Christmas gift. There was nothing more to say except, "Happy Holidays, my love."

Paolo and I shared a long kiss.

THE FIRST NOEL

BOBBY
AND PAOLO'S
HOLIDAY
STORIES:
BOOK THREE

JOE COSENTINO

To Fred for everything over all these years, my Italian-American family,
the staff at Dreamspinner Press,
the readers who begged for another Bobby and Paolo novella,
and to everyone seeking a happily ever after ending over the holidays.

"MOM, I'M worried about the planet we're leaving behind for your grandchildren too. It's horrible how our air, water, soil, and food are polluted because of lobbyists from wealthy corporations who control conservative politicians."

"You're wrong, Bobby. The environment is polluted because nobody cleans as good as I do."

I sighed.

Mom said, "I'm also concerned about the economy your son and nieces and nephews will inherit. It's sluggish and getting worse because people go out to eat and travel too much. They should stay home and cook, like me."

"It's sluggish because average people don't get any 'trickle-down,' unless we pee on ourselves by accident."

"No, people who work too hard, like you, are the reason there's a bad economy."

"Little did I know that defending clients being evicted from their apartments, losing their medical insurance, and getting fired from their jobs was destroying the country's economy."

"Well, now you know, Bobby. That's what mothers are for. To educate their children."

I needed a break from Mom. Hi, I'm Bobby McGrath. Since you can't see me, I'll tell you I'm twenty-six, tall with frizzy red hair, green eyes, and a swimmer's build. That is whenever I get to the gym for a swim while my husband of two years, Paolo, hits the weight room. I'm also a lawyer, specializing in civil rights cases. My husband and I live with our adopted son in the city with the greatest cheesesteak in the US. Philly is also the city with the most lactose intolerant people. That dichotomy perfectly sums up my mother's reasoning.

I sat on the turreted window seat overlooking the department store my father manages. Gazing out the window, I enjoyed the late-night shoppers illuminated by the candy cane–decorated street lamps. As they trudged through the snowy street, some people disappeared into Dad's store with hopes of finding the perfect holiday gift.

"How does me working too hard hurt the economy, Mom?"

"Because you're too tired to go out and buy anything," Mom replied.

"I just bought Paolo's Christmas gift: a gold watch with sapphire stones that match his eyes."

"And what did Paolo get you?"

"Nothing… yet."

"How do you know?"

"I know his hiding places. They're all empty."

"See! That's why the economy is in a slump."

The marigold, violet, and burgundy flames danced in our fireplace, surrounded by the white marble mantel and gold lions on each side. I wished Paolo was next to me. "Paolo's been incredibly busy. He's designing a new line of men's sportswear that his boss Edgar is calling, 'The Edgar Line.'"

"Why not 'The Paolo Line'?"

"Good question."

"I have another question."

"I assumed you did." Clad in my red nightshirt, I took a sip of hot cocoa and rested against the baby-blue pillows.

"You know I adore Paolo, and I trust him implicitly."

"But?"

"He's been working every night this month."

"And?"

"Don't you think that's strange?"

"Strange how?"

Mom said, "I remember you telling me Paolo's father told Paolo's mother he was working nights. Then he'd visit one of his girlfriends."

"Paolo is nothing like his father."

"Of course." Mom sighed. "Still, Paolo's mother looked the other way at his father's shenanigans with other women. So many spouses do."

I choked on my drink. "Do you think Paolo is cheating on me?"

"I didn't say that, Bobby."

"Then what are you saying, Mom?"

"I'm saying that some men cheat. Especially men who work at night. Like when Gavin cheated on your sister, Roseann."

I glanced over at a silver framed picture on our antique cherry wood end table. The photo of Paolo, Geoffrey, and me was taken the day our eight-year-old foster child became our adopted son. After three years with Paolo, his olive skin, wavy chestnut hair, Roman nose, and sculpted muscles still caused my heart to skip a beat and my nightshirt to tent. The joyous look on Paolo's handsome face whenever he is with Geoffrey and me confirmed my faith in him and in us.

"Wasn't Paolo a playboy when you first met him in his family's villa in Capri?"

"Where *you* sent me to meet my distant cousins. And *you* conspired with Paolo's mother to get Paolo and me together. And then *you* and Dad hosted our wedding in *your* backyard summerhouse!"

"And aren't *you* glad I did?"

"Yes. Because my husband is loving and loyal. Like Dad, who by the way works *nights* in December playing Santa Klaus."

"I don't think Dad's cheating on me in a Santa suit."

"I don't know. Some of those elves *are* pretty cute." I giggled.

"Where was all this wit when you were in college and law school, and I sat up nights worrying about your celibacy."

I followed the gold swirling molding of our Victorian-era apartment. "You worried about me not having dates in college?"

"Of course. I didn't want to die and leave you all alone in the world."

"Nobody is dying, Mom."

"Except your father." She sighed.

I slid to the edge of my seat. "What's wrong with Dad?"

"He has a heart condition. Did you forget?"

"Of course not."

"So I told him he needs to find someone else to play Santa at the store, and come home at five o'clock. Take a hint from your mother, Bobby. Keep your man at home after dark."

The brushed nickel doorknocker tapped lightly as our large cherry wood front door opened. "Paolo's home."

"Finally."

"Good night, Mom."

"Remember what I said!"

Paolo looked more amazing than the models of his menswear. He hung up his long black leather coat in the entryway closet and then walked toward me with his muscles bulging out of a tapered sapphire dress shirt and gray dress slacks. After sitting next to me, he rested his head on my shoulder. "I have never felt so tired in my whole life." His Italian accent still made me shiver with delight.

I smelled lemons—and cologne. "Did you eat dinner?"

"Edgar went home to his wife and kids. I had to take out a client."

"Is that why you smell like cologne?"

He nodded. "The scent must have rubbed off in our handshake."

I put Mom's cautions in the back of my mind. "Paolo, there are only a few days left before Christmas. You shouldn't be working so hard." Hoping he would take the hint, I added, "Most people are out shopping."

"Are Geoffrey's gifts all hidden in our bedroom closet?"

I nodded. "He tried to wait up for you, but he fell asleep. I nearly did too."

"Forgive me." Paolo wrapped his arms around me and everything was right with the world. "I miss you both so much."

We shared a long, wet kiss.

"Can't you tell Edgar that you need to work from home on your laptop?"

Paolo exhaled. "He wants to check up on me, and for me to show each draft to the sportswear client."

"Then Edgar will take credit for *your* work."

Paolo massaged his forehead. "Edgar is the boss—at work. But I am no longer at work. Time to play." The devilish spark in Paolo's eyes caused me to forget the fact that many men do play at work. We kissed again. Our bodies sizzled like the flames in the fireplace illuminating us. Careful not to knock over our white Christmas tree laden with gold bulbs, Paolo took my hand and led me into our bedroom. The minute I shut the door behind us, we stripped off our clothes and leapt onto our four-poster.

When we were in each other's arms, I said, "Are you trying to have your way with me?"

He chuckled. "I am not trying. I am succeeding."

"Serves me right for being so easy."

"It serves me right too." Paolo lay back on our white sheets, looking like a Greek god. "You are the love of my life, Bobby."

"You are love to me." I lay on top of him and kissed his forehead, eyelids, nose, cheeks, and mouth. He gasped in excitement and then licked and nibbled on my neck. When I squeezed his round shoulders, high-peaked biceps, and full pecs, I felt ready to explode. I licked down his chest and flicked at his erect nipples, and Paolo let out a shriek of delight. He ran his fingers through my hair, pushing my head slowly down his stomach until my breath brushed close to his manhood, where he clearly wanted more. I licked his black pubic hair, and then took each of his balls in my mouth. After licking his long, thick shaft, I tickled his foreskin with my tongue. When Paolo moaned, I kissed his mushroom-like head, and finally sucked until Paolo cried out. Tasting his precum, I released him and lay on my back. Paolo was quickly on his knees, next to me. After he kissed and sucked every inch of my long, thin dick, I was dizzy with desire. He lifted my legs.

"I need to be inside you, Bobby."

"Always, Paolo. Inside my heart."

He entered me cautiously. After I relaxed, he leaned into me, possessing what was his and I pushed back in acquiescence. As I massaged his rippling back, buttocks, and thigh muscles, Paolo slid his warm tongue into my mouth and showered me with warm wet kisses. The thrusts in my mouth matched the thrusts down below. I happily gave myself to the man I love as our bodies became one. He whispered in my ear, "*Sei il mio cuore.*"

"You are my heart too, Paolo."

He rested his body on top of mine, and I prepared myself for the warm river of his released love inside me. Instead, Paolo's thrusts became slower and less intense. When they stopped altogether, Paolo rested his face on my shoulder, and I heard a soft snore. Surprised, I wrapped my arms around him and stared at the wall.

I WOKE the next morning to the smell of kale goat cheese frittatas, cinnamon apple nut muffins, and apple cider with cloves. After a quick shower, I tossed on my dark-blue suit and headed out of the bedroom. I passed our living room window filled with a gorgeous sunrise painting the sky in shafts of vermillion, gold, and violet. Geoffrey sat at the cherry wood dining room table looking adorable in the turquoise dress shirt and black chinos my best friend Jared had bought him on their last mall outing together. I kissed the top of Geoffrey's blond hair, careful not to ruin his layered style—also courtesy of Jared. "Sleep well?"

Geoffrey nodded, his blue eyes glistening in the early morning sun. "How come my bed is called a sleigh bed?"

I sat at the head of the table. "Because it's shaped like a sleigh."

"Then can I go sleigh riding in it?"

"I took my old sleigh from Grandma and Grandpa's basement. We'll go sleigh riding soon."

"Yeah!"

I placed the napkin on my lap. "Did you do your nebulizer this morning?"

Geoffrey played coy. "Is going sleigh riding predicated on me doing my nebulizer?"

"Asthma under control. We did it earlier this morning." Paolo served our breakfasts, sat across from me, and dug into his food. He looked good enough to eat in a tight pineapple-colored dress shirt and black slacks.

Raising my cup and inhaling the wonderful aroma of apple, cinnamon, and cloves, I asked Geoffrey, "How does an eight-year-old know the word 'predicated'?"

"Uncle Jared used it when we got our manicures." Geoffrey's dimples were on display.

Knowing Jared, I was afraid to ask. "Use the word in a sentence."

Geoffrey finished his muffin and imitated Jared. "This manicure is predicated on you introducing me to your male friends when you're twenty-one."

I buried my head in my frittata and ate. "Did Uncle Jared help you pick out holiday gifts?"

"No fishing, Dad. Everything's cool," Geoffrey said. "But since we're talking gifts, I could use a bigger laptop. Just saying. Can we go to see Santa at the department store tonight?"

I did a doubletake. "I already took you to see Santa at the department store. You asked for so many things, the other kids started taking notes on their phones. Their parents shot me dagger eyes."

"I like seeing Grandpa in the red suit and white beard."

Paolo cleared his throat. "Geoffrey, did you tell the other kids that Santa was your grandpa?"

Geoffrey nodded.

"That garnered me death threats," I explained.

Paolo groaned.

"We'll see about visiting the department store again." Once we finished breakfast, I cleaned up in the kitchen while Paolo helped Geoffrey put on his coat, scarf, hat, and gloves at the entryway closet.

"Did you do all your homework?" Paolo asked him.

Geoffrey replied under his scarf, "Dad helped me last night."

"Even with math?"

"You weren't here, Papa. I took the best I could get."

I joined them and handed Geoffrey his bag—laden with lunch, books, and laptop. "Thanks for the vote of confidence."

Geoffrey grinned. "No worries. If I get any problems wrong, I'll tell Ms. Carlyle *you* helped me instead of Papa."

I threw up my arms. "I have a reputation with the third-grade faculty!"

Paolo put on his coat and kneeled next to Geoffrey. "Will you hold Dad's hand on your walk to school?"

Geoffrey nodded.

"And will you be good in school?"

Geoffrey nodded again.

"And do your inhaler with Dad when you get home after late school activities?"

"If I don't, Dad will remind me."

"You got that question right," I said.

Paolo kissed Geoffrey's cheek. Then he rose and kissed mine. "I am sorry about last night. I was so exhausted. The designs are taking much longer than I had thought. You know how demanding Edgar can be."

"Your new sportswear client sounds pretty demanding too. When will you be home tonight?"

He looked at me like a puppy caught with a slipper. "Late again. It will just be until the designs are finished and approved." Paolo's eyes begged for affection. "I will make it up to you both."

"We'll hold you to that, Papa."

I seconded that emotion.

Paolo and I each grabbed our laptops from the antique coffee table, and then we all went out. At the front door of our apartment building, Paolo waved to us and turned left for the gym and work as Geoffrey and I headed right. As we walked along the city streets with Geoffrey's small hand in mine, he pointed out the huge decorated Christmas tree, market booths brimming with handmade items for sale, and eccentric-looking snowmen at Dilworth Park. Then he smiled at the garlands on doorways and gave a thumbs-up to Santas with donation buckets on street corners. When we arrived at the entrance of his school, I stopped him at the front gate. "Do you know how much Papa and I love you?"

Geoffrey nodded.

"More than the earth, moon, and sky." I hugged him into my stomach as he craned his neck to make sure none of his friends were watching. "I'll be here at five."

"Cool. So will I."

I waved as he hurried through the gate, up the stairs, and disappeared into the school hallway. Then I continued on to my office building, where I hurried through the marble hallway, and up the elevator into my law firm's wing. After making my way past the private offices of the partners and the glass-enclosed conference room, I came to my small office, located just before the closet I had previously been assigned as a junior lawyer. The moment I rested my laptop on the desk, my best friend and colleague, Jared Schenken, stood at the doorway with his thin hand on his thinner hip. "It's about time you got here."

I looked up at the clock on the wall. "I'm not late."

"Don't be so defensive. You sound like an eighteen-year-old girl in an abstinence-only program being asked about her period."

We shared a smile.

"Thank you for taking Geoffrey shopping." I hung up my coat. "I exchanged the leopard coat you bought him for a bomber jacket."

"When he identifies as straight, don't blame me." Jared plopped himself down on the chair opposite my desk and then straightened the crease in his gray suit. "Though I'm far too young to have a son Geoffrey's age, I love being an uncle."

"He loves you too. Almost as much as you love yourself."

"You won't be mocking me when I tell you what I know."

"Is your wicked stepmother preparing to cook you for Christmas dinner in Maine?"

"I'd be sweeter than anything she could ever make, including my father. But that's not what I have to tell you." Jared leapt to the doorway, looked both ways, shut the door behind him, and resumed his seat. With a sober look on his face, he said, "I feel like an oncologist with a terminal patient."

I sighed. "Stop being a drama queen and tell me what's going on."

After taking in a deep breath, he said, "I met the man I'm going to marry."

I laughed. "Every weekend since I've known you."

"But *that* isn't the big news."

"I didn't think so." I opened my mail.

"Noel and I—

"His name is Noel?"

Jared nodded.

"How fitting for the season." I couldn't resist teasing him. "Will you date someone named Peter for Easter?"

He narrowed his eyes and the blue contact lenses nearly flew out. "Laugh clown, laugh. But you won't be laughing when I tell you my news."

"Which is?" I leaned forward.

Jared ran a hand through his blond-tipped hair. "Bobby, do you promise you won't hate me."

"Jared!"

As if guest-starring on a courtroom television drama, he said, "Noel and I went to that new little restaurant around the corner. The one at the end of the alleyway."

"How was the food?"

He waved me away like a fly. "Who cares? I don't go out to dark, out-of-the-way restaurants for the food."

"How did you and Noel meet?"

"He might have just been released from prison, and I could have found him on a website. He maybe wanted someone to play dress up with."

I raised my eyebrows. "Dress up?"

"He's been playing punishing Santa to my naughty elf."

"At least you keep it in the holiday spirit."

Jared folded his thin arms over his narrow chest. "Will you let me tell my story?"

I motioned for him to continue.

"Noel and I were sitting at our table. I was licking my lips at the sight of his meatballs, and he seemed equally interested in my breadstick."

I groaned.

"And I noticed a familiar silhouette sitting in the darkest corner of the room."

"Whose?"

Despite Jared's constant facials, a line formed on his forehead. "Paolo's. And *your* husband was with another man. So, I accidentally threw my napkin on the floor, and checked my knee reflexes—kicking the napkin across the room. After getting down on all fours, I chose my friendship with you over advances from Noel and made my way over to Paolo's table to retrieve my napkin." He placed his hand over his heart. "And I glanced up at Paolo having dinner with Noel what's his name."

"I thought *you* were having dinner with Noel."

"Paolo's Noel is a lot more important in my story. Let's call him 'the first Noel,' and mine 'the second Noel.'"

I smiled. "You don't know your date's last name, do you? And having 'sewn your wild oats,' you're thinking about marriage?"

"This isn't about *me*, pal! It's about Paolo having a romantic, late-night dinner with the first Noel! I rest my case." He smiled hopefully. "Do you hate me?"

"Jared, I already know about Paolo's dinner. The first Noel is Paolo's client. He owns a sportswear line, and Edgar assigned Paolo the new designs."

"Bobby, do you know who the first Noel is, or rather, was?"

I shook my head.

"A professional quarterback whose totally delicious milk chocolate-colored face and body filled billboards all over the city. Billboards by the way that nearly got me run over by a bus, a taxi, a bicycle, a young mother with a stroller, an old man with a walker, and a blind nun with a stick."

"Well, he must be opening a sportswear line."

"And you're okay with Paolo, the ex-Latin lover, designing gorgeous and hunky the first Noel's bicycle pants, tank tops, and jockstraps?"

"It was a business meeting."

"In the corner of a dark, secluded restaurant?"

"You sound like my mother. She thinks Paolo is cheating on me."

"Listen to your PFLAG mom, Bobby."

"Edgar has been throwing a lot at him. Paolo's been pounding his head against the wall at work."

"He's been pounding his head, but not against the wall. Bobby, the first Noel is about six-feet-five inches and two-hundred-and-fifty pounds of solid muscle, dreamy hazel eyes, and crewcut macho black hair."

"Paolo's been exhausted."

"I'm sure."

"He even fell asleep while we made love last night."

Jared gasped as if he had been shot. "That's the sign that your lover is cheating! Take it from one who has never fallen asleep in bed during sex."

"*You* had sex lying down?"

"I won't take offense to that, because I know you are hurting. And as your best friend, I am here to help soften the blows. Pun intended."

I opened my laptop and started to check my messages. However, I'd taken Paolo's by mistake. Since we used the same security code—the date of our wedding anniversary and a combination of our first names—Paolo's messages appeared on the screen. My stomach dropped.

"What's wrong?"

"Nothing."

Not buying it, Jared hurried over my shoulder and read the email from the first Noel to my husband. *P, thanks for last night. You're amazing. I want you. And I totally understand about not telling anyone. Let's keep this our little secret… for now. N.* Jared wrapped his arms around me. "My poor divorcee!"

I pushed him away. "I'm sure there's a logical explanation for this."

"Of course there is. Paolo is having an affair with the first Noel!"

A message from Paolo appeared.

"Watch him try to cover it up." Jared smirked.

We took each other's laptops. Text me if you need anything from yours. No need to forward anything from mine. My designs are all on the office computer.

As if exhibit A in court, Jared pointed to the computer. "'No need to forward anything from mine' is clearly a plea not to read Paolo's emails, especially the one from the first Noel."

I glanced at my watch and stood. "I have a meeting in the conference room."

"Is that all you can say at a time like this?"

"Go to your office and text the second Noel about your sneaky Scrooge and Tiny Twink costumes for tonight."

He held me in his arms. "I'll be here for you pal when the Italian stallion bucks off the runway."

"Goodbye, Jared." I picked up my, or rather Paolo's, laptop and hurried to the conference room.

My first interview was with a gay couple who had been thrown off a bus for holding hands. The driver, an evangelical Christian, stated it was "religious discrimination" against him to drive with the couple onboard. I had done some research and found another passenger, an ex-convict imprisoned for raping a little girl, had not caused a problem for the driver's belief system—despite a woman recognizing the pedophile. I explained to the couple how I would use that information during their upcoming court case.

Next, I met with a client on an employment discrimination case. After he had married another man, my client had been terminated from his job due to "religious discrimination" against his manager's orthodox Jewish beliefs. To prepare my client for court, I shared the information I had collected for the trial: my client's excellent evaluations, and the nontermination status of other employees including a divorcee, a spousal-abuser, and a convicted felon.

My third appointment was with a lawyer who had been relatively nondescript on the phone about his reason for wanting to meet with me. I recognized the group he represented—The Adam and Eve Forever Organization—a wealthy, powerful, anti-LGBT, evangelical Christian organization with close ties to the Republican Party.

A thin Asian man of about thirty-five entered the conference room, wearing a designer dark suit. He took me in like a fisherman spotting a whale. My gaydar signaled "another friend of Dorothy's." The man snapped a rubber band on his wrist and then cut off eye contact with me. I'd heard that technique was used in so-called gay "conversion" therapy.

He was accompanied by a small, thin blonde woman looking uncomfortable in a beige dress that failed to hide the ends of her numerous tattoos. She appeared to be in her twenties with a deer-in-the-headlights gaze.

I rose and shook the man's limp hand.

"Mr. McGrath. I am David Tong. This is Calista Simon."

I shook her tiny, cold hand. "I apologize to you both. I left my laptop at home, and my office laptop doesn't list the reason for our meeting."

"May we sit down?" David asked.

"Of course."

David and Calista sat on spacious white chairs across from mine at the long, glass conference table. "Mr. McGrath, we are here on a legal as well as personal matter."

Calista's leg bounced up and down nervously under the table. He handed me a court brief and a court order and said as I read, "As you can see by Judge Stoll's order, Ms. Simon receives immediate visitation rights. After you submit your brief, the judge's office will schedule the hearing. My organization believes custody of Geoffrey will revert back to his mother at that time."

I dropped the paper on the table and stared into Calista's blue eyes. Unable to stop my shaking hands, I said in a dry, raspy voice, "You're Geoffrey's birth mother?"

"That's correct." David slid to the edge of his seat. "And since Geoffrey's mother is obviously alive, your adoption papers are invalid."

The room spun around in circles and my heart pounded in my ears. As the sweat dripped down my back, I tried to gather my thoughts. I remembered what Cynthia Hamilton, the social worker at the foster care office, had said about Geoffrey's parents. "Geoffrey's father died of a drug overdose. You left Geoffrey as a baby. You were a prostitute and a drug addict."

Calista opened her mouth, but David spoke over her. "Ms. Simon faced some difficult personal challenges at that time. She did the right thing by requesting voluntary termination of custody for Geoffrey. However, she has more recently received the help she needed from The Adam and Eve Forever Organization's rehabilitation center, and now she would like to rejoin with her son."

David definitely had that gay "conversion" therapy dullness in his dark eyes, no doubt from receiving shock treatments in the basement of some fundamentalist church. I turned to Calista. "Geoffrey needed a great deal of medical attention as a child. He still does, due to his asthma. He was with a different foster caretaker every year." I swallowed hard. "One of them abused him. My husband and I became his foster parents last year. Geoffrey wanted us to adopt him. Mr. Tong, since Geoffrey's father is dead and his mother had relinquished custody then disappeared, we were awarded the petition for adoption. Geoffrey is happy with us."

"A child is never truly happy without his mother," David said as if instructing a child in basic mathematics.

I couldn't stop the tears from brimming in my eyes. "Geoffrey has two fathers now, and grandparents, and aunts, uncles, and cousins. He's doing well in school, and he has friends there." Rage churned in my stomach and rose to my throat like acid. "Where were you the last eight years?"

Calista tried to speak, but David raised a finger for her to be silent. "According to the staff at the treatment center, she is now fully recovered and ready, willing, and able to raise her son." David sat back in his chair. "Ms. Simon's parental rights are being stomped on by your adoption of Geoffrey. And as a Christian, Ms. Simon's religious liberty is violated by you and Mr. Mascobello raising her son in an environment that her religion, and she, consider sinful and unfit for an impressionable child."

I asked her, "Why are you doing this?"

She answered in a small voice, "I made a lot of mistakes. But now I miss my son. The people at the organization promised to help me get him back."

"There you have it, Mr. McGrath." David rose, pulled back Calista's chair, and she stood. "After you submit your brief, you will be hearing from Judge Stoll's clerk about the custody hearing date. Ms. Simon would like to visit with Geoffrey tomorrow evening at seven. She is willing to come to your home, unless you prefer another location."

Feeling numb, I heard myself say, "Home is fine."

"Thank you for your time." He offered to shake my hand.

I declined.

When they were gone, I sat alone in the conference room, unable to move. As the tears streamed down my cheeks, I thought about the last year with our son: Geoffrey asking Paolo and me for a chestnut at Germantown Avenue in Chestnut Hill, the fun he had with us at Peddler's Village and Morris Arboretum, becoming Geoffrey's foster parents, registering him for school, showing him off to my family and friends, helping him with his homework, teaching him how to eat properly and take his medicines, tucking him in at night, and officially adopting our son. But he wasn't our son. He was Calista Simon's son, and she was coming to visit him the next evening.

The survival instinct took over: the survival of Paolo, Geoffrey, and me. I ran down the hallway as I phoned Paolo. No answer. After sitting at my desk and opening Paolo's laptop, I researched everything I could find on The Adam and Eve Forever Organization, David Tong, and Calista Simon. It came as no surprise that the organization hired antigay lobbyists in Washington, DC, and had branches all over the country. David Tong was a graduate of one of the organization's "Christian centers for youth," i.e. a gay "conversion" therapy center. The organization also owned a local

Christian drug rehabilitation site, which Calista Simon had attended. She had given up her baby boy for adoption shortly after Geoffrey was born.

Next, I checked the adoption laws in Pennsylvania. Foster parents are allowed to adopt if the birth parents are proven deceased and/or give their permission for adoption.

I phoned Paolo again on his cell. Still no answer. When I called his office, the receptionist said Paolo had just left for dinner with a client. I realized I hadn't eaten lunch.

Jared appeared at my doorway. "It's five o'clock. Don't you have a husband at home. Oh, that's right. You don't." Seeing the look on my face, he asked, "What's wrong, pal?"

"What's the name of that new restaurant, where you saw Paolo and the first Noel?"

"Down Under."

I grabbed my coat—remembering how Paolo bought it for me because he said the color matched my hair. Shortly afterward, we had met Geoffrey.

"Are you going to Down Under to find Paolo and serve him divorce papers on the grounds of adultery? Since fifty percent of straight marriages end in divorce, you'll help gay people start to level the playing field. Accent on the word 'playing.'"

I closed the laptop. "Geoffrey's mother wants him back. The Adam and Eve Forever Organization hired a snake lawyer named David Tong to do their gardening."

Jared sank into the chair across from my desk. "Who's the judge?"

"Stoll."

"He was appointed by a Republican." His face drained of color. "What can I do?"

"Pick up Geoffrey at after school activities and bring him to my apartment. Make sure he does his nebulizer." I called out over my shoulder as I ran out the door, "Tell him I'll be home for dinner."

I made my way out of the building with my heart nearly exploding in my chest. When I hit the cold air, my head began to clear, and I ran to Down Under. Entering the small, dark restaurant, I said to the host, "I'm meeting Noel here, the football player."

The young, thin man licked his lips and smiled. "Lucky you." He winked at me. "And lucky Noel for having two such attractive dinner companions." Pointing to the far corner of the restaurant, he said, "I'll ask Carmen to set another place. They haven't ordered yet."

I squinted in the dark and made my way to their table.

Jared wasn't exaggerating about the first Noel. Sitting across from Paolo was the best-looking man I had ever seen in my life. Smooth, light chocolate-colored skin was highlighted by piercing hazel eyes, a straight nose, and full red lips. His perfectly sculpted muscles were housed beneath a tight white sweater and black slacks. As I approached their table, Noel looked at me like a celebrity expecting an autograph seeker.

Paolo, in a canary dress shirt and navy slacks, did a doubletake. "Bobby!"

"Why haven't you been answering your phone?" I asked, out of breath.

Paolo retrieved the phone from his pocket and examined it. "I accidentally shut it off."

"Is there a problem?" Noel asked Paolo.

"Actually, there are two problems." I sat at their table uninvited.

When Noel seemed confused, Paolo said, "Noel, this is my husband, Bobby McGrath. Bobby, Noel Samson."

Noel offered a large, strong hand. "A pleasure."

Not shaking his hand, I said, "I don't have time for formalities or good manners, I'm afraid."

Paolo's face showed concern. "Bobby, what's going on?"

"First, why are you two having private dinners in the secluded corner of a restaurant so underground it's called 'Down Under'?"

"May I?" Paolo asked Noel. After Noel nodded, Paolo said, "When I was designing the sportswear for Noel's company, I mentioned that Edgar puts his name on my designs. I also complained about working such long hours, keeping me away from you and Geoffrey. Noel offered to finance my own line of clothing. But we aren't telling Edgar, or anyone, until we've worked out the deal."

"Even your husband?"

Paolo blushed. "I didn't want to get your hopes up in case the deal fell through. I know how upset you and Geoffrey have been about my overtime at Edgar's."

"Jared and my mother are convinced you're having an affair."

Paolo and Noel shared a laugh.

"Your husband talks constantly about you and Geoffrey," Noel said. "Besides, I generally like Asian guys."

Paolo took my hand. "Did you really think I was cheating on you?"

"No. But I had to be sure."

"Are you sure now?"

I squeezed his hand. "I'm sure. But we have a much bigger problem. Geoffrey's mother has surfaced. Calista and her lawyer came to see me today. She wants Geoffrey back!" I grimaced. "Or rather, I suspect the staff at the local Adam and Eve Forever Organization have convinced her she wants him back."

Paolo collapsed into his chair. "But we legally adopted Geoffrey."

"With the information that Geoffrey's father was dead, and his mother had voluntarily terminated her parental rights then disappeared into a life of drugs and prostitution. Unfortunately, now she's claiming rehabilitation and a change of heart," I explained.

"Does she and this organization have a chance of taking Geoffrey from us?"

My throat tightened. "I'm afraid they have a very good chance, especially with a Republican-appointed judge."

Noel rubbed his square jaw. "The Adam and Eve Forever Organization, huh?"

"Have you heard of them?" I asked.

Noel revealed a row of straight pearl white teeth. "They've heard of *me*. When I was a football player. The group led protests trying to get me fired from my team, and boycotts to take away my endorsements. I'm not surprised they're after your son. Is there anything I can do to help?"

"Thank you, Noel, but Bobby is a lawyer."

I had an idea. "Noel, would you be willing to come to our apartment for dinner tomorrow at six? It's not far from here."

"Sure."

"Paolo, please give Noel our address. See you at home. Thank you, Noel!"

I hurried out of the restaurant. As I ran the few blocks home, the sky enveloped the tall buildings around me in a blanket of peach, burgundy, and marigold. White cottony snowflakes landed on my face like manna of hope. No longer feeling panic and fear, like a bear protecting its cub, I resolved to protect our son from The Adam and Eve Forever Organization.

I entered the apartment to find Geoffrey sitting on the living room sofa, next to Jared. Looking like auditioners for the musical *Wicked*, their faces were green. I hung up my coat and joined them, trying to act as if my world hadn't been blown apart.

"Hi, Dad." Geoffrey came to me for a kiss.

I opted for a hug. "What's going on?"

Geoffrey explained, "It's never too early to start masking. Otherwise, your skin will be as dry as a Republican woman's—"

"Sense of humor," Jared said quickly.

"Did you do your nebulizer?" I asked Geoffrey.

Geoffrey nodded.

Jared winced. "It nearly ruined his facial. Is that thing really necessary?"

"Yes. It keeps Geoffrey healthy."

"What good is health without beauty?"

I offered Jared a stern glance. "I'll fix dinner."

"Make my favorite. Chicken, spinach, and oyster mushroom brown rice risotto." Jared blew me a kiss.

"And lemon squares for dessert!" Geoffrey blew me an identical kiss.

Over dinner in the dining room, I blinked back tears, thinking about Calista Simon. Spearing a mushroom with my fork, I asked Jared, "How are things going with the second Noel? Are you two playing Santa and his elf again tonight?"

Jared giggled. "Tis the season to be jolly."

Hearing the name Santa, Geoffrey asked, "Can we visit Grandpa at the store tonight?"

Unable to stop thinking this might be our last Christmas with Geoffrey, I wanted my father to kiss my wounds away. "As a matter of fact, that's exactly what we're going to do."

"Yeah!"

Jared whispered in my ear, "Did you catch Paolo and the first Noel at Down Below?"

I whispered back, "I sure did—at their business meeting. Noel is coming over tomorrow night to help us with Geoffrey's custody case."

He rubbed his manicured hands together. "The plot thickens. I can't wait to meet him—in the flesh—someday soon. And yes, that's a hint."

"I thought you were going to marry the second Noel."

"I am. But that doesn't mean I can't enjoy the first Noel—appropriately first."

Geoffrey dug into a piece of chicken. "Uncle Jared, can I be the ring boy in your wedding?"

"Only if you exfoliate and moisturize your face every night." Jared lifted his green chin. "You see, Bobby. That's how you instill good habits in a child."

I swallowed hard, praying Paolo and I would have the chance to continue raising Geoffrey.

I cleared the table and loaded the dishwasher in the kitchen while Jared and Geoffrey washed their faces in the bathroom. Then we put on our winter things and headed over to the department store. The window displays of Victorian-era families leaving out cookies for Santa, sleigh riding, and making a snowman made me think how lucky those parents were not to have someone threatening the custody of their child.

We entered the department store, passing decorated Christmas trees and hollies, as the smell of evergreen filled my nose. Though Geoffrey had seen it many times before, he gaped at the large toy section. Finally, we arrived at the sign for Santaland. The plastic reindeer were lined up in front of the plastic sleigh, but Santa's large gold and red chair was empty. Two elves were trying unsuccessfully to calm down the anxious parents and even more anxious children in line. I recognized one of the elves, a short middle-aged woman who worked in the shoe department. "Where's my dad?"

She pointed to his office and then continued arguing with a well-dressed man threatening a law suit if his son didn't get to sit on Santa's lap.

The other elf, a tall, thin young man I didn't know, said to a female customer, "Santa had a bit of a dizzy spell. I'm sure he'll be back soon."

The woman's daughter screeched, "I want to go home, Mommy!"

"You're not leaving this store until you tell Santa what you want," the woman screamed face-to-face with the little girl. Then the woman turned on the young elf. "If you don't get Santa out here in one minute, I'll have you arrested for false advertising!"

"Don't bother! I quit!" He threw his green elf hat in her face, and then his pointy shoes and green and white striped socks led him out of the store.

"Watch Geoffrey. He likes to go up and down the escalator." I left Geoffrey under Jared's charge. Then I made my way to the door marked

Manager, knocked, and walked inside. I found Santa, rather Dad, laying on the leather sofa next to his desk with Mom standing over him.

Mom clutched at the collar of her long coat. "Bobby, thank goodness you're here. Maybe you can talk some sense into him."

Dad's cottony beard parted. "It was just a dizzy spell."

"Says the man who had a heart attack last Christmas." Mom ran a hand through her high-teased dark hair. "You aren't thirty years old any longer."

"I haven't been thirty years old for centuries." Dad took off his red cap and wiped the perspiration off his bald head.

I kneeled next to the sofa. "What happened, Dad?"

Mom sighed. "What happened was your father passed out after working all day as manager and all night as Santa—just like I predicted." She sniffed. "Even Santa didn't work day and night. He drank hot cocoa during the day while the elves made the toys."

"Are you all right?"

"Of course he isn't all right." Mom sat on the arm of the sofa. "He fainted from exhaustion. And now he won't go to the emergency room."

"I don't need to go to the hospital. My heart is fine," Dad said.

Mom paced the room to make her case, as I've done in court. "It has to stop, Bobby. Tell him he can't continue playing Santa. If he won't do it for me, maybe he'll save his life for you, Colleen, and Roseann. Not to mention his five grandchildren."

Contemplating whether or not this was a good time to tell them about Geoffrey, I rested a hand on my father's sagging shoulder. "Maybe Mom's right. Can you find another Santa to take your place?"

"This close to Christmas?" Dad laughed, and his belly jiggled under the red suit. "Any Santa worth his weight in cookies at the fireplace is booked."

Mom sighed. "I offered to play Mrs. Klaus. I can sit out there and have little kids spit up, vomit, and pee on *me*. I have experience from raising you, Bobby."

Dad groaned. "The kids come here to sit on Santa's lap, not his wife's."

"You'll also need a second elf, since your male elf just quit," I said.

"What?" Dad sat up.

Mom pushed him back down. "Where are you going?"

"To try and find another elf."

As if starring in an Italian opera, Mom grabbed a letter opener from the desk. "Since you don't care about your health—here! Take this knife and ram it into your heart, Robert. And as you're dying, stab me too. It will be less painful for me than watching you die of a heart attack and becoming a widow, completely alone and penniless."

"It's a letter opener, not a knife, Mom."

"And it's pretty dull." Dad grinned.

She threw it back onto the desk. "Then give me a knife!"

"I don't have one," Dad said.

"What store manager doesn't have a knife? What if you get held up?"

"I'll pull the alarm."

"Then pull the alarm. Because we have an emergency!"

"Maybe not." I hurried to the door, opened it, and waved for Jared. He and Geoffrey entered the office.

"My baby!" Mom kneeled, threw her arms around Geoffrey, and wept.

Despite Mom's dramatics, thinking about Geoffrey's mother, I choked back tears.

Mom cried out to my father, "How can you do this to our grandson?"

Geoffrey patted her on the back. "What's wrong, Grandma?"

"Nothing's wrong, Geoffrey," Dad said.

I turned to Jared. "Can you and the second Noel play an elf and Santa at the store tonight, and each night until Christmas?"

Jared's eyes sparkled. "Sure. We'd love to go public."

Dad asked from the sofa, "You have the costumes?"

"Not a problem." Jared whispered to me, "I'll tell Noel to leave the red sling at home."

Mom rose and kissed his cheeks. "You're a good boy, Jared."

"You don't know the half of it." Jared winked at her. "I'll call Noel and ask him to come over with the costumes, pronto." He moved over to the window and used his cell phone.

I put my arm around Mom and feigned calmness. "Everything's okay now."

She plopped into the chair next to the desk. "Thank goodness." Then waving her finger at Dad, she said, "You're going home and marching straight to bed. And I'm calling your doctor."

Finished with his phone call, Jared said, "Noel will be here in five minutes. Give us three minutes to get into costume, and we'll be ready for our public debut."

Dad sat up again. "As Santa's elf, you can sit on Santa's lap."

"I'm good at that." Jared giggled.

"After the kids see it's safe—"

"We're always safe."

"—Line them up and tell each kid to sit on Santa's lap and tell him what they want for Christmas. And warn Noel about the cell phone pictures."

Jared smiled. "We like taking pictures—and videos."

"Good." Dad added, "Then as the elf, you can dance around Noel's North Pole."

"My favorite pastime." Jared looked like the Cheshire Cat.

Geoffrey turned his ear at the mention of Christmas costumes, and he walked over to Dad. "Can I play an elf too, Grandpa?"

Dad threw his arms around him. "You'll always be my favorite elf." He kissed his grandson's cheek.

Jared said, "Noel and I have this one covered, kid. But you can come back outside and help me wait for Noel. Sometimes I hide from him and play naughty elf who needs to be disciplined by Santa."

"Cool!"

Jared took Geoffrey outside.

I called out after them, "No naughty Santa!"

Dad stood and took off his Santa outfit, revealing a green and blue flannel shirt and jeans. "Thank you, Bobby."

"Thank Jared," I said.

Dad smirked. "I have the feeling Jared will have a good time." He sat behind his desk. "How's my boy?"

Mom replied from her chair, "Better, now that his father isn't going to kill himself by working day and night."

"Actually, there's something I need to tell you." I sat on the sofa with my heart pounding in my chest. "A lawyer came to see me today."

"Is that unusual?" Mom rested a hand on Dad's arm.

"No. But this one brought Geoffrey's mother with him."

My parents glanced at each other nervously.

Dad gave a distracted pat at Mom's hand. "What did they want?"

"Geoffrey. The Adam and Eve Forever Organization is funding her."

"What's that?" Dad asked.

Mom tsked at him. "You know from PFLAG, Dad. They're the antigay, so-called family group. But they haven't met *this* family yet."

"Who heads their organization?" Dad didn't look like friendly Santa now.

"An ex-televangelist." I shook my head at the irony.

Dad nodded. "That means they have lots of tax-exempt money 'for God.'"

"And they have a board of fundamentalist ministers and Republican politicians."

Mom was surprisingly calm. "What's Geoffrey's mother's name and the lawyer's name?"

"Calista Simon and David Tong. Why?"

"You'll see." She rose and picked up the phone on the desk.

Dad cocked his head. "Who are you calling?"

"Someone who can take care of Simon and Tong." Mom smiled proudly. "I always knew working as a bookkeeper for a sanitation engineering company in Philly would come in handy one day."

Dad leapt up and returned the phone to the receiver. "Sit down."

Mom resumed her seat disgruntledly.

A crease deepened on Dad's forehead. "Where has Geoffrey's mother been for eight years?"

"She came from one of the organization's Christian rehab centers, where she was treated for drug addiction."

Mom shook her head. "These young people nowadays with their drugs. They say they get started because they're nervous. If they're nervous, they should do what your father does: take a tranquilizer."

"Says the woman who won't even take an aspirin," Dad said.

"That's where it starts!" Mom bellowed, "Gateway drugs!"

Dad sat back down. "Bobby, can they take Geoffrey away from us?"

Mom glanced over at the phone. "Not as long as Carmella Mascobello has a pulse!"

"Will there be a court case?" Dad looked as worried as I felt.

"The custody hearing will take place in the judge's chamber without a jury." I swallowed hard. "The judge has a history of siding with the birth parents."

"If we lose, can you appeal?"

I nodded. "But the judge can place Geoffrey with his mother during the process."

Dad's voice broke. "What can *we* do?"

"I know what *I'm* doing." Mom pointed to the phone.

I stood. "When the time comes, can you both be witnesses for us?"

My parents leapt to their feet and placed their arms around me.

"There are no better parents than you and Paolo," Mom said.

"We'll tell that to the judge, son."

I hugged them. "Paolo and I learned from the best."

My father placed a hand on my shoulder and I felt like a child again. "Your mom and I were given the gift of three wonderful children. We thought each of you was a miracle, and we still do. It was also a special kind of miracle when Geoffrey came into your life."

Mom put a hand on my cheek, the gentle touch never aging even though the lines around her eyes had. "It doesn't matter how we get our children. What matters is how much we want them and love them. This woman wanted nothing to do with Geoffrey for eight years. You and Paolo are Geoffrey's parents. He chose you and you chose him. Use everything you've got as a lawyer and as a parent to hold on to him." She smiled. "And if all else fails, remember your mother can take out the garbage!"

Mom, Dad, and I left the office and made our way over to Santaland. I was relieved to see Jared in his elf costume, dancing with children and their parents. Geoffrey ran over to me. "Uncle Jared is a big hit!"

"So I see."

Cell phones raised for selfies with Jared as if he were a celebrity.

On Santa's chair sat Noel the second, a dark-skinned, round-faced young man with a hearty laugh. Though his red costume was a bit form-fitting, his black boots quite modern, and the black chain dangling from his waist jarring, he seemed to be a favorite with the children and their parents.

A young girl was just getting off his lap. She said to her mother, "Santa said I'm going to get everything I want this year."

The mother beamed. "That's wonderful, honey."

The girl added, "And he told me I have a very handsome father."

"What a nice thing for Santa to say." The mother smiled at the father who happily checked himself out in the store mirror.

A young woman holding a little boy's hand approached Jared. "Excuse me, my son wants a doll for Christmas. My husband and I believe he should have what he wants. Will there be a problem with Santa?"

Jared put his arm around the little boy. "Honey, you've come to the right Santa." Then he danced with the elated child as his mother took pictures.

When it was time for a break, the second Noel, or rather Santa, approached Geoffrey and me. "Ho-ho-hello!"

"Hi, I'm Bobby McGrath. This is my son, Geoffrey. Thank you for doing this."

"I'm Santa. It's my job!" Noel kneeled next to Geoffrey. "And what do you want this Christmas, Geoffrey?"

"Another facial with Uncle Jared. That was fun."

He rubbed Geoffrey's hair, then stood, offering a smile. "Jared is teaching him well. He loves Geoffrey."

"And Geoffrey loves him," I replied.

Geoffrey nodded his agreement.

The second Noel said to me, "Jared plays the role of the wild queen, but inside he's a sweet, caring, and kind human being."

"I'm glad you found that out."

"And he's also a lonely soul longing to be loved."

"Are you the one to give him that love?"

He saluted. "Santa, reporting for duty."

"Are you in for the long haul, Santa?"

"The longest."

Jared joined us, met with a discreet brush of the hand from Santa. "What do you think of my boyfriend, Bobby?"

"I think you've met your match, pal."

Noel and Jared gazed at each other adoringly.

"Congratulations to you both." I turned to Noel. "Sorry I didn't ask this before. What's your last name?"

The second Noel winked at me. "Klaus."

I did a doubletake.

"Seriously. And I hope you get what you want for Christmas, Bobby. I know Jared will."

Jared laughed excitedly.

We waved goodbye to Jared and Noel as they headed back to the line of children.

Geoffrey eyed the computer games as we made our way to the lobby. Meeting us there, Mom and Dad kneeled next to Geoffrey.

"Geoffrey, whatever happens in the future, never forget that you are part of *our* family," Mom said.

Dad added, "Your Papa, Dad, and you are *our* boys, and nothing will ever change that."

Since Paolo and I hadn't yet broken the news to Geoffrey about his mother's visit, I motioned for Mom and Dad to stifle the drama. Then we kissed Mom and Dad good-night, bundled up against the cold night air, and hurried across the street. Paolo met us in the entryway of the apartment.

"Where were you?" he asked as we hung up our winter things in the closet.

"Uncle Jared is an elf. He's friends with Santa."

I explained to Paolo and ended with, "I'm sorry I didn't call you. How did things go with Noel Samson?"

"We're close to working out a deal."

"What kind of deal, Papa?"

Paolo asked Geoffrey, "Would you like me to be home at night again?"

"Yes!" Geoffrey threw his arms around Paolo's waist.

"And would you like me to have my own line of clothing?"

"The Geoffrey Line?"

Paolo laughed. "Competition from my own son."

"It will be called 'The Paolo Line,'" I explained. "If all goes well Papa will have a boss who was a professional football player. His name is Noel Samson."

"Another Noel?"

"It's Christmas time." I forced a smile.

"I will tell you all about it while we do your nebulizer."

A faster run of young feet led to, "TV for an hour or two, Papa? Or skyping with my friends?"

Paolo's slower, more confident walk followed. "You have until I get there, kid, then it is nebulizer and lights out."

I smiled at their usual nighttime battle played out for a year and looking like it was set to continue for a few more... if we had a few more years together. At the thought of losing Geoffrey, a hard tug pulled at my chest.

They disappeared into Geoffrey's room with echoes of laughter that might soon fade from our home.

Head down, heart already trying to stockpile moments like this, I headed into my bedroom to do some more research at my desk and begin writing my brief for the custody hearing.

When Geoffrey called me into his room, Paolo and I sat on the side of his sleigh bed and tucked the sky-blue comforter over his small body. I didn't know where to begin. Paolo's sad eyes told me he was at a loss for words too. Finally, I heard myself say, "Geoffrey, somebody came to see me in my office today."

"Who?" he asked.

After taking a deep breath, I said, "Your mother."

Geoffrey looked to Paolo who sadly nodded his affirmation. "She is coming here to visit you tomorrow after dinner."

"Why?"

I moved a tuft of blond hair off his forehead. "I guess she misses you."

"Then why did she give me up?"

"Maybe you should ask her," Paolo said.

Geoffrey shrugged.

"What is it?"

"Don't you want to meet your mother?" I said.

Geoffrey seemed to ponder it. "When I was in the foster homes, I used to think about her every night before bed. Sometimes I'd wish on a star that she would come and get me. But she never did."

"She's come now."

He looked out the window at the charcoal sky. "I'm all out of wishes."

My throat tightened, and I couldn't go on pretending it was all right to lose my son.

"Geoffrey, your mother wants to take you with her," Paolo said.

"But that's not what *we* want." I needed our son to know we would fight for him.

"Can she ask a judge to take me away from here?"

I couldn't lie. "Yes. But we can ask to keep you."

Geoffrey took our hands. "No matter what my mother wants, I won't leave you guys alone. Like Grandma and Grandpa said, '*We're a family. Nobody can break us up.*'"

I kissed Geoffrey's cheek and hurried out of the room before he saw me crying.

After washing my face and putting on my nightshirt, I climbed into our four-poster. Paolo came into our bedroom, stripped to his boxers, and took his place next to me in bed. As his welcoming arms wrapped around me, so did the scent of lemons. I spoke the truth. "Geoffrey is wise beyond his years."

Paolo kissed my neck. "He has been through a great deal."

I sighed. "And now he has to go through this."

"With us by his side."

I hugged Paolo closer and his pecs pressed against my chest. "I'm glad you're by *my* side."

"Always. You are the only man for me."

"Let's keep it that way."

"That sounds like a good plan."

We shared a long, passionate kiss.

Paolo broke contact. "Why did you invite Noel Samson here for dinner tomorrow?"

I smiled. "You'll see. If my plan works."

"What are you planning?"

"To keep our son."

"I like your plan." He ran his fingers through my hair. "Bobby, this woman abandoned Geoffrey. Look at the life she has led. She is no role model. We cannot lose him."

"We won't." I didn't sound very convincing.

We shared another kiss and Paolo fell asleep in my arms. I kissed his forehead and moved his head onto his pillow. Then I tiptoed over to our roll top desk, opened my laptop, and continued writing my brief. I fell asleep at my desk with the room bathed in early morning sunlight.

THE NEXT morning, Paolo, Geoffrey, and I sat at our dining room table eating breakfast: whole wheat blueberry pancakes with maple syrup. Paolo looked terrific in a lavender dress shirt and black slacks. Geoffrey was adorable as usual wearing a sunflower colored shirt and blue pants.

I sipped my strawberry smoothie, dreading the conversation ahead. Finally, I summoned up my courage. "Remember what we talked about last night before bed?"

Geoffrey nodded.

Paolo tried unsuccessfully to sound pleased. "Your mother will be visiting you after dinner."

Geoffrey asked over a lump in his throat, "Will you guys be here too?"

"Of course." I plastered on a smile. "Are you excited about meeting your mother?"

Geoffrey's face hardened. "Can we go sleigh riding before school?"

Paolo and I shared a glance. I checked my watch. "We can have a quick ride across the street."

"Yeah!" Finished with his breakfast, Geoffrey rose and took his plate and glass to the kitchen sink.

I followed with mine. "She's your mother. I hope you'll be polite to her."

He avoided my gaze. "I'll be polite."

Worry lines appeared on Paolo's face. His kiss to Geoffrey's forehead lasted longer than usual. We kissed goodbye and Paolo left for the gym and work. I bundled up Geoffrey and myself and then took my old sleigh from the closet.

When we got outside, the sun enveloped us in its golden glow. The air bit our cheeks and nose, so I adjusted Geoffrey's scarf around his mouth. Then I took his gloved hand in mine and we crossed the street. Since it was early morning, the parking lot behind my father's store was nearly empty. I sat Geoffrey on the sleigh and pushed him around the lot, amidst his shouts of joy.

After returning the sleigh to our apartment, I packed Geoffrey's lunch in his bag, and walked him to school. When we arrived at the front entrance, he took the bag and looked up at me. "I'm glad I found you and Papa."

"We're glad you found us too." When no other kids were watching, I kissed his cheek. As he walked through the gate and into his school, my fear over the return of Geoffrey's mother turned to anger. I was ready to fight for my son.

When I arrived at work, Jared was waiting for me in my office.

"The reviews are in. Noel the second and I were a smash hit at the store!"

"So I saw last night." I hung up my coat and rested my laptop on the desk.

"We're all ready for our encore engagement tonight."

I rested a hand on his shoulder. "Thank you, Jared."

He squeezed my arm. "My pleasure, pal." Giggling, he added, "And since Noel is playing Santa, I do mean 'my pleasure.'" He sat on the chair without wrinkling his suit. "Are you ready for Geoffrey's big visitor tonight?"

"As ready as I'll ever be. Luckily I'm not due in court today and I don't have any appointments. So, I'm finishing some briefs, including mine. Then heading out early."

He slid to the edge of his seat. "You're going to get through this, pal."

I nodded. "But will I still have my son?"

Jared rose, patted my hand, and left my office.

When I finished my work, I put on my coat, and grabbed a tuna sandwich on oatbread from the cart in the hallway. As I ate, I walked through the late afternoon passersby on the busy streets. In my mind, each led a happy life free of the stresses and horrors Paolo and I were facing. I wondered if any of them might have gone through a similar personal crisis in the past, and if so, how they had survived it. I dropped off my brief, requesting continued sole custody of Geoffrey, at Judge Stoll's office.

My next stop was our gym, where I changed into my bathing suit and did ten laps in the pool to clear my head. When I was back in my suit and coat, I hit the cold air again.

The moment I saw the old stone church with its tall steeple, stained glass windows, and rainbow flag out front, I breathed easier. I pulled open the heavy wooden door, walked through the lobby, and stopped at Rev. Jillian's office doorway.

"Bobby. It's good to see you!" She moved pamphlets, brochures, and flyers from the chair onto her already overflowing desk. Most seemed to announce social justice causes and activities. "Take a seat."

"Thank you for seeing me, Reverend Jillian."

"It's always a pleasure." She sat behind the desk and adjusted the black jacket over her white shirt. "Geoffrey is a favorite with the Sunday School teachers."

I unleashed a sad smile.

"Bobby, what's wrong?"

I cleared my throat. "Geoffrey's mother has emerged."

"I thought she was out of the picture before you and Paolo became foster parents."

"So did we."

"Why has she surfaced now? A mother's love for her son? Regret? Trying to make amends?"

"I met her in my office yesterday, and she didn't seem to be feeling any of those things."

"What did she seem to be feeling?"

I thought about it and answered honestly. "Fear."

"That doesn't sound like a mother craving reconciliation with her son."

"She seemed to be craving something. I should know more after today."

"Why?"

"She's coming to our apartment for a visit, prior to the custody hearing." I grimaced. "Funded by The Adam and Eve Forever Organization."

She fell back into her chair. "Open and affirming congregations like ours have been in holy battle with that group for years."

"How can they use books written two thousand years ago, that have been rewritten for political reasons over the centuries, to try and render LGBT people second-class citizens? And according to the story, Adam and Eve lived for nine hundred and thirty years! Who would believe that?" I remembered I was talking to a minister. "Sorry."

"No need. As you know, in our church we see the books of the Bible as a source of spiritual inspiration, not as literal facts or law. And we never quote passages out of their historical context. In their zeal to persecute LGBT families and gain wealth and conservative political clout, the people running the organization supporting Geoffrey's mother have forgotten Jesus' message not to judge others, to take care of those in need, and to love your neighbor as yourself. Unfortunately, unlike our denomination, they are incredibly well-funded."

"It gets worse. I haven't come before this judge in the past, but he hasn't been sympathetic to gay families."

She sighed. "What can I do to help?"

"Will you be a witness for us?"

"Of course. I married you and Paolo, and I baptized Geoffrey. The entire congregation will support you in this."

I exhaled. "Thank you. We'll need all the help we can get."

"And you've got it." She ran a hand through her short dark hair. "Bobby, do you remember the Bible story where Jesus asks the little children to come to him?"

"Sure. Luke 18:16. It's a beautiful story."

"I believe the message of that passage is children are not only the responsibility of their birth parents. As another sage said many, many years later, 'It takes a village.' Our children are exactly that—*our* children." A crease appeared between her thick eyebrows. "The Bible stories tell us that Jesus was unmarried, and he traveled with twelve men, including John, his 'most loved disciple.' He had no children of his own, but he welcomed other people's children, and he valued his role as teacher, rabbi, and caregiver. Even more importantly, Jesus welcomed everyone and strove for social justice. Bobby, you and Paolo are wonderful parents. Along with Geoffrey, you make a beautiful family. I believe God looks proudly on the three of you, and as the saying goes, 'What God has joined together, let no one put asunder.'" She took my hands. "Let's pray."

After my meeting with Rev. Jillian had ended, I thanked her and then walked briskly to pick up Geoffrey at school. Despite my attempts at conversation, he was pensive and quiet on the way to our apartment. The moment we got home, he hung up his winter things and ran past my open arms into his room to do homework and Skype with his friends.

At six o'clock, Paolo led Noel Samson through the front door. As I welcomed them and hung up their coats, I couldn't help noticing the first Noel looked amazing in a tight gold sweater and black slacks that revealed each of his muscles. His onyx hair, charcoal eyes, and cocoa complexion glowed. Geoffrey came out of his room, and Paolo introduced Noel to Geoffrey as Paolo's "new boss."

"It's nice to meet you, Geoffrey."

As they shook hands, Geoffrey said, "You're even stronger than my papa."

The first Noel laughed. "Your papa is pretty tough. You should see the contract he negotiated."

Paolo laughed.

"Are you going to keep my papa out working late at night?"

"Not if I can help it," Noel replied.

"Good."

"Thank you for coming, Noel," I said.

He released a radiant smile. "It's my pleasure."

"I don't mean to impose on you, but when David Tong arrives, I wonder if you can keep him occupied."

"How?"

"By talking to him for a bit, so Paolo and I can speak with Calista."

"Who's David Tong?" Noel asked.

"A lawyer for The Adam and Eve Forever Organization."

"I'll do my best." He sighed. "Based on his line of work, I'm guessing David Tong is a total bore."

I couldn't disagree.

Paolo had gotten up early and made eggplant rollatini, manicotti, chicken primavera, and Cesar salad. After we enjoyed dinner in the dining room, Paolo, Noel, and Geoffrey sat on the sofa and talked while I cleaned up in the kitchen. Given the circumstances, the air was rife with tension.

When the doorbell rang at exactly seven o'clock, my heart skipped a beat. I opened the door to Calista Simon in the same beige dress and David Tong wearing a blue pinstriped suit. After I made the introductions, they handed me their coats and I rested their things over the ottoman. David took one look at Paolo and snapped a rubber band on his wrist. When he saw Noel, he gasped and snapped again and again. In turn, Noel focused on the young lawyer. Paolo offered Calista, David, and Noel a seat on the chaise, and then he sat on the sofa, with Geoffrey between us.

After an uncomfortable pause, I said, "Geoffrey, Calista is your mother."

Calista smiled weakly. "Hello, Geoffrey."

Geoffrey stared at her, not uttering a word.

David stopped gaping at Noel. "Geoffrey, I hope you enjoy this visit with your mother. Because you two will have a lot more time together. She would like you to live with her again."

"Which we are challenging in court," Paolo said.

I put my arm around Geoffrey. "We'll all talk to Judge Stoll soon. He'll help us figure this out."

Geoffrey rose from the sofa and walked slowly toward Calista. She opened her arms and embraced him to her chest.

"You aren't my mother." He ran into his room and slammed the door.

My jaw tightened. "I knew this would stir up Geoffrey's fears of abandonment."

David smugly folded his arms over his chest. "Judge Stoll ordered the visit."

"Geoffrey should not be forced to do something he does not want to do." Paolo disappeared into Geoffrey's room and closed the door behind him.

I took in a few deep breaths to calm down. Then I tried to explain. "This is quite uncomfortable for Geoffrey, and for us. He was moved from foster home to foster home over the years until finding a family with Paolo and me. He's happy here. This is his home."

Calista turned pale. She excused herself to use the bathroom.

David cleared his throat. "Judge Stoll ordered an hour of supervised visitation this evening for Geoffrey and his mother."

"I'm sure Paolo is trying to get Geoffrey out of his room," I replied with venom in my voice.

Still taking in David, the first Noel said, "In the meantime, can we talk a little business?" He smiled. "I'm Paolo's new boss."

David returned the smile. "Weren't you a football player?"

"I was." Noel held David's gaze. "It's nice of you to mention that."

David snapped the rubber band around his wrist. "I was a fan."

"Is that right?"

David nodded, and snapped.

"I'm flattered."

"You had many fans." David licked his lips. "I'm sure you still do."

"Not as many now that I'm selling activewear for men." He whispered in David's ear, "The couch potatoes hate me."

They shared a laugh.

The first Noel was certainly keeping David occupied as I had requested.

"Bobby, my lawyer will be sending you Paolo's contract to look over." Noel winked at me. "Be easy on me. Paolo is a terrific clothing designer, but I don't want to lose my shirt."

David snapped his rubber band wildly.

Noel winked at me. "My lawyer is a bit of a pussycat, I'm afraid."

David spoke up. "I'm a lawyer too."

Noel nodded. "I figured that out."

David was practically salivating. "I could look at the contract, if you like."

"You'd do that for *me*?" Noel asked.

David nodded like a ragdoll.

"I don't know, David. I wouldn't want to impose on you."

"It wouldn't be an imposition. I'd enjoy it." He snapped his rubber band. "I'm happy to offer you legal advice."

"It would be helpful if you could check the contract for any loopholes," Noel said.

David snapped the rubber band again. "Sure. I can take a quick peek."

"Great." Noel rested an arm around the back of the chaise. "I'd really appreciate that."

"I'm glad." David snapped.

They gazed at each other like homeless men offered a mansion. Though still upset about Geoffrey, the irony of The Adam and Eve Forever Organization's lawyer being attracted to another man didn't escape me.

David asked, "When would you like me to see it?"

Noel's square jaw dropped. "See it?"

"The contract."

"Right."

I followed my own plan. "As the saying goes, 'There's no time like the present.'"

David cleared his throat. "But since I work for The Adam and Eve Forever Organization, we'll have to keep this strictly confidential between us."

"Sounds like fun." Noel played his role like a pro. "How about walking with me to my office and checking it out right now? It's only a couple of blocks from here." He leaned over with his pecs swelling like melons. "I can also show you some of Paolo's sportswear designs—if you're interested."

David looked like a starving man spotting a banquet through a ring of fire. "I'm interested. Very interested." He tried to cover with, "Sportswear has always been important to me."

"I'm not surprised. You're in great shape." The ex-athlete asked, "What sport do you play?"

A crease formed on David's smooth forehead. "I go to the gym, but I'd like to start playing a sport too."

"Which sport?"

"How about… tennis? Yes, tennis. A great sport. But I'll need to buy some… tennis sportswear."

"You came to the right place." The first Noel stood. "Shall we go?"

Calista rejoined us, still looking sallow.

David's voice cracked as he rose. "Agh, I was told not to leave Calista."

"I'll make sure she sees Geoffrey," I said.

David pried his focus off Noel. "Calista, will you be all right without me for a while?"

She nodded and then stared at the hardwood floor.

"Paolo should have Geoffrey out of his bedroom soon," I said.

"I think you'll really like the swimwear Paolo designed, David." Noel's abs curled. "I can't wait to wear one myself."

David wiped the sweat off his forehead and onto his straight black hair.

"Let's go." As Noel offered a hand to David, Noel's bicep nearly tore his shirt.

David said to Calista, "Remember what we discussed."

She nodded again.

Noel walked David to the door. "I think you'll like my company's assets."

David snapped wildly.

I handed them their coats. "Show him the entire line," I whispered to the first Noel.

As they left, David craned his neck back toward Calista.

"Enjoy!" I closed the door behind them.

Paolo exited Geoffrey's bedroom, the strain showing on his handsome face. "We did Geoffrey's nebulizer. He won't come out. So he is getting ready for bed." He sat on the sofa across from Calista. "Geoffrey is usually a happy, social child."

"Until tonight," I added.

Calista squirmed. "I'm shy myself. My son probably gets that from me."

"This is more than shyness." I joined Paolo on the sofa. "No little boy should have to live in a household where he isn't wanted, where he is put to work and receives contempt instead of love. Geoffrey survived that for seven years."

Calista's large blue eyes clouded. "I'm so sorry to hear that."

"Are you?" I couldn't stop myself. "What did you think would happen when you voluntarily gave up a child with severe asthma?"

She took a tissue from her purse. "I wish I could explain everything I did and why, but you wouldn't understand."

"Try us." Paolo was at the edge of his seat.

"Don't you think we deserve that?"

"Yes." She pulled back her small shoulders. "What would you like to know?"

Paolo was stern. "Where are you from?"

"Philly. But not a nice place like this." Calista gazed around the room.

"Where in Philly?" I asked like an investigative reporter.

"In a housing project." She winced. "As a young girl, I remember hiding under my bedsheet from the rats, until they gnawed through it. Then I hid under the bed with the roaches. I did a lot of hiding, especially from my father after he lost his job at the steel mill and my mother died of cancer."

Paolo's face saddened. "Why did you want to hide from your father?"

"He was a simple, kind man." She looked away. "Until he drank. Then he became angry. He called me by my mother's name, and he…. I begged and pleaded, but it didn't help. He kept on…. When I met Bill on the street one day after school, I thought he was my ticket out. He was twenty-five, handsome, and nice to me. Bill took me to restaurants and movies. And he gave me pills to dull the pain." Her face hardened. "But when I wanted more pills, and I couldn't pay for them, he put me to work."

I was surprised at my feelings of empathy for her. "How old were you?"

"Sixteen. I was one of Bill's girls for a year. When I became noticeably pregnant, Bill said he would drive me somewhere to get rid of it. I couldn't do that. And I told him so. He became enraged, and he kicked me out of his apartment. I didn't have anywhere to go, so I followed a homeless woman to a shelter." She shuttered. "It wasn't much better than living with my father."

"You had Geoffrey there?" Paolo also seemed to be warming up to her.

"In a nearby clinic." She laughed ironically. "How could all that horror produce such a beautiful little boy?" She smiled. "I named my son after my grandfather. I loved him so much. Before Grandpa died, when I was a little girl, I remember how he gave me candy and called me his 'pretty girl.'"

She wiped her eyes with the tissue. "At the shelter, I loved holding my baby and talking to him. But he was sick. He kept coughing and gasping for air. I didn't know what was wrong with him. So I went back to the clinic. The doctor there ran some tests, and then he said they needed to keep him there and do more tests. I was so afraid my baby would die. And what kind of mother could I have been, given all my… problems? So I talked to a social worker at the clinic. She helped me make the arrangements with the state agency." She wept bitterly. "To give away my baby. After that, I couldn't go to the shelter. I missed my boy too much. So I went back to Bill. For five years." She made eye contact with me. "When people say Hell doesn't exist, they're wrong. I know firsthand."

Paolo reached out for her trembling hand. "Then what happened?"

"I couldn't do it anymore."

"Do what?" I asked.

"The drugs. The men. I felt like I was dying." She sighed. "And I was. Outside and inside. I told Bill I wanted out. He got angry and hit me. Then he dragged me into his car, drove for a while, pushed me out to an alleyway, and took off. I got up and walked for I don't know how long. It was a cold, windy day and I didn't have a coat. I was freezing. Suddenly, the sun came out, and there was a ray of light in front of me. I followed it to a building with a cross in front of it. I went inside, and a woman asked me why I was there. After I told her, she led me to a room with a bathtub, and she gave me clothes to wear and food to eat. Then she took me to an office. The minister and I talked for an hour. Nobody had ever listened to me like that. He said he could help me get off the drugs, protect me from Bill, and even put me in a school. And he made good on his promises. After two years, when I was recovered, I told him about my baby."

"And The Adam and Eve Forever Organization paid for an investigator to find your child, and a lawyer to sue for custody?"

She squeezed Paolo's hand. "But you have to understand something. Those eight years, I thought about my son every day. I had dreams at night where he called out for me, reached his little hands to me, and told me he loved me."

Paolo released her hand. "You received quite a different reception from Geoffrey."

She offered a bleak smile. "I understand why Geoffrey doesn't want to speak to me. What kind of mother doesn't see her son for eight years?"

The lawyer in me was revived. "Why are you seeking custody of Geoffrey now?"

"Pastor Rosario at the clinic said the Lord forgives sinners, and if we are born again in his son's name, God makes all things new again." Her eyes filled with tears. "I'm not the person I was when I left my son. It took me a long time, but I've finally forgiven myself. I hope my son will one day forgive me too. I want that second chance with my son."

"So you hope to pull Geoffrey out of the only home where he's ever felt loved, protected, and secure?" I asked.

She clenched her fists to her chest. "I know that with the Lord's help my son will one day be happy with me. That's what I'm holding on to."

Paolo rested his elbows on his knees. "We thank you for giving birth to Geoffrey. And we would like you to be a part of his life. I believe one day he will come to understand why you left him."

"But we've provided a loving home for Geoffrey. He sees us as his parents, and we see him as our son. Geoffrey is now a healthy little boy who is doing well in school. Changing his routine will only hurt him."

Calista tented her fingers. "It's clear that you two have been conscientious guardians for Geoffrey. But The Adam and Eve Forever Organization believes a child's place is with his mother." She wiped a tear off her cheek. "I believe that too."

"Can we work out a schedule of regular visitation for you?" I asked.

Calista shook her head. "That's not what The Adam and Eve Forever Organization wants."

"What do *you* want?"

"I want my son. That's the only reason I'm here."

Paolo rose. "Let's try this again." He motioned for us to follow him into Geoffrey's bedroom. When we got to the doorway, we found Geoffrey feigning sleep in his sleigh bed. Paolo and I stood on one side of the bed and nodded to Calista.

After moving to Geoffrey's other side, she rested a hand on his head and smiled. She whispered, "He looks like an angel. I can't believe I lost out on precious moments like this with my son."

"It was your decision."

Calista met Paolo's defiant stare. "And I've regretted it every day of the last eight years." Then she said, "Geoffrey?"

Clearly not interested, Geoffrey rolled over onto his stomach and placed his hands over his head.

Secretly pleased, I led Paolo and Calista out of the room and closed the door. "I delivered my brief to Judge Stoll today. I'm sure we'll hear soon about the hearing date."

She seemed to speak from the heart. "I wish it didn't have to be like this, but I need my son."

"So do we." Since David and Noel hadn't returned, I walked Calista to the hallway and offered her coat.

"I hope you gentlemen both don't hate me."

I took Paolo's hand for support. "We don't hate you. We love our son."

"I love my son too."

After she left, Paolo leaned against the front door. I rested my head on his shoulder, and he hugged me to his chest. "What a horrible life she has led."

"And now she's trying to make our lives horrible too," I said.

"I feel sorry for her."

"Yes, and I feel sorry for us, and for Geoffrey."

We checked in on Geoffrey who was really sleeping this time. We placed the sheet over him, each kissed his cheek, and then we continued to our bedroom. When we were under the white sheet of our four-poster in our undies, Paolo smelled like a lemon grove after the rain. He said, "This is difficult enough for *us* to process. Geoffrey is a little boy. How will he get through it?"

"With our help and support."

"I wonder why Noel and David didn't return."

"I think I know."

We shared a giggle and wrapped our arms and legs around each other.

Starlight from the window twinkled in Paolo's sapphire eyes. "This will all soon be just a memory."

"Hopefully one that the three of us will soon forget."

As the moonlight filled our bedroom, we cuddled in each other's arms until sleep overcame us.

THE NEXT morning, while Paolo made breakfast—vanilla buckwheat waffles, I did Geoffrey's nebulizer with him in silence and then he dressed for school. He also didn't speak as I straightened out his lime dress shirt and black slacks. Then as I watched him tie his shoe laces, I brought up Calista. His response was the same: "She's not my mother."

After breakfast, I wished Paolo a good day, and then walked Geoffrey to school. He held my hand tightly all the way, and he didn't wince once when I kissed his cheek near one of his classmates.

Upon reaching the gym, I tried to get in some swimming before work. The visions of Calista in my head psyched me out and I gave up after two laps. At my office, I hung up my coat and looked through my mail. The first Noel had sent over Paolo's contract. Upon perusal, it seemed quite generous to me.

Then I noticed the letter from Judge Stoll's office:

Having received the briefs from both parties, the custody hearing of Geoffrey McGrath Mascobello is scheduled for December thirtieth at three p.m. in the judge's chambers. Counsels are welcome to bring witnesses. The child's presence is required as are the presence of the birth mother, Calista Simon, and the adoptive parents, Robert McGrath and Paolo Mascobello. Until that time, the child will remain with the adoptive parents. The birth mother will have visitation rights any evening or evenings of her choice from seven p.m. until eight p.m.

I sank into my chair feeling sorry for myself—and for Geoffrey. I texted Paolo the date and time of the hearing. Then I opened my laptop and emailed my parents, Cynthia Hamilton the social worker, Rev. Jillian, Geoffrey's teacher, and Geoffrey's doctor, requesting them as witnesses. When I looked up, Jared was standing over my desk. "The custody hearing?"

I nodded. "It's set for December thirtieth."

"I'm not surprised Judge Stoll put it on the fast-track. Hopefully he won't let his narrow-minded conservative beliefs cloud his judgment." He smirked. "If he does, I'll pay him a little visit, give him a big kiss, and take a selfie for the internet."

Even Jared couldn't make me laugh. "If Stoll follows the 'family values politician' mold, he'll be caught in a public restroom with another man."

"Or a young boy."

I changed the subject. "How are things going in Santaland?"

"Amazing!" His creamed complexion glowed. "Having an audience has invigorated the second Noel. And being with Santa is truly a winter wonderland for me!"

I smiled.

"How's your dad?"

"Fine. Thanks to you."

"Thank Santa." He winked at me. "*I* do often."

THAT EVENING at dinner—baby hens with rosemary new potatoes and broccoli in a lemon garlic cashew sauce—Paolo opened his laptop on the dining room table. "Here are some of my new designs for The Paolo Line."

Geoffrey gazed at the terrific photos of colorful men's swimwear, summer clothes, and sportswear. "I still think 'The Geoffrey Line' has a better ring to it."

"Do your own designs." Paolo kissed Geoffrey's nose.

I took his hand. "Geoffrey, next week you, Papa, and I have an appointment with a judge. Your mother will be there."

"She's not my mother." Geoffrey ate his dinner.

Paolo placed a hand on my elbow and then said to Geoffrey, "Judge Stoll will ask you some questions."

"Just answer them honestly," I added.

"Do I have to?"

"Yes, I'm afraid you do."

He drank his almond milk. "I don't care what that judge says. I'm not leaving you and Papa."

Paolo and I shared a hopeful glance as we cleaned up from dinner.

"Come on, let's forget about the judge for tonight and celebrate the new fashion line."

"Where?" Paolo and Geoffrey asked in unison.

"Follow me."

Paolo and I bundled Geoffrey and ourselves up and took the bus to the Longwood Gardens Christmas in Kennett Square. Geoffrey's smile nearly touched his eyes watching the twinkling lights, colorful fountains dancing to holiday music, steel band, and giant trees adorned with red and green festive decorations. Stimulated but exhausted, we took the bus back. We all headed to bed, having quickly forgotten about the holiday festivities, and focused back on the upcoming hearing.

SINCE THE next day was Christmas Eve and Geoffrey was off from school, after breakfast Paolo and I took him on the bus to the Reading Terminal

Market Holiday Railroad. Geoffrey perked up watching the toy trains choo-chooing through the seventeen train lines and miniature scenery of Center City and the Pennsylvania countryside. He then pulled us over to the counters of food.

When Geoffrey complained of being tired from turning on the childhood charm to get tastes of the shopkeepers' delicacies, we ate lunch at a table, and then headed back on a bus to a matinee of *A Christmas Carol* at the Walnut Street Theatre. At first, he tried to behave like a sophisticated adult. However, Geoffrey soon gave in to giggling at Tiny Tim's antics, gasping at the three ghosts, and applauding wildly at Scrooge's metamorphosis from selfish miser to compassionate advocate of social justice. When the performance was over, he turned to Paolo, sitting on one side of him. "Edgar is like Scrooge, and you're like Bob Cratchit."

Paolo laughed. "Not any more. Noel is a far more understanding and generous employer. I have lots of time off over the holidays to spend with you and Dad."

"Yeah!" Geoffrey and I said in unison.

After an early dinner at Geoffrey's favorite restaurant, we attended an evening performance of The Philadelphia Ballet's *The Nutcracker*. Geoffrey dozed off during the initial party scene. Getting his second wind, he was mesmerized by Drosselmeyer's magic tricks. Sitting at the edge of his seat, he cheered on the Nutcracker and the toys at their war with the Mouse King and the mouse soldiers. He snoozed again during the Candyland dances. Then during the curtain call, I smiled with pride when he applauded wildly and said to me, "I don't need a mother to take me to ballet shows."

While caught in the crowd during the slow exit through the lobby, we ran into Noel Samson and David Tong, looking spiffy in black tuxedos.

I said, "Hello, Noel, David."

Paolo hid his face behind his program. "My new boss just caught me away from my design software."

Putting an arm around David, the first Noel said, "We spotted you at *A Christmas Carol* too. Great story, huh, David?"

David nodded uncomfortably.

Noel explained, "David and I are enjoying a day and night out on the town too."

David's face hardened. "Actually, I have been giving Noel some legal advice."

"Meet my new lawyer, and date." Noel squeezed his shoulder. "When the Sugar Plum Fairy danced with the Cavalier, I snuck a kiss."

David snapped the rubber band on his wrist.

Stopping near the box office, Geoffrey asked the first Noel, "What do you think of selling 'The Geoffrey Line'?"

Paolo and I shared a laugh.

Noel kneeled next to him. "I think I can't afford you, so I'll have to stick with your papa."

Geoffrey nodded.

Rising, Noel asked, "What are you folks doing for Christmas?"

I replied, "We're going to church and then to my parents' house."

Noel waved a thick index finger in the air. "Ah, that's the church Paolo was telling me about. I walked by the other day. It's really beautiful. Would you like to go with me, David?"

The lawyer shuffled from foot to foot. "I was going to my own church."

"Of course." Noel was clearly disappointed.

David seemed to notice. "But it wouldn't hurt to attend another church, just this once."

Noel released his famous smile, reached out his hand to David, and his bicep practically burst through his suit jacket. "Then you'll join me?"

"All right." David snapped the rubber band.

"Great. We'll both see you there." The second Noel shook our hands. "You folks have a wonderful Christmas Eve."

Paolo glared at David. "That is going to be difficult this year… under the circumstances."

David blushed. "We each have our business to attend to."

I recalled *A Christmas Carol*. "Mankind should be our business."

As they were leaving, Noel pulled me aside. "Lay off David. I'm not pretending any longer. I really like this guy."

"Remember he works for The Adam and Eve Forever Organization."

"Bobby, it's Christmas. A time for miracles and happy endings. Believe." The first Noel hooked David's arm and they were gone.

When we got home and hung up our winter things, Paolo made hot cocoa with cinnamon and turned on the golden lights of our Christmas tree. The three of us sat under the tree and exchanged gifts. Paolo loved my watch and Geoffrey's handmade angel—named the First Noel. I adored the leather wallet Paolo gave me, and the elf Geoffrey had made for me at school—aptly named Jared. Geoffrey jumped up and down when he opened the polo shirt and shorts Paolo had designed and made for him, and the computerized space station from me.

I thought about Geoffrey's toys carefully hidden in my closet. "I wonder what Santa will bring you in the morning?"

Geoffrey looked at me as if I had said the earth was flat. "Just ask Grandpa or Jared's Noel."

Paolo and I shared a smile.

After we tucked Geoffrey into bed, Paolo and I snuggled in our four-poster. I placed my head on his thick neck. "It was a wonderful Christmas Eve, but I couldn't shake the nagging suspicion that it could be our last together as a family."

"I am afraid too. We need to have Geoffrey's certainty and resolve."

"I think Geoffrey is in denial, insisting Calista isn't his mother."

"Maybe you and I should be in denial too."

We shared a long kiss. Paolo slipped off my nightshirt and his boxers, wrapped his arm around my waist, and spooned in close, releasing the smell of lemons. I felt warm, protected, and loved. As he kissed my neck and shoulders, I said, "Is this to make up for conking out on me the other night?"

"Oow, make-up sex. It sounds kinky."

I giggled as Paolo blew into my ear and gently bit my earlobe. Then Paolo massaged and pinched my erect nipples. I gasped in delight as the thickness of his girth eased inside me. After a while his gentle thrusts grew in intensity and speed, as did our desire. He grasped my bobbing erection and toyed with it, which caused me to cry out in ecstasy. When he buried his Roman nose into my hair, we both shouted our release—Paolo filling me with his essence and me exploding into his hand. As we kissed, he said, "You, Geoffrey, and I will always be a family. Nothing can change that."

After we cleaned up, Paolo spooned me again. As he snored softly, I repeated Paolo's words in my head like a mantra until sleep finally came.

PAOLO AND I woke early Christmas morning to Geoffrey's screams. I panicked, remembering Geoffrey's past nightmares about his days in foster care. However, we raced into the living room and found him sitting on the floor, surrounded by his opened presents from Santa. Sitting next to him, we oohed, aahed, and yawned as he showed us each of his wardrobe, toy, and electronic treasures.

After we all washed up and did Geoffrey's nebulizer, the three of us put on dress shirts, dress slacks, and red and green sweaters. Then Paolo made popovers, Greek yogurt, and mixed berries for breakfast in the dining room.

Afterward, as I loaded the dishwasher in the kitchen, Geoffrey disappeared into his room to text his friends in a one-upmanship on their Santa stash. Paolo sat on the chaise in the living room and phoned his mama, papa, nonno, nonna, and sister Francesco in Capri, thanking them for the usual carton of *limoncello*. Then I called my grandparents in California, always early risers, and thanked them for the crate of oranges—a yearly ritual.

Checking the time, I bundled us up, grabbed the shopping bag of gifts in the hall closet, and we all headed down the stairs. The Victorian carolers in front of Dad's store serenaded us, and the light snow landed on our noses as we walked along the city street. For one day of the year, passersby smiled and said, "Merry Christmas." Cars waited for pedestrians, and people held open doors for each other.

When we arrived at our church, we hurried inside. Geoffrey led us to our usual pew next to the stained glass window of Jesus holding up a stone, beckoning others to stone the "sinner" to death if any in the lynch mob were without sin themselves. Poinsettias and tall white candles filled the historic building with a floral and vanilla scent. We enjoyed singing the traditional hymns accompanied by the antique pipe organ that filled most of the sanctuary. I gazed around the church and spotted the first Noel and David Tong sitting toward the rear.

Rev. Jillian delivered a heartfelt sermon on believing that baby's birth so many years ago can still bring peace on earth and goodwill to all who demonstrate acts of love and compassion for others. She went on to speak passionately about Jesus' ministry of equality for all. I couldn't help wondering how taking Geoffrey away from a loving home could possibly be considered a "Christian value" by The Adam and Eve Forever Organization.

After the service, Geoffrey greeted some of his friends. While we kept an eye on him, Paolo and I approached Noel and David. "Did you enjoy the service?" I asked.

"Yes, thank you for inviting us." Noel put his arm around David. "I also enjoyed being with this guy."

David gazed at Noel. "It's been a wonderful Christmas morning." He snapped the rubber band on his wrist. "The sermon provided a different perspective of Christianity than I've heard in the past."

I couldn't resist. "Yes, we don't advocate taking children out of loving homes, hating ourselves for being born gay or lesbian, judging others, and screaming 'religious discrimination' as we persecute those who are different."

David stiffened. "I was brought up to believe certain things."

"Perhaps now is the time to question those beliefs," Paolo said.

Noel squeezed David into him. "Are you willing to open yourself up to something new, David?"

David melted and snapped. Paolo and I stifled giggles.

Rev. Jillian shook hands with her congregants in the lobby as we exited the small church. Paolo and I regrouped with Geoffrey. When it was our turn, Geoffrey said, "You talked really well, Reverend Jillian. My dads didn't even fall asleep this time."

She laughed. "Thank you, Geoffrey. And thank you for keeping an eye on your fathers for me."

He nodded.

As I shook her hand, Rev. Jillian said, "Keep your eyes on God's love. Know that everything will be all right."

I whispered back, "Please speak with the gentleman behind us."

She nodded.

Paolo, Geoffrey, and I chatted with a few other church members. As we were leaving, I heard Rev. Jillian say to David, "As for Adam and Eve, there are two other creation stories in Genesis that don't mention them. And Sodom and Gomorrah is a cautionary tale against greed and rape, not homosexuality. The correct English translation of Leviticus 18:22, 'You shall not lie with a male as with a woman,' is actually, 'You shall not lie with a boy as with a woman.' And if being gay is a sin, why didn't Jesus ever mention it?"

You go, girl.

Paolo, Geoffrey, and I took the bus to my parents' house, where we were greeted with hugs and kisses from the usual swarm of relatives as we took off our coats. Since I'm allergic to my parents' dog Bella, she ran over to me and lay over my feet. When I moved, she growled and showed her fangs.

The kids opened their gifts under the tree. Then Paolo gnashed his teeth, trying to start up the "easy to operate" electronics that would stump a mechanical engineer.

My little niece Zoe was decked out in a red velvet dress with a white lace trim. She took Geoffrey by the hand and led him to a dining room window. "You see that glass house out there?"

Geoffrey nodded at the all-glass structure in my parents' backyard.

"That's where your fathers got married. I was there."

"I want to get married there too," Geoffrey said.

Zoe shook her head, and dark hair sliced the air. "We can't get married. I'm your cousin."

"My dads are cousins."

I said quickly, "We're *distant* cousins," and then steered Geoffrey back to the living room.

As the children screamed in delight at their new toys, my sister Colleen flicked back her long auburn hair and stood next to me. "Mom told us about the custody hearing."

"I assumed."

"I wish somebody would try to take Zoe and Lucas."

"No you don't."

"You're right." She took in a deep breath and the Santa on her stomach expanded. "You know I'm here for you and Paolo."

"I know."

"There are no parents better than you two." She ran toward her daughter. "Zoe, stop waving that doll! You nearly poked your brother's eyes out!"

My other sister, Roseann, appeared, and the eight reindeer on her dress stared up at me. "Geoffrey belongs with you and Paolo. What mother leaves her kid for eight years? I'd never leave Franco and Nicola. Unless their nanny quit."

"Thanks, Roseann. How's everything going with you and Gavin?"

"Not as good as with you and Paolo."

"Maybe that's because I'm not hot for my personal trainer."

She slapped my shoulder. "The way Paolo looks, you don't need a personal trainer." We shared a laugh, and then I walked into the kitchen with

Bella at my heels. As is Mom's way, she had made enough food to feed the homeless—all over the world. In a red dress that was snug around the hips and with her hair teased even higher than usual, she moved platter after platter from the refrigerator onto the counter. "Hosting this will kill me one day. I'm sure of it. You know I'm not a young woman. And I never signed up to be a caterer."

I sneezed, and Bella rubbed her head against my leg. "Why don't you stop doing this, Mom?"

She looked as if I had asked her to murder the Pope. "It's tradition!"

"Paolo and I could have brought something."

"Nobody brings food to Carmella Mascobello's house."

I laughed.

"You think it's funny that your mother is about to drop dead on the floor with a house full of people here?"

"I find it interesting how you use your maiden name when you want to be Italian."

"I *am* Italian. And so are you. At least half of you. The *good* half."

I looked over at the kiddie table. "I married an Italian. Does that graduate me from the kiddie table this year?"

"You can sit with the adults in the dining room—if you make sure your father doesn't eat anything with a drop of cholesterol in it."

I pointed to the dishes full of pasta, meat, and fish covered with rich sauces. "I don't think that's possible."

"Fine. Then your father and I will *both* drop dead. Good luck finding a priest to bury us on Christmas."

"I'll check the altar boys' locker room."

She glared at me with mascara-laden dark eyes. "Hey! I told you we don't talk against priests or the Pope in this house."

"They talk against *us*, and they lobby in Washington, DC, to take away my rights."

"That's why I work so hard as a PFLAG mom to make sure they don't succeed."

I threw my hands up and then helped Mom carry the platters out to the dining room. She made circles around me like a tornado.

When we were through, she said, "How is my grandson's case going?"

In honor of old time's sake, I sat at the kiddie table in the kitchen. Bella rested her head on my lap and I sneezed. "I'm as ready as I can be. Soon it will be in the judge's hands."

She looked upward. "Not only in the judge's hands."

"You mean in God's hands?"

"Not exactly." She pointed to the phone. "You sure you don't want me to call one of our clients at my company to... take care of things."

"Yes! I'm sure."

"I'm hungry!" one of the kids whined from the living room.

Mom sprung to action. "Bobby, your father's watching the ballgame in his den as usual. He thinks I don't know he snuck a scotch and two meatballs in there. Tell him to put on the clothes I left on the bed, and then come to the dining room to say grace. It's his place as the man of the house. And hurry up, so I can tell him what to say before everyone starts eating."

I made my way to Dad's study with Bella following. When I knocked on the door, I heard a shuffling noise. Then my father called out, "Come in."

I opened the creaking door. "Hi, Dad."

"Bobby. How's my boy?" He swallowed fast.

"Mom knows you smuggled in the scotch and meatballs."

He displayed a cannoli in his palm. "But she doesn't know about this." He laughed as he ate.

"How are you feeling, Dad?"

"Great." He sat on his worn, brown easy chair. "Thank your two friends again for helping out at the store."

"They're having a ball. Literally."

He laughed and shut off the television. "Sit down."

"There's no time. Mom wants you to change out of your flannel shirt and jeans and say grace in the dining room."

"Rest for a minute."

I sat on the frayed ottoman across from him. Bella sat on my lap. When I tried to move her, she showed her teeth.

"How are you three guys holding up?"

I sneezed. "Geoffrey keeps insisting that Calista isn't his mother. I guess it's his way of avoiding the whole issue. Paolo and I are putting up a brave front, but we're both scared to death of losing Geoffrey."

Dad rested back in his chair and drank his scotch. "Bobby, when you were three years old, you had a very high fever."

"I don't remember that."

"I do. We took you to Dr. Columbo, and he didn't know what was wrong. Antibiotics, cold baths, and children's aspirin didn't help. Needless to say, your mother and I panicked. Friends and relatives offered us all kinds of frightening scenarios of what could be wrong with you. When you got sicker and you wouldn't leave your bed, we started to believe each scenario. Then suddenly one morning you woke up fine."

"What did I have?"

Dad shrugged. "We never found out. But I learned some things aren't what they seem at first. And our minds can be our worst enemy, or our best friend. So instead of thinking about the worst, ponder on the best. And know that you, Paolo, and Geoffrey deserve it."

I hugged my father and he patted my back like he did when I was a boy. When Bella growled, I said, "Come on, Dad. Let's get you ready for dinner."

We stuffed ourselves at dinner—Paolo and I in the dining room and Geoffrey at the kiddie table in the kitchen. Then Paolo, Geoffrey, and I hugged and kissed my parents, and said goodbye to my relatives. Finally, we bundled up and boarded the bus for home.

When we reached the apartment, Paolo did Geoffrey's nebulizer and then we all dressed for bed. Once Geoffrey was tucked in, Paolo and I lay on our backs with the sheet over us, staring up at the wall. We heard laughter and singing from the street below, passersby enjoying the last few hours of Christmas. They echoed the laughter we'd left at my parents, but then took on the shapes of the shadows on the wall, warning me my family was in serious danger of being destroyed.

THE NEXT few days seemed like years. I numbly went through the mechanics of washing, dressing, cooking, eating, swimming, working, and taking care of Geoffrey, never once able to stop thinking about the upcoming custody hearing and the possibility of losing our son. We were home every night at 7:00 p.m. After Geoffrey refused again to see her, Calista never took the judge up on his offer of visitation rights.

The thirtieth finally arrived. Paolo, Geoffrey, and I spent the day at home silently contemplating the hearing. Then we rode on the bus to the courthouse as I offered Geoffrey words of hope and encouragement that I didn't fully believe myself.

At 2:45 p.m., the three of us sat uncomfortably in our suits, waiting on a bench in the courtroom. Paolo stayed with Geoffrey as I rose and thanked each of our arriving witnesses for attending the hearing.

Mom said, "Where else would I be when someone is trying to take away my grandchild?"

Dad added, "Take one wave at a time, son."

Geoffrey's teacher, doctor, and social worker offered their full support.

Lastly, Rev. Jillian squeezed my hand. "I've been praying for justice."

Calista entered in a white dress with a man I hadn't seen before. Mom lowered her fingers and gave Calista the Italian horns.

The court clerk entered. I introduced myself.

The man with Calista did the same. "I'm counsel for Ms. Simon."

I offered my hand to the short, middle-aged lawyer wearing a drab blue suit. "I'm Robert McGrath."

Shaking my hand limply, he replied, "Allen Arnold." He adjusted his horn-rimmed glasses. "Counsel with The Adam and Eve Forever Organization."

"Where's David Tong?"

Before Arnold could answer my question, he excused himself to welcome Calista's witnesses: a counselor and a minister from the local taxpayer-funded Christian drug rehabilitation center, owned by The Adam and Eve Forever Organization.

The court clerk informed Arnold and me, "The judge will interview each of your witnesses, and then they may depart."

I called each of my witnesses, and the clerk led them into the judge's chambers individually. Arnold did the same. Though they were through testifying, Mom and Dad and Rev. Jillian remained in the courtroom.

The clerk announced, "Judge Stoll would like to speak with Geoffrey."

I nodded to him, and Geoffrey followed the clerk into the judge's chambers. Then she exited the chambers and left the courtroom. Since the chamber door was open a crack, I stood nearby and watched—pretending to be on my cell phone.

Judge Stoll's black robe hung off him. Sitting behind a huge desk, the short and thin man looked even smaller. With a forced smile on his sunken face, the elderly justice spoke like the host of an old children's television show. "Hello, Geoffrey, can you please take this seat next to my desk?"

Geoffrey did so, and his back faced me.

The court reporter sat at a smaller desk.

Judge Stoll asked, "Do you know where you are, Geoffrey?"

Geoffrey said, "I'm in a judge's office."

"And do you know who I am?"

"You're the judge."

"Right." Stoll leaned forward. "And do you know what a judge does?"

"My papa said you're going to ask me questions."

"That's right. Did he go over the questions with you, and ask you to answer them?"

"How could he do that? They're *your* questions."

"Yes." Stoll examined a sheet of paper in front of him. "You've lived with Robert McGrath and Paolo Mascobello for a year." He looked at Geoffrey. "They were your foster parents and now they are your adoptive parents. Is that correct?"

Geoffrey nodded. "I call them Dad and Papa."

"Do you like living with 'Dad and Papa'?"

Geoffrey nodded.

"What kinds of things do you do with them?"

"Papa does my nebulizer with me. He designs some of my clothes. And he cooks for us. Dad brings me to school and to see Dr. Sherman. He also takes me swimming, and he plays games with me."

"What kind of games?"

"On the computer. And we go sleigh riding."

"What else do you do with them?"

"They buy me what I need, and let me Skype with my friends. And they tuck me in at night."

"Do they take you to church?"

"Every Sunday. If you don't believe me, you can ask Reverend Jillian. She's out there with my grandpa and grandma. Reverend Jillian wouldn't lie."

Stoll stifled a smile. "How are your grades in school, Geoffrey?"

"All A's except for math."

"What did you get in math?"

"A B-plus."

"A B-plus is good."

"That's what I told my dad, but he said after all the hours Papa has helped me with my math homework, I could do better."

"Maybe so." The judge continued. "Are you involved in any activities after school?"

Geoffrey nodded. "Chess, the choir, and gymnastics. My Uncle Jared told me to try out for the school play. We did *The Wizard of Oz*. He was hoping I'd be the Wicked Witch of the West because that's his favorite role. But Ms. Santillo cast me as a Munchkin and a talking tree."

"As they say, 'There are no small roles, only small actors.'" He sighed. "Bad analogy in this case." Stoll folded his small hands over his narrow chest. "Geoffrey, you received two visits from Calista Simon. As I understand it, you wouldn't speak with her on either occasion, which hurt her feelings. Do you know that?"

Geoffrey nodded.

"And do you know that she is your mother?"

"She's not my mother."

"Yes she is. And like most mothers, she would like to have her son live with her. I think that is a good thing. What do *you* think about living with your mother?"

"I found my dad and papa last year. They're my family. I'm staying with them."

Stoll rested back in his wide chair. "You are a remarkable little boy."

"I don't know what 'remarkable' means. But if it's good, thank you."

Stoll nodded. "All right, Geoffrey. Can you please go back into the courtroom?"

As Geoffrey rejoined us, Mom sat him next to her and then held up her cell phone toward me. "Let me know if I should make the call to 'you know who.'"

Dad gave me a hug. "Love always wins."

Rev. Jillian squeezed my shoulder. "Godspeed."

The clerk returned and asked Paolo, Calista, Arnold, and me to enter the judge's chambers. Once inside we were directed to sit across from Stoll's large wooden desk. Paolo and I took seats on one side, and Arnold and Calista sat on the opposite side.

Stoll said, "This is the case of Robert McGrath and Paolo Mascobello versus Calista Simon over the custody of Geoffrey McGrath Mascobello on December thirtieth at 3:00 p.m. in the chambers of Judge Jeremiah Stoll. All parties are present. Let it be noted that Robert McGrath has decided to represent himself, and I have already interviewed the child and each of the witnesses from both counsels." He looked up at Arnold. "Where is David Tong?"

Arnold cleared his throat. "Mr. Tong filed the initial papers, but he has since relinquished himself from the case. I am replacing him."

Stoll raised an eyebrow. "Let it be noted that Allen Arnold will be representing Ms. Simon. Welcome back to my chambers, Mr. Arnold."

"Thank you, Judge." Allen nodded.

Stoll took a moment to review the papers in front of him. "I've read the briefs on both sides, heard testimonies from your witnesses, and read the medical and financial statements from both parties. As I mentioned, I spoke with Geoffrey. All right, gentlemen. This is your time." He motioned to me. "Mr. McGrath."

I cleared my dry throat. "Judge, my husband and I were Geoffrey's foster parents for three months. Our social worker, Cynthia Hamilton, wrote a report about our progress."

"Yes, I read it," Stoll said. "And I spoke with Ms. Hamilton."

"During that time, Geoffrey asked if we would adopt him. My husband and I wanted that very much. As you read in my brief, and I assume you heard from my witnesses, Paolo and I take care of all of Geoffrey's needs, including the special activities revolving around his medical condition. Geoffrey had led a life of instability prior to last year. But he is doing very well now in school and at home. Conversely, Ms. Simon voluntarily gave Geoffrey up for adoption eight years ago when she was having problems with drugs and living a life on the streets. My husband and I are pleased that she went to rehabilitation, and we are certainly open to visits from Geoffrey's birth mother, but we believe it would be a reckless decision that would harm all parties concerned if she were given custody of Geoffrey. Most importantly, Geoffrey wants to stay where he is, in the place he calls his home with the family he loves. Please don't break his heart and ours. Please keep our family a family."

Paolo rested his hand on mine. I took in a deep breath and sat back.

Judge Stoll nodded. "Thank you, Mr. McGrath. I appreciate your brevity and clarity."

"Thank you, Judge."

Stoll added, "Mr. Arnold. Please see if you can do the same."

Arnold rose and addressed the judge. "There is nothing more natural and important than a mother's love for her child. Calista Simon gave life to Geoffrey, and she has thought about him every moment of every day since. Rather than risking possible damage to the child, she gave him to a state agency who could help him, while she sought much needed assistance for herself. And the moment she was rehabilitated, this woman came back for her son. You read my brief and heard testimony from a licensed professional and a clergyman both touting Ms. Simon's progress. In their expert opinions she is able to care for her son. You also heard their quoted research on how the homosexual lifestyle is in direct opposition to child-raising."

"The results of the studies I submitted show the opposite."

Stall glared at me. "Mr. Arnold did not interrupt you. Please award him the same courtesy."

"Thank you." Arnold leaned over the judge's desk. "Mr. McGrath and Mr. Mascobello live a deviant lifestyle in the same home as an eight-year-old boy. Ms. Simon, our studies, and frankly I, find this behavior to be detrimental to the well-being of the child. In addition, not awarding Ms. Simon custody of her child would be a case of religious discrimination, given Ms. Simon's religious beliefs and the nature of Mr. McGrath's and Mr. Mascobello's unnatural sexual proclivities."

"We've never made love in front of Geoffrey!"

Stoll raised a finger. "You'll get your turn, Mr. Mascobello."

Paolo sat back in his seat.

"And what do homosexuals do in bed? It goes much further than the sodomy condemned in the Bible." Arnold spoke as if there were rotten eggs in his mouth. "Fisting, golden showers, whipping!"

"Maybe *you* do those things, but we've never done them," Paolo shouted.

Stoll waved a hand. "Mr. Arnold, we don't need a lesson in alternative sexual practices. And Mr. Mascobello, I won't caution you again."

"We apologize, Judge." I shushed Paolo.

Arnold ended with, "These two men have chosen their abnormal lifestyle. Geoffrey is an innocent boy who has not. I beg this court, please don't subject this child, Ms. Simon's child, a moment longer to the homosexual agenda of child abuse and recruitment."

Paolo seemed ready to explode.

After Arnold sat, Stoll turned to me. "I get the feeling Mr. Mascobello has something he wants to say."

Paolo slid to the edge of his seat. "Bobby gave you the results of a study showing children brought up in gay households generally fair the same or better than children brought up by heterosexual parents. And in most cases the children do not turn out to be gay themselves. This man and his so-called 'family' organization are the perverted ones as they lie and deceive others, distorting words like 'religion' and 'family.' Bobby, Geoffrey, and I are a family."

I held Paolo's hand.

Stoll turned toward Calista. "There's one person in this room we haven't heard from. Mr. Arnold, will Ms. Simon speak to us this afternoon?"

After Arnold nodded, Calista rubbed her palms against her dress and took in a deep breath. "I made a lot of mistakes. I should have never given up my son. I know you can't go back. But what I've learned at The Adam and Eve Forever Organization is that you *can* ask God for forgiveness and to begin again." She turned to Paolo and me. "You both seem like nice people who have taken good care of Geoffrey. I won't judge you, and I thank you for not judging me." She made eye contact with the judge. "But I want my son back, and the people at The Adam and Eve Forever Organization said they can help me do that. In addition to rehabilitation and schooling, they've found me an apartment and a job as a church secretary. I believe with their help, I can make a good home for my son." She took a tissue from her purse and wiped her eyes. "That's all I want. My son. Please let me have my son."

Judge Stoll shuffled his papers. "I've heard all your testimonies. Now it is my task, based on the laws of Pennsylvania and my own judgment, to decide what is in Geoffrey's best interest." He rested on his elbows. "I scheduled this case quickly because of its high importance. The life of an eight-year-old child with Geoffrey's history vitally needs resolution. It is clear to me that Mr. McGrath and Mr. Mascobello have done a fine job as foster and later adoptive parents. Geoffrey seems like a happy child whose needs have been met. However, my life, my time as a judge, and my religion have taught me there is nothing more sacred than a mother's love for her child. We are all sinners who fall short of God's will for us. Can we not forgive those who have erred in the same way we are forgiven? And this mother has certain religious beliefs that we cannot ignore. Doing so would be religious discrimination against her."

Paolo rose with a trembling body. "No!"

I joined him. "Judge, please—"

"So I am awarding temporary custody of Geoffrey for one month to his mother. After that time, we will reassess Ms. Simon's progress with her rehabilitation and with Geoffrey."

"You can't do this!" Paolo shouted.

"Yes, I can." Stoll added, "Mr. McGrath and Mr. Mascobello, you may visit with the child one evening a week for one hour when Ms. Simon is at home."

The room was spinning around me. I heard myself say, "We're appealing."

"That is your prerogative." Stoll made a note. "Please have Geoffrey's things packed and Geoffrey ready to leave tomorrow at 10:00 a.m."

The chamber door opened.

Arnold said, "My organization will have a car to take Ms. Simon to pick up her son."

"No, you won't." Noel Samson rushed in with David Tong and the court clerk following.

"I apologize, Judge, but—"

Stoll waved the clerk away. "Mr. Tong, you finally arrived. I've already pronounced my judgment."

"I'm Noel Samson."

"I know who you are," Stoll said.

"I believe you will reconsider your decision about Geoffrey after hearing what David has to tell you." Noel nudged David toward Stoll's desk.

"Well, Mr. Tong?"

David averted Arnold's glare and handed Stoll a packet. "Judge, this is proof that Ms. Simon is not Geoffrey's mother."

Calista rested her head in her hands.

Arnold turned beet red. "This is outrageous!"

Stoll offered Arnold his palm. "Just a moment."

As Stoll read, David said, "The Adam and Eve Forever Organization employs researchers to investigate gay couples who adopt children. Then they hire lawyers like me on staff to use legal avenues to remove the children from those households. If no legitimate method of obtaining the child exists, they fabricate a scenario by which to accomplish their goal."

Noel nodded, and David continued. "Calista Simon gave birth to a child eight years ago when she was involved with drugs and prostitution. Five years later, she wound up on the doorstep of The Adam and Eve Forever Organization. They sent her to drug rehabilitation and classes, and got her an apartment. When she told them about her son, they investigated, and eventually offered legal services to try and take her son from his adoptive parents: a heterosexual couple. The organization did all this with one stipulation. Ms. Simon first needed to pose as Geoffrey's mother, who in reality died of a drug overdose six years ago. When Ms. Simon agreed, the organization paid someone working at the state agency to forge Geoffrey's birth certificate and list Calista Simon as Geoffrey's mother."

Arnold replied, "Lies! It's all fake news from the liberal homosexual lobby. This is religious discrimination against—"

"Stop!" Calista slowly got up from her seat. "I've done enough harm to this family." She turned to Arnold. "I appreciate what you and your organization have done for me, but I can't go on with this."

Arnold's veins bulged out of his neck. "Think about what you're doing!"

"I am. For the first time in my life." Calista walked toward Paolo and me. "I wasn't lying when I said I'm doing this to get my son back. That's all I wanted. But after watching you both with Geoffrey at your home and here today, I realized that destroying your home won't help me get mine." She addressed Stoll. "Your Honor, Geoffrey isn't my son. Everything Mr. Tong said is true. Geoffrey belongs with his fathers."

Stoll waved David's packet. "I am forwarding the papers from Mr. Tong to the district attorney's office with my recommendation for a full investigation of this matter."

"Judge, I can explain."

"My assumption is that you will be explaining to another judge in a disbarment hearing, Mr. Arnold. You too, Mr. Tong." Stoll glared at Calista. "And I will not be surprised if you land in prison."

"We aren't pressing charges against Calista."

Paolo joined me. "But we *are* pressing charges against The Adam and Eve Forever Organization and Mr. Arnold."

Stoll said, "Regardless, the district attorney's office will take things from here. Mr. Arnold and Mr. Tong, I hope to never see you in my chambers again. Ms. Simon, I recommend you get your life together. Mr. McGrath and Mr. Mascobello, though I disapprove of your chosen lifestyle, and I don't believe you should be raising a child, legally, I have no recourse but to rule that Geoffrey's custody remains with you. Case closed."

As we left the judge's chambers, Calista said to me, "My little boy had asthma too. I hope one day you'll understand."

I took her hand. "You're a brave woman. I hope your son knows his mother soon."

"Not on *our* dime." Arnold glared at her. "You've angered some very wealthy and incredibly powerful people.

"So much for Christian love," Paolo said.

I slipped Calista the card of a well-known secular organization that I thought could help her.

When we reached the courtroom, Calista and Arnold flew out the door. I gave everyone the good news. Paolo, Geoffrey, Mom, Dad, and I shared a long hug. Then I turned to Noel. "Thank you! How did you do this?"

Looking amazing as usual in a tapered peach dress shirt and slacks, the first Noel unleashed his dazzling smile. "When I had *my* run-in with The Adam and Eve Forever Organization, they had hired 'offended customers' to complain to the companies about using me as the businesses' spokesman. When Geoffrey insisted Calista wasn't his mother, I paid someone to do a little research, and I started suspecting the organization was doing the same thing with your case."

"That is so generous of you," Paolo said.

"Not really. The fee is coming out of your pay checks." Noel faced him. "When David admitted the truth, I wanted to give this guy the boot. But I've been spending a lot of time with him. And, especially after what he did today, I'm ready to get a lot better acquainted." After kissing David's cheek, he added, "Wasn't he terrific in there?"

Paolo said to David, "We appreciate what you did at the hearing."

David hung his head. "Better late than never."

I raised his chin. "You helped our family stay together. Thank you."

"Thank *you* for introducing me to Noel." David added, "And to Reverend Jillian."

While Paolo continued talking to the first Noel and David, I kneeled at Geoffrey's side. "You were only a baby when your mom brought you to the state agency. How did you know Calista wasn't your mother? When she hugged you at our place, did you somehow remember something?"

Geoffrey shook his head. "As I said, I don't have a mother. I have two fathers. And that's fine with me." He took our hands. "Let's go home."

Rev. Jillian whispered in my ear, "And the little child shall lead them."

We left the office with our son.

THE NEXT evening, Paolo, Geoffrey, and I stood in our coats on the Delaware River Waterfront watching the New Year's Eve Fireworks preshow. The sky was full of rainbow umbrella bursts of pink, gold, teal, and blue. To our right were Jared and the second Noel.

Jared held Noel Klaus's hand. "My heart feels like the sky. Can I tell them?"

The second Noel nodded.

"Noel and I are engaged!"

Paolo and I hugged them.

"Congratulations, pal."

"You showed me how, pal." Jared giggled. "You have to help me pick out a bouquet and garter, Best Man."

"You got it." Then I said to the second Noel, "You'll have quite a handful with Jared."

The second Noel's dimples emerged. "No problem. I'm keeping Santa's whip."

On our left side, Noel Samson put his arm around David Tong. David said, "You're a wonderful man. Thank you for helping me see the light."

"My pleasure," the first Noel replied.

"And mine." David grinned.

They shared a passionate kiss.

The first Noel said to Paolo, "My lawyer boyfriend and I may be following Jared and Noel, and you and Bobby someday."

David's face lit up like the fireworks. "Do you really mean it?"

The first Noel nodded.

David swooned. "You're so amazing!" He pulled the rubber band off his wrist and threw it into the water.

"You're pretty amazing yourself."

The first Noel and David shared a long kiss.

I kneeled next to Geoffrey. "You understand that Calista was playing pretend about being your mother, like Uncle Jared and Noel pretended they were the elf and Santa?"

Geoffrey nodded. "Play pretend is fun. But I'd rather have the real thing with you two guys." He took our hands in his.

Paolo turned to me. "Happy Anniversary, *mi amore*."

I rested my head on his shoulder. "The first of many more to come, my love."

We all looked out at the fireworks, ready to welcome in a new year.

JOE COSENTINO began as an actor appearing in principal acting roles in film, television, and theater, opposite stars such as Bruce Willis, Rosie O'Donnell, Nathan Lane, Holland Taylor, and Jason Robards. Watching him on YouTube, his students said, "You were cute when you were young." He moved on to playwriting and directing, where his plays were published and produced in NYC, regionally, and on tour. Upon writing fiction, his mother said, "Don't you have anything better to do than write books?" He replied, "I wonder if Shakespeare's mother said that to him?" All's well that ends well, as his mother, other family members, and friends love his published books. He hopes this book is made into a movie and he wins an Academy Award, so he can make a too-long acceptance speech. Writing is all in the family since his spouse is an audio book performer.

Joe received his MFA from Goddard College in Vermont and MA from SUNY New Paltz. He is currently Chair of the Department/Professor of Theatre at a college in upstate New York, where he and his spouse designed and had built an environmentally friendly home. Joe is a member of an open and affirming church, and does fundraising for GLSEN.

He hopes people will find this book to be the perfect gift for the holidays, and he loves to hear from readers.

Website: joecosentino.weebly.com

Cinder, a poor and beautiful young man who designs clothing, makeup, and hair for his stepmother and stepsisters, offers his clothing and slippers to a naked stranger in the woods, who turns out to be none other than Prince Charming. Follow Cinder and Prince Charming in this twist on the classic Cinderella tale as they discover their inner strengths and find their very own happily ever after.

Enjoy *The Naked Prince* and three other reimagined tales from Fairyland, each with a unique spin on stories we all know and love, including *The Golden Rule*, where eighteen-year-old Gideon Golden, after being thrown out of his home in Fairyland by his homophobic parents, breaks into the cottage of three burly men on Bear Mountain.

In *Whatever Happened To...?*, friction ensues between a celebrity with a growing appendage and a reporter who has a thing for giants.

And in *Ice Cold*, young Gaelen must save his love, Kieran, after a handsome but evil prince freezes Kieran's heart and bewitches him into being the prince's slave.

www.dreamspinnerpress.com

An
INFATUATION

Joe Cosentino

An In My Heart Novella

With his ten-year high school reunion approaching, Harold wonders whether Mario will be as muscular, sexy, and tantalizing as he remembers. As a teenager, it was love at first sight for Harold while tutoring football star Mario, until homophobia and bullying drove Mario deep into the closet. Now they're both married men. Mario, a model, is miserable with his producer wife, while Harold, a teacher, is perfectly content with his businessman husband, Stuart. When the two meet again, will the old flame reignite, setting Harold's comfortable life ablaze? How can Harold be happy with Stuart when he is still infatuated with his Adonis, his first love, Mario? Harold faces this seemingly impossible situation with inimitable wit, tenderness, and humor as he attempts to reconcile the past and the future.

www.dreamspinnerpress.com

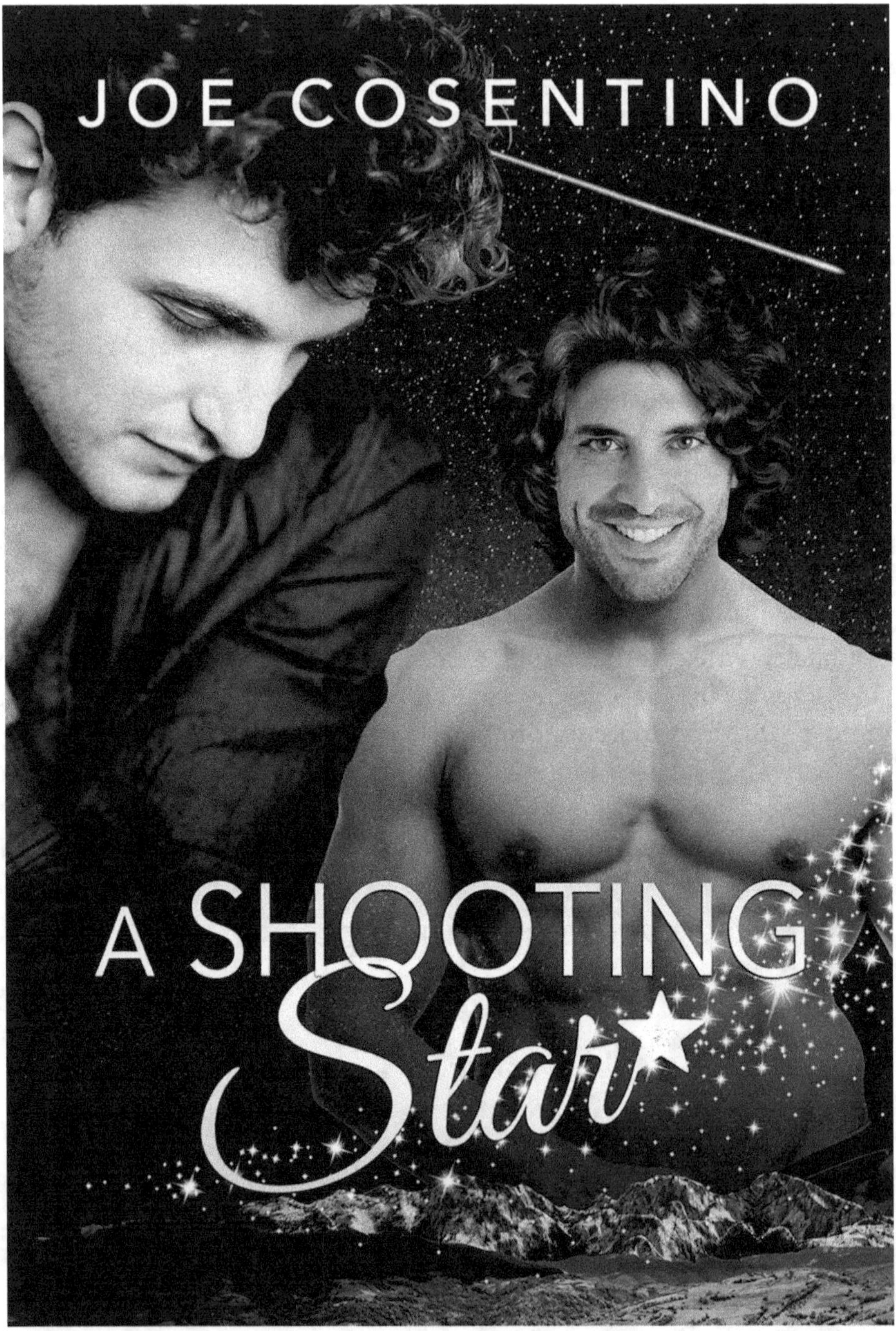
JOE COSENTINO
A SHOOTING
Star

An In My Heart Novella

On the eve of the best night of his life, winning an Academy Award, Jonathan Bello thinks back to his one great love, David Star.

Flipping back the pages of time, Jonathan recalls his handsome, muscular, and charismatic college roommate. Since Jonathan was a freshman and David a senior in the Theatre Department, David took Jonathan under his wing and molded him, not only as an actor but as a lover. With every wonderful new adventure, David left his joyful mark on anyone with whom they came in contact, but Jonathan soon uncovered David's dark past, leading to a shocking event. Undaunted, Jonathan celebrates the captivating man who will always hold a special place in his heart.

www.dreamspinnerpress.com

FOR
MORE
OF THE
BEST
GAY
ROMANCE

DREAMSPINNER
PRESS
dreamspinnerpress.com